Song of the Atman

Song of the Atman

Ronnie Govender

JACANA

Related titles by Ronnie Govender

Wrote and directed the following plays:
Beyond Calvary
The First Stone
His Brother's Keeper
Swami
The Lahnee's Pleasure
Off-Side!
In-Side!
Back-Side!
Who or What is Deena Naicker?
At The Edge
Your Own Dog Won't Bite You
1949
Too Muckin' Futch
The Great R31m Robbery
New plays still to produce:
Song of the Atman
1949 – A Dance Drama
Short stories:
At the Edge & Other Cato Manor Stories

First published in 2006 by Jacana Media (Pty) Ltd.
10 Orange Street
Sunnyside, 2092
Johannesburg
South Africa

ISBN 1-77009-186-6
978-1-77009-186-3

Cover design by Michiel Botha
Set in Bembo 12.5/15.5
Printed by Pinetown Printers

Ronnie Govender, himself a second-generation descendant of Cato Manor's indentured labourers, wrote *Song of the Atman* as a fictionalised account of the life of his uncle, Chin Govender. Winner of the Commonwealth Writers' Prize for Best First Book, Ronnie Govender is renowned for several award-winning plays, including South Africa's longest running play of the 1970s, "The Lahnee's Pleasure". His internationally acclaimed play, "At the Edge" was nominated for South Africa's Best Play in 1991. It was described by London's *Stage and TV Today* as "a resounding hymn to humanity".

This is CHIN GOVENDER, *uncle of the author, Ronnie Govender, and the inspiration for this novel.*

Acknowledgements

This story might not have seen the light of day had it not been for the support of my family, Kay, Dayanandan, Pregaluxmi, Pathmanathan, Paul and Radha.

It was a pleasure working with the accomplished writer Henrietta Rose-Innes during the final edit.

The staff at Jacana, especially Maggie Davey (whose faith in the novel was a strong motivating factor), Mike Martin, Serusha Govender and Sahm Venter.

Various family members helped with the recall of family history, mainly my eldest sister, Mrs Gonapushini Pillay, who lived at Govender's Hotel when she first moved to Cape Town and was close to Uncle Chin, especially during the last years of his life.

To all these people go my heartfelt thanks.

for

karlind, parusha, yashodan, triya,
disha, kamil, nirvana and saien

1967

Dear Devs,

I hope, by God's grace, that this letter finds you in good health. The last time we spoke, you said it was too late, and that it was too easy to say sorry. You were angry but you were right. It was late and it is easy to say sorry. Sorry's just a word, but I have no other way to show what is in my heart. Remember when I took you for walks at Sea Point? You loved to run after the seagulls … I remember the way you laughed when the birds scattered.

That was a brave thing to do. You have always been very brave. I'm told that I was just like that when I was small.

But I was not brave when it counted.

I wanted so much to be close to you, especially when you were growing up. You must believe me. It was painful, but it had to be that way.

Even now, I hear you cry, "You were not there!" No, I was not, and I curse myself that I wasn't, and for that I'm saying I'm deeply sorry. Just words, but I'm hoping that for once words will get past the walls we shut ourselves behind.

With all my love,
Pops

THE CHOPPY SEAS shot spray into his face. Chin's face was almost frostbitten, and he huddled into his thick woollen overcoat. Like a sullen, drawnout silent movie, where the music, dubbed words and action don't quite synchronise, the events of the recent past had been dreamlike in their unfolding; he felt like a powerless player, manipulated to fulfil some distant karmic drama.

It had begun when Guru had dared to confront him about Devs. The north-wester had been blowing with all its relentless fury. Inside the large, high-ceilinged kitchen, which had given such welcome refuge from the harsh Cape winters over the years, the coal stove had failed to dispel the chilly emptiness he'd felt. Suddenly there'd been a hollowness, a bottomless pit: the nothingness that swallows you when your life is no longer in your own hands.

He wouldn't have confronted his elders in similar fashion when he was a youth, no matter how justified the indignation or the anger. Respect was the strong foundation on which families were nurtured. Time was when family was you and you were family.

Chin hadn't realised how much things had changed. Young people these days spoke their minds – even if they didn't know all the facts or have complete understanding, even if families went to pieces, even if they drowned in the high seas of their rashness. He'd wanted to say, "You've got it all wrong. It's not like that." Anything to avert the look of contempt and pity that had replaced the deep respect, even hero-worship, that had once been there in Guru's eyes. Instead, he'd said brusquely, as he walked back out into the north-wester, "Nothing, nothing gives you the right … this is none of your business."

They had at last acceded to his request to visit Devs. Visitors were finally allowed, but only very close relatives. Thank God for the many contacts he'd made over the years.

And Stomps Diederichs, a senior police official, was more a friend than a "contact".

For all their closeness over the decades, Stomps had been taken aback when Chin approached him. "Wragtig! Now you're asking me to do the impossible. That place is very strict. It's only for communists and agitators. You know I'd do anything for you, but this … man, I really don't know. Why go to all this trouble anyway? What's he to you?"

Repetition had given it some plausibility. He was the son of a very good employee, Chin said. Not a troublemaker. She'd worked hard and had served him well. The whole business had shattered her. This was the least he could do.

On the form he was asked to fill in, he'd identified himself as "employer of mother of prisoner". Stomps had told him to say that his reason for standing in for her was that she was very ill and had no next of kin. Leave the rest up to him, Stomps had said.

Now, on the ferry, Chin clutched the letter in his pocket. Stomps had told him that all letters were scrutinised before passing between visitor and prisoner, but he was hoping to smuggle this one in. It was a risk he had to take. The letter was quite innocuous as far as the authorities were concerned, but it had the potential to disrupt the course of his life – which up to now had been so ordered, so jealously private. The danger lay in its being made public. He'd managed to conceal this side of his life from the small group of people whom he valued. It would hurt, for example, if Stomps got to know its contents. A closeness had grown between them. Things wouldn't be the same if the news leaked out. And he was not yet prepared for that, not now, not for a long time – although he hoped one day to be able to say: This is my life, this is the way it is, this is what I want, there's nothing wrong with it. For God's sake, there's nothing wrong with it.

The spray continued to badger his face. He could have sought refuge behind the pilot's cabin, but his troubled thoughts had immobilised him.

The Island heaved into view. How would Devs react? Would he ignore him, the way he'd done in those last few months before the bomb blast? Where there once had been instant reciprocation, there was now a painful gulf. Years ago, at Sea Point on a sunny day, he'd thrown Devs into the air. He hadn't minded the stares of people then. They'd been admiring the happy little boy. As he'd caught a gurgling Devs, he'd vaguely noticed the Island. There were days when the Island stood out serenely on the horizon, in the azureness of the Atlantic, signifying its presence like a shy child.

Now the Island was a petulant, neglected child, derelict, abandoned, decaying – rust everywhere. Rust, rust even on those once-sturdy sentinels, the steel girders which supported the bleached wooden jetty.

The heavy iron gates clanked open. He clutched the letter.

The search was thorough. They found the letter and it was confiscated. Its secret was hidden no more. The guards were unsmiling strangers, but he felt exposed, vulnerable. And worse, he dreaded the ultimate rejection towards which his uncertain steps were taking him.

Yepadi paadenaro

How shall I sing thy praises, teach me

Adiyaar

My supreme master

Apadi pade naan

That's the way I want to sing

Sivene, apadi pade naan

Almighty Siva, that's the way I want to sing

Aasai konden

Thus to convey my love for you

The voice of DK Pattamal, the timeless essence of Carnatic music, sliding through the senses, through the mind, through the soul, in tune with the rhythms of the universe, celebrating the unity of life, of non-dualism. Humility before the unfathomable depths of being. The urge to live the melody.

Instead, watching it flit before him like the firefly, the nimtampootch.

Chapter One

1930

THE SIGN-WRITER had done a splendid job on the shop window. "BAIJNATH'S BOOK-KEEPERS", it said, in gold and with a flourish. And it was right there in Umbilo Road – the first, if not the only, Indian business among all the tidily ordered shops and houses. Baijnath was like that. He took his chances and he did things in style – which for him meant green or brown suits, bright floral shirts and equally bright, severely contrasting ties. He was never without his tie, his coloured braces, his imitation gold cufflinks and tiepin. Strangely, his choice of clothing didn't jar. It seemed to go with his gentle, disarming smile. His handwriting, besides being eminently legible, was a thing of beauty. Its symmetry and shape, its swirls, curls and twirls were so precise that it looked like it came off a printing press.

Baijnath had finished his standard four and everybody looked up to him. If there'd been a higher standard, he would have been in it, but at the time the villagers could only build an English school up to standard four. There were imposing schools not far from where he'd stayed, built by the government, which had up to standard six, then up to standard ten – but the law hadn't allowed him to attend such schools. His father had come to South Africa from Bihar in India, where he and others like him had been fed stories of gold nuggets being picked up on the streets of Durban. It was a different story, of course, when they arrived, aching to get away from an India impoverished by waves of Arab and British imperialism. The word "indenture", as he and his fellows were to discover, was a polite word for slavery.

Baijnath's father had saved enough to pay a small deposit on a piece of land in Cato Manor, practically mortgaging himself for life. He'd started a market garden and had built up a steady trade selling vegetables and fruit to the housewives on the Berea. He'd hoped that his son would follow him. By the time Baijnath was a grown man, the land would be free.

But Baijnath couldn't see himself spending the rest of his life trudging along the wide, tree-lined streets of the Berea with his baskets of greens, constantly sucking up to haughty madams. After four years of working for the old man, nineteen-year-old Baijnath had made his move. He'd trudged all over Durban, visiting Indian shops and urging them that if they didn't keep books, the government would take action against them. "Why cause more trouble for yourself? One day the tax man will come, and if you don't have your books they will throw you into jail. Besides, how will you know exactly how much profit you're making or how much you're losing if you don't keep accounts?" He was a persuasive youngster and soon he had three book-keeping accounts. Within a year he had over twenty, including those of two white factory owners, who found the likeable, smiling Indian to be efficient and trustworthy – and, above all, much cheaper than white book-keepers.

Baijnath astonished the Cato Manor community when he moved into an office in Umbilo, the area just over the hill where whites lived. Umbilo Road was the main arterial road to the South Coast, and Baijnath's keen business sense told him that if he could get a place there, he'd be on the right track. Baijnath approached Mr Cohen, who owned a building on the corner of Francois and Umbilo Roads. Baijnath was like that – he took his chances. The worst that the white man could say was no. As it turned out, Mr Cohen said, "Okay – but if you miss one month's rent, you're out!" He was a different kind of white man. At least he had given Baijnath a chance. Of course, no one else was prepared to pay the rent that Cohen wanted.

Baijnath consulted a pandit, who gave him an auspicious date and time to have a small ceremony, after which he could move in. The ceremony was conducted in hushed tones, so as not to offend the white neighbours. The pandit, who was used to intoning the mantras over the sacred fire of the havan in loud, piercingly nasal tones, was not at all pleased at having to appeal to the Gods in such a muted fashion. The Gods would not be happy; but Baijnath was more prepared to incur the wrath of the Gods than that of his new neighbours. In any event, he had only agreed to perform the ritual on the urging of his mother. There was little point in upsetting her at this high point in his life.

Now, many years later, Baijnath was an established businessman, still in the same premises. Baijnath kept in touch with his old standard-four teacher, Mr Peters, who spoke much like an Englishman except for the occasional dropped "h" and rapid delivery. Mr Peters had a fine bearing and grey sideburns, and always looked well groomed and distinguished in his dark suit and tie, despite Durban's hot, humid weather. He seemed to have a built-in thermostat, because there was never a bead of sweat on his brow, even in the hottest weather and no matter how busy he was. He was a born teacher and had been the first to spot Pradeep Baijnath's talents, his stylish handwriting and his skills at arithmetic. Although they were no longer master and pupil, Baijnath couldn't stop calling him "sir".

Every Friday, when Baijnath closed the shop and sent the staff home, he would pull out a bottle of cane spirits and share a drink with his old schoolteacher. It was illegal for Indians to have liquor in their possession. They could drink at the "Indian" bars of white hotels, but could not buy liquor at bottle stores to take home. It cost far more to drink in a bar, and the white hoteliers made a fat profit. But Baijnath had a way of obtaining his weekly bottle of cane spirits, and once he'd closed his front door, nobody could enter. Mr Peters would bring along some slices of roast beef for bites – although Baijnath was in many ways a good Hindu, he saw nothing wrong in having beef. He was a practical man; he felt people should not follow customs blindly, but should ask why they were there – although, strangely, he did not feel the same way about caste.

When he'd been at school, he'd had the impression that Mr Peters was a very religious man. Every morning at assembly, the schoolteacher led The Lords Prayer, "Our Father which art in heaven …", closing his eyes and tilting his head heavenwards. Now, after a few drinks, Mr Peters would look back and have a good laugh. "I closed my eyes to keep out the hot sun!" Then, after another drink, he would say, "You know, Pradeep, we give God a hard time – doing so many stupid things in his name. All we have to do is just be good." Baijnath would agree enthusiastically and pour out more drinks.

Baijnath would often bring masala-fried shad, which was plentiful off the coast of Natal. At that time, whites looked down on the fish, as they did on cane spirits. "Those are for the coolies, my deah!" Baijnath mimicked. "Sir, it's good. The idiots don't know what they're missing. We'll have the shad all to ourselves."

In winter, when the sardine run was on, Baijnath's wife would deep-fry the sardines in a light batter made of masala, ginger, green chillies, curry leaf and dhania, all crushed and mixed with flour into a paste. "Delicious, absolutely delicious!" Mr Peters would say after four canes and a couple of crispy sardines, sweating for once.

They had much to talk about. "That young lawyer from India was a very brave man," Peters remarked as he tucked into another sardine snack, washing it down with a sip of cane and water. "I mean, he got kicked out of a train for refusing to move to third class, and he was prepared to go to jail."

"Yah, he can be brave. They sent him back to India what will happen to us? These people are too powerful."

Mr Peters believed that the young lawyer, Gandhi, had been on the right track. "This Natal Indian Congress is something we need. We have a lot of grievances. Thumbi Naidoo thinks so too. He gave his support."

Baijnath said, "Without Thumbi's support, the NIC will be nothing. You think it's good to join the passive resistance?"

Mr Peters was adamant. "Of course. I am ready to join."

Baijnath was sceptical. "I'm not so sure. Who'll run my business if I go to jail?"

Baijnath's business was doing very, very well, and he needed a clerk who was good at figures and had good handwriting. Somebody he could train, with the aim of making him a junior partner in the business – he wasn't going to overwork himself and die of a heart attack like his father. But God had not blessed him with a son. He had two daughters, lovely, obedient girls, but they would one day marry and leave the home. How he longed for a son … this was man's work.

One Friday, when Mr Peters walked into the shop with his parcel of roast beef, Baijnath noticed he was unusually excited. Even when he'd had a few drinks, Mr Peters was normally very composed and correct in his manners and speech. It was something he'd inherited from his father, a South Indian without a caste name who had converted to the Roman Catholic faith. He told Baijnath, "I think I have found the right young man for you. I've been keeping an eye on him for some time now. He has just passed his exams with flying colours. He is bright and his handwriting is very good. I've never known him to make a mistake in his writing exercises – never used a rubber once. He is also very good at arithmetic."

Baijnath sat up. This was the kind of youngster he was looking for. Maybe this chap would even marry one of his daughters, and keep the business in the family.

The following Friday, Mr Peters arrived at three o'clock, two hours earlier than usual. He introduced Baijnath to a lanky, nervous Chin Govender. Chin was a Tamil – not quite what Baijnath had in mind. No matter how good Chin was, he could never marry one of his daughters. The prospective bridegroom had to belong to the same caste as Baijnath – which was a stratum above the chamar, or leatherworker's caste, which in turn was just above the pariahs, whom Gandhi called the harrijans, the "children of God". Ironically, among the Tamils, the Govenders were a middle caste, which put them above the Baijnaths. But the Baijnaths, of course, were fairer in complexion than most Tamils.

Never mind. The most important thing was that Mr Peters had said this youngster was very good.

Chapter Two

After a lengthy interview, Chin left, pretending to be walking to the bus stop. Mr Peters had brought him in his old Ford, on the understanding that he would find his own way home. Chin had no money for bus fare, but had not told Mr Peters this.

As he left the shop, he started trudging up Fenniscowles Road. The four miles to his home in Montile Road, just off Cato Manor Road, were no problem. All of seventeen years old, Chin was tall and sturdy and had the stride of an athlete in prime condition. The walk was no burden, particularly because happy thoughts occupied his mind. He'd found work, all on his own. Mr Baijnath had even hinted that if he was satisfied with him, Chin could become a partner in the business. For the last half mile, he broke into a trot, anxious to tell his mother the good news. The prospect of seeing her eyes light up made Chin's spirits soar; Amurtham would be thrilled. The coolness of the gently invading dusk heightened his exhilaration.

Amurtham, so hard-working, so devoted to her brood. Amurtham, always praying, always working, always smiling – except when the children and grandchildren got on her nerves. Then the "children must-behave" side of her got going – the stern matriarch, like Mariammen, the unyielding Goddess of discipline. "Aravelli, suravelli, alangaravelli, neeye thiya!" The song echoed through Chin's memories of childhood: the sambrani smoke, the marigold-bedecked kavadi, the sudden eerie trances. "Queen of all Life, Queen of Destruction, Queen of Retribution, that's what you are, oh Mother!"

Amurtham had come to South Africa as a young girl to marry Karupanna Govender, many years her senior. He himself had come to the country as a young man with his parents from Thanjaoor. The surly, half-baked English clerks at the Immigration Offices had distorted the surname. Instead of "Gounder" they had entered "Govender" – just as Nayager became Naicker, Mudaliar became Moodley, Nyar became Nair and so on.

Karupanna loved people. People must laugh, and a few drinks made people laugh more than normal. There was little time to laugh. You got up at four, your wife filled the billycan with kulli or sangiti (similar to the putu made by the Zulus), dhall, herbs braised with chillies and garlic cloves or sometimes chicken or fish if you were lucky; then you trudged into the cane fields, hoe in one hand, cane knife in the other, your wife carrying the billycan alongside you. The cane fields were owned by the mulungus, as the few Pondos who worked alongside them called the sugar barons, many of whom had escaped the slums of London for a better life in the colonies. Karupanna, whether he'd had a few drinks or not, laughed, joked and played, even as his hoe dug into the rich, red soil. He sang his favourite Carnatic songs as he cleared the thick subtropical undergrowth to make way for the sugar cane, occasionally slicing off the head of a harmless grass snake – or that of an aroused green mamba, seconds before it could sink its deadly fangs into his vein. Karupanna, smiling even as he stood his ground before the tall Irish foreman.

Karupanna had taken a break to wipe the sweat off his brow after some backbreaking hoeing when the Irishman shouted at him, "You're not on holiday, coolie!"

Karupanna shot back, "My name is Karupanna Govender, not coolie."

It was the first time anyone had spoken back – and in

full view of the others. The Irishman got off his horse to whip this insolent coolie into line. Just one backhand sweep across the cheek would do. The hand flashed. The cheek wasn't there. What was there was a toe in his groin. As he doubled up, an uppercut exploded on his gaping jaw. The lights went out.

George Cato, former barrow boy from Covent Gardens, sugar baron and first mayor of Durban, sent for the coolie. "You know what the sentence is. Why did you do it?"

Karupanna did indeed know what the sentence was: twenty lashes with a whip dipped in brine, and then time in solitary – the terrible punishment that had driven dozens to take their lives on the Hanging Tree in Umhlali. Karupanna looked Cato in the eye and, although he knew English, spoke in Tamil: "He left me with no choice. It was him or me."

Cato listened to the interpreter in astonishment and grudging admiration. He hesitated. This was a simple case of insubordination, and the coolie knew the consequences. Yet he had stood his ground. Cato was fully aware that the Irishman was hard – that was the only way. You wanted results, you cracked the whip. Cato admired strong men. He himself had had to be very strong to get where he was. The world was no place for weaklings. This little coolie was far stronger and braver than he looked. An insolent smile was backed by a sharp native intellect. Such men were as dangerous as they were rare. You won such a man to your side, you won an army – a strategy that had built empires. He could use such a man – but first he had to be disciplined. Solitary confinement for one month; stale bread and water.

On Cato's instructions, Karupanna was promoted to sirdar or overseer. Quick to learn, he soon became fluent in English. The other sirdars were harder on the workers than their employers were, but Karupanna was a different kind of sirdar, winning small concessions to lessen the tedium of the workers' oppressed lives. Yet he was far more productive than his sycophantic peers, like Mudaliar. (Not unlike colonised African chiefs, the Mudaliar sirdars were an institution – the name literally means "first in line".)

When his contract was over, Cato urged Karupanna to stay on, offering him an increase. But Karupanna was a free man and he wanted to stay that way. He got a job as a court interpreter. With his teenage bride, Karupanna settled in Cato Manor, land immediately to the west of Durban given to Cato by the municipality. Karupanna and Amurtham erected a wood and iron house and planted a market garden, which Amurtham kept going while her husband was away in court. They raised a family of eleven boys and a girl before diabetes, the silent killer, struck Karupanna down. His liking for cane spirits didn't make it any easier. First his left leg had to be amputated, after a small wound on his toe had turned gangrenous. Then he went blind. Mercifully, hypertension led to a massive coronary, relieving him of further suffering.

Chin was third in line. When Karupanna died, Madramuthoo, the second eldest son – or Jack, as he was more popularly known – became the head of the family at twenty-three, stepping into the breach like he was born to it. The eldest son, Chidambaram, a strapping young man, had become a soldier and had died on the battlefront in the First World War. Jack was a clone of his father, inheriting his sinewy leanness and hard-as-nails toughness. You felt it when you shook his hand – his grip was iron, quite unconsciously; a calling card that immediately established his extraordinary physical strength, belying his small stature.

Karupanna had been easy-going; Jack took his role as head of the family much more seriously than the old man had done. He didn't smile as much, and had inherited a streak of bossiness from Amurtham. Not that he was humourless; at work, he gained a reputation for being companionable and at times even charming. He started work as a filing clerk at the stationery firm, Davies and Barrow in Umbilo Road. Competition for the few jobs available was stiff. At the mere sniff of a vacancy, long queues formed immediately, and you had to do some fast talking to get noticed. Whether it was English, Zulu or Tamil, Jack placed great store by proper speech – he hated sloppiness – and his facility with English impressed his employers. Jack was conscious that his job put him a cut above his fellows.

One lunch hour, a quarrel broke out between two of the labourers, Samson and Petros. Samson was much bigger, and was pushing Petros around. Jack stepped in, trying to placate the two. Samson made the mistake of pushing him away, as he might a troublesome fly. Jack reacted instinctively with a full-blooded punch to Samson's jaw. Samson fell. He got up groggily, holding up his hands in shock.

The managing director of the firm, Mr Davies, had just come on the scene. Wally Davies had been an amateur boxer and he realised that he had a potential boxing champion on his hands. He took Jack to his boxing school. The others in the school thought it was a big joke. A coolie as a boxer? Coolies were coolies, working automatons that jumped to attention when you spoke to them. They were not fighters. Wally said, "You wait and see." He patiently instructed the more than eager Jack in the skills of the "noble art" – straight left followed by a right hook, right cross or right swing; how to feint, bob and weave; how to dance around the ring without losing balance or power. Jack was a natural. A bantamweight, he had a punch like a mule-kick – the bigger boxers in the gym were reluctant to spar with Jack after one of them lost two front teeth. Jack treated sparring sessions with the same intensity as he did his actual fights in the ring.

His first pro fight didn't live up to expectations. It was a four-round bantamweight preliminary in the tournament that featured the international fight between Kid Mothi Singh of Guyana and Kid Veeran of Durban. Jack had trained hard. He was ready. The dressing room was a short distance from the ring. As he stepped out of the passageway into the crowded hall his muscles, normally taut on such occasions, suddenly loosened. This was the biggest crowd he had experienced. So many eyes fixed on him, such a huge din. They were shouting his name but he couldn't hear them. He was desperate not to make any mistakes, not to make a fool of himself. It wasn't fear but a crippling self-consciousness that almost immobilised him the moment the opening bell sounded. In the other corner, Johnson Mkize, another newcomer to the pro ranks, was equally nervous. The first two rounds saw both fighters clinching at every opportunity; the referee warned them sternly. The next round was no better. The referee stopped the fight, calling it a no-contest.

Wally was mad. "You want to be a fighter, you fight!"

That night, Jack hardly slept. He had never felt such humiliation before. For two months before his next fight, he shut out everything else from his mind. He kept to himself. Wally had to force him off the punch bag. He flattened two of his sparring partners. Wally had a word with him: "Save it for the fight. Don't be so hard on the guys or you won't have sparring partners." Jack was a different fighter in the next bout, against the experienced Speedy Tshangase. He won by a knockout in the third round.

There was no stopping him after that. He won all of his amateur fights, eventually winning the Natal non-European Amateur Bantamweight Title. Wally thought it was time to turn pro. Jack's fighting name was Kid Jack Govender. He won the next ten fights, all by knockouts. He was soon lined up for the South African non-European Bantamweight Title against the champion, Jim Slasher from Cape Town. Wally was at first reluctant to sign for the fight. As Wally agonised, Jack begged: "I know I can take him. Please give me the chance, I won't let you down." Even as he signed, Wally wasn't sure he was doing the right thing. He'd grown quite fond of this youngster, whom he'd come to regard as a son. A deeply religious man, Wally said a prayer as he signed.

Slasher, a fair-skinned, blue-eyed Capetonian with long, straight hair, who could have passed for white and often did, made it known that "no coolie was going to take away my title."

The fight was held at the Royal Bioscope in Victoria Street in the heart of Durban's "Casbah", a patronising name coined by white journalists to describe the area around Grey and Victoria Streets. The bioscope was a bughouse which showed mostly B-grade Westerns.

Twenty of Slasher's thirty-one challengers had been rendered comatose for a little more than a full minute of their lives, mostly by roundhouse rights. Mind you, he was not averse to dispatching his hapless victims with a left hook or a hammer-like uppercut whenever the opportunity arose. Not many had dared challenge him in recent times. The fight-hungry Slasher camp was therefore only too happy to entertain Jack's challenge. They signed the contracts with great bonhomie and enthusiasm – this was a rookie with just ten fights.

The only Indian paper at the time was the *Indian Opinion*, which had been founded by Gandhi to further the cause of satyagraha or passive resistance. It did not cover sport, least of all boxing, which contradicted the newspaper's ethos of non-violence. Other newspapers did not write about "non-white" sport, for far more mundane reasons. But the grapevine got to work, and soon people were talking about the fight everywhere. Pre-fight talk for this encounter went beyond the buses and pubs, spreading to weddings and religious ceremonies. A small community, battling to survive, experiencing all kinds of racial humiliation, needed its heroes – even a clear underdog like Jack. Even those who'd never seen a prizefight or were not given to violence were behind him. Jack became the centre of attraction and he couldn't say he didn't like it.

Came the big night. Standing room only. You were lucky if you got breathing space in the stuffy Royal Bioscope. The promoters ignored fire regulations and let in far more people than they should have. Kid Jack Govender was the first to step into the ring. When he took off his white gown, his blue satin trunks with a white waistband and two white stripes down the sides glistened in the arc lights. His fans gave him a rousing reception, but the applause was even more deafening as Jim Slasher, wearing a red sequined gown with the legend "Jim Golden Boy Slasher" emblazoned on its back, stepped into the smoke-filled arc lights. Jack didn't hear them, neither did he hear the final instructions from the referee. Slasher's broad, supremely confident smile had more than a touch of arrogance. Jack's eyes were downcast, fixed, cold, revealing nothing. Wally, constantly rubbing his shoulders to abate the tension, kept talking: "Just keep that left in front of you – jab, jab, jab – don't rush him, this guy's too experienced. Jab and move, jab and move. Most important, keep your right hand up. Cover your jaw and jab, jab, jab …" Jack's nod was mechanical and Wally knew he wasn't listening. He desperately hoped that the big occasion hadn't overwhelmed his fighter. "Don't rush the guy, don't rush him, keep your left in his face, jab, jab …"

"Chairs and seconds out – round one!"

Slasher hadn't finished preening himself in his corner, and the sound of the bell had hardly died down, when Govender was out of his corner like a little terrier. He was fighting his own fight. Instinct had taken over. Wally, crouching in his corner, yelled, "For God's sake, don't rush him, don't rush him!" Slasher had barely lifted up his arms in combat stance when three punches thudded into his ribs. The fourth dug into his solar plexus, knocking the wind out of him. He doubled up and a fifth, an upper-cut, scythed through the air. The timing was pin-point, the power deadly. Slasher hit the canvas, out to the world. They had to take him to hospital with two broken ribs.

It was such a sensation that the media could not ignore it. Jock Leyden, then a young rookie cartoonist for the *Daily News*, just out of Scotland, was moved to draw a cartoon of the sensational event. He showed the Indian fighter, in a turban, flooring the well-built Slasher, with the caption, "Well done, Sammy!" He was new to the country, but Leyden had already absorbed local customs. His caricature of Jack was true to the stereotype, hooked nose and spindly legs, when in fact Jack had lean but muscular legs and, unusually for a prizefighter, a well-shaped nose.

A new champion was born and with it a newly cocky Jack. He didn't throw his weight around, but he was now the king and you had to respect that. If you didn't, the consequences were not at all pleasant. Discipline, respect, correct speech and behaviour, especially in front of elders: this was the unwritten code, and you didn't dare break it in his presence. As long as you stuck to the rules you had no problems; in fact, you would find Jack on your side. But at home, there was no mistaking who was the boss.

Chin looked up to Jack, always anxious to please him. By getting a job, he was living up to the expectations of his famous perianna – his big brother. Chin's ego would have ballooned had he heard the conversation behind closed doors between Amurtham, Jack and Archee, Jack's wife of two years.

"He went by himself. He's only seventeen!" Amurtham said proudly.

Jack replied, "Getting a job is fine. The thing is to keep it."

"He got a job, that's not a small thing," Archee chipped in. "Give him credit."

Amurtham agreed, "Yes, such a young man – no, he's still a boy – to get a job when it is so hard to find one. That's something."

Eventually Jack gave in to both women. "Yes, it's a big thing. He's a clever fellow."

That evening, the family celebrated. A chicken was brought from the coop and slaughtered. The spicy aroma of chicken biryani was soon floating through the household, the handiwork of two splendid cooks, Amurtham and Archee. There was also braized gadra and double beans, dry-fish chutney, dhosai and dhall garnished with fresh dhania. Amurtham brought out the big jar of mango pickles from the pantry – fruit harvested from their three faithful mango trees, salted and left for some months to soak in mustard oil spiced with pickle masala. There was even some payasu, liberally sprinkled with diced almonds, normally reserved for big occasions or ceremonies.

Jack was full of praise for Chin. He was a bright lad who'd done well at school, but they couldn't afford to send him for further studies. Jack regretted that they couldn't do for Chin what had been done for a family friend, Mogamberry Naicker. A determined effort had been made to send

"Monty" to the imposing new high school, Sastri College, named after the Agent-General from India, Srinivasa Sastri. After school, the comparatively well-off Naickers would have just enough money to send him to Edinburgh to study medicine – and so become one of the first South African Indian doctors. Indians were not allowed to enter South African medical schools, no matter how well they fared in the exams. Chin was forced to abandon any such ambitions; Sastri College had been built too late for him, and anyway his family would not have been able to afford it. He was just happy he'd got a job. That, for the time being, was an achievement.

The family talked well into the night about the family's progress and lamented that three brothers, Chindambaram, Murugase and Loga, all older than Chin, were not around to share in the celebrations with the rest of the family. Chidambaram had gone off to the war, much against Amurtham's pleading, and never returned. Murugase had succumbed to tuberculosis, for which proper treatment had not yet been found and which had scythed its way through the poor community. Loga had died while trying to save a young lady who had fallen into the village well. Revelling in his blossoming manhood, Loga had had an eye for the girls, and they no doubt had had an eye for this good-looking, ever-cheerful young man. He'd also been a daring young man – too daring for his own good. He hadn't hesitated when he heard the scream, but had dived into the well, fully clothed. He'd managed to push the girl over the brim to safety and would have saved himself too, but for the slimy lichen on the cement walls of the well.

At that very moment, over the hill, quite a distance from the well, his little sister Chellamma became suddenly hysterical. She was running around shouting, "Where's the rope? Where's the rope? Unnah needs a rope!" Before they could get a rope to him, he had slipped down the algae-ridden walls of the deep well.

At the mention of her late sons, Amurtham tried to leave the room without attracting attention. They let her walk out into the night. Prayer had been her constant staff since Karupanna died. There'd been many times when she'd been convinced that God had heard her prayers – and many times it seemed he hadn't. There were times when everything seemed lost. Times when she clutched at the last strands of hope. Even then, she refused to lose faith. When Karupanna died, only her Madramuthoo, Jack, had been working. Amurtham had turned to the soil with steely determination. It was backbreaking work, toiling in the small market garden through the long day. The children helped out whenever they could, but she was determined that they attend school. Education was a sacred duty.

Life's demands, however, went beyond food, clothing and shelter, and Amurtham's little temple had become her lifeline. Fervent prayer would give way to long moments of meditative silence, or to an almost hypnotic trance-like state, both of which nourished her soul and created an aura of caring spirituality around her. She had come to see that the ways of God were beyond understanding, and there were times when much more than prayer was needed to cope with life. Despite her strong beliefs, she could never come to terms with the deaths of her husband and her children.

The day's humidity was receding before the evening's descending coolness. Crickets chirped close to the corrugated-iron walls of the kitchen. In the outhouse behind the umdoni tree, Gugu, the maid, was softly singing a Zulu lullaby to Bongi, her newly born fifth child. Her soft, comforting voice with its touch of melancholy floated out of the kaya. The fireflies – nimtampooch – darted through the long grass, through the curry-leaf shrubbery and the clump of banana plants, punctuating the darkness with tiny stabs of light. The nimtampooch always made their appearance just before Deepavali: a time of rededication and spiritual regeneration, a time for the cleansing of souls. Amurtham lifted her arms to the heavens, remembering her husband and three sons, repeating softly, "Aum Naamasivaya."

Chapter Three

BAIJNATH'S BOOK-KEEPERS continued to flourish. This was abundantly clear the moment you entered the large office, actually a small hall. There was no reception area; you just walked straight into a buzz of activity. Four tables, laden with well-worn brown files, dominated the room. The walls were also lined with shelves stacked with files. Baijnath's office was in the far right-hand corner behind a wooden partition, the top half of which was glass. Sitting behind his busy-looking table, on which sat a Remington typewriter and a telephone, Baijnath had a clear view of his domain. Baijnath always wore a benign smile, not giving the impression that he was in any way spying – but the moment any of his staff were seen to slacken, he would walk over and have a friendly word or two, which was enough to keep them on their toes. After three such friendly chats, an errant staff member was given his marching orders, again in the friendliest manner possible. No amount of contrite protestation and reassurance would help. You put your foot in it and you took your medicine, which, bitter as it was, was at least administered without a touch of rancour.

Nearly all the Indian businesses in Durban, and several white firms, were now handled by Baijnath's Book-keepers. The staff had been increased by two more clerks, again introduced by Mr Peters and placed under the supervision of Chin. Baijnath was able to afford a second-hand Model T Ford and a double-barrelled gun for hunting. Buck and guinea fowl were still in profusion in places like Merebank, just ten miles out of the city centre. Guinea fowl would often scamper across the South Coast highway, which was flanked by tall gum trees. Across the road to the west lay lush, rolling hills of sugar cane.

Chin sometimes went hunting with Baijnath and Mr Peters, who was a crack shot, but he preferred fishing. Amurtham had come from a fishing family – hardy folk, seine netters who went out past the harbour breakwater in their rickety little boats, often battling the strong tides and winds to ply their trade – and all her sons possessed a passion for the sport. Durban harbour was less than a mile away from where Chin worked. Depending on the tide, Chin would often spend two hours after work, fishing. It was a bit of a distance, but transport was no problem. Baijnath had bought him a second-hand bicycle, mainly to visit big clients, which he was allowed to take home.

Straight across from the Congella, the dry docks were being set up. The harbour itself teemed with fish, especially grunter. The coastline's abundant shoals were ignored by the Zulus, who had a traditional aversion to fish. The fisher folk as well as ordinary people looked forward to the annual sardine run around May and June, when huge shoals of the small fish beached themselves on the South Coast shoreline. The boiling shallows, with hundreds of the little fish thrashing wildly, held people in hypnotic thrall, and a mad scramble followed as they scooped up the sardines in their dresses, saries, baskets, and whatever makeshift containers were available. The bonus was that, while the sardines themselves were a sought-after delicacy, they were followed by shoals of game fish such as tunney, barracuda and the prized seventy-four, which made for an excellent fish biryani.

Fish curry was cooked on a kadai in the open and left to cool overnight in the unpolluted air, covered with a muslin cloth. Tamarind gave fish curry its peculiarly exciting taste. Mind you, fish curry was not fish curry if it did not contain the right amount of green chillies and thin, long brinjals. One's palate had to be chilli-literate before one could enjoy its distinctive flavour. In the absence of refrigeration, the tamarind was an excellent preservative and, despite the heat, the curry could last for several days. The Govender pantry was never short of fish, either dried or salted. Some days, they were even able to give some of the fish to grateful neighbours and relatives.

Now that Chin had a steady job, Amurtham suggested it would be nice if he married and settled down. Karupanna had left them over a third of an acre of land, and there was enough space to attach two more rooms to the building, if not to build another home.

"You don't get on with one daughter-in-law, how are you going to deal with two?" Chin joked.

He was teasing her, but Amurtham was hurt. "How can you say such a thing?"

Chin tried to soothe her ruffled feelings. "It's only a joke, Amma."

When Amurtham was upset, she busied herself. With quick movements, she tied and untied the mundhani – the free end of the sarie – around her waist, a sure sign that she was annoyed. Doubling up on her work in the kitchen, rattling the pots and pans, Amurtham continued to grumble. "Sometimes people say things in jest, but they mean it. I do not quarrel with Archee, but it's a mother-in-law's duty to instruct her daughter-in-law on how to cook and care for her husband."

Chin wisely refrained from continuing with the now slightly strained conversation. Fortunately, Archee was out of earshot – or so they thought.

Marriage was the furthest thing from Chin's mind. He'd set his sights on owning his own accounting business one day, if not some other business. The seeds of his aspirations had been sown at a tender age, when most kids had no real understanding of what life held for them or what they wanted from it. He'd been quick to notice things that escaped the attention of others. He'd been conscious, for instance, that his father's job was very different from the jobs that others were doing. Most were either subsistence farmers or labourers, with the spectre of unemployment hanging over their lives. The handful who were business people were generally either Gujerati or Moslem. His father, the court interpreter, was always well dressed and dignified. It had dawned on Chin, even then, that his father had broken new ground and hadn't allowed the obstacles that faced his community to thwart his progress. He'd had heard the story of how his father had beaten up his big white foreman, and this had made a lasting impression on him.

He made up his mind the day he stood on the wharf, waving goodbye to his friend Monty, going to Scotland to study medicine. It was then that he firmly decided he would be like his father, not allowing himself to be sucked into the weary ordinariness of the downtrodden. He would've loved to have studied further, but the family could not afford it. That was that. There was no point in crying about it. He'd told himself that he would somehow make it in business on his own.

Although Baijnath had promoted him to senior bookkeeper, he hadn't again mentioned the prospect of making him a junior partner, as he'd hinted in their first meeting. Although Chin was earning far more than many of his colleagues, it had become obvious that Baijnath had passed much of the responsibility of the business onto Chin's youthful shoulders, without a commensurate increase in his salary. Chin decided that he would bide his time until the right moment came to branch out on his own.

He'd mentioned it to Jack, who dismissed it out of hand.

"Rubbish! You can thank your lucky stars that you have such good, regular employment. Don't push your luck. You're too young for all that." Jack knew it was risky for a young man to go into business without any capital. Besides, Chin's steady income was indispensable.

At such times, Chin felt that there was a growing distance between his brother and himself.

Jack's family was increasing: Archee was expecting their third child. Jack was also spending long hours at the gym. That year he defended his title, winning against the Transvaal champion, "Engine" Twala, and the hard-hitting Border Champion, Moses Mabide, both inside the distance. He was that rare combination, a skilful boxer and a knock-out specialist.

In boxing, you have to outwit your opponent. Once you've sized him up in the first few exploratory minutes – or rounds, depending on your powers of perception – you have to decide whether to go on the offensive or shore up your defences and bide your time. You have to think fast and move fast. But the biggest challenge is that the ring can be dauntingly lonely under those searing arc lights. Not for Jack. When the gong sounded, he didn't have the slightest hesitation. His muscles became taut and he went into a slight crouch, like a gun being cocked. There was little or no fear. In a brutal contact sport, this might be a serious weakness – such fearlessness can result in the absorption of damaging punishment, especially to the head. But thanks to speedy reflexes and a well-honed defence, Jack had an uncanny ability to avoid taking full-blooded punches to the head, and unlike many other prizefighters, he had retained his razor-sharp mental faculties. But the intensive training it took to keep in shape and the demands of caring for his extended family occasionally led to some frayed nerves and a loss in concentration.

Chin never broached the subject of starting his own business again, but he didn't give up the idea. He would retire to his room early to spend time building his dreams, taking flights of exhilarating fancy or reading Zane Gray – except when his little sister Chellamma barged into his room, which was quite often. His smallish room was at the back of the house, which had begun life as a one-bedroomed wood and iron cottage. Karupanna had almost single-handedly put up the structure, choosing the best second-hand corrugated iron for the walls and the roof. He'd been able to afford timber for the ceiling and the floor and for lining the walls of the bedroom and lounge. Over the years, as the family grew, the cottage had been further improved by Karupanna. The kitchen floor, which had once been regularly daubed with cow dung mixed with straw, was cemented. He had even added a concrete verandah, which greatly enhanced the appearance of the already pretty cottage, surrounded by roses, dahlias, marigolds, carnations, snapdragons and pride-of-Indias.

All three working brothers had their own rooms, while those still at school shared a single large room. Of course, Jack's room was the largest, adjacent to the lounge. Chellamma slept in Amurtham's room.

Chellamma had just turned twelve but looked as if she was in her teens. There were signs that she would soon be reaching puberty. Amurtham, after talking to Jack and Archee, took her out of school. It was time to prepare her for marriage.

Unlike other girls in the district, Chellamma spoke openly to her mother. "Why are you stopping me from going to school?"

Amurtham was patient. "You are going to be a woman soon. We have to prepare for that."

Chellamma couldn't see the point. "Why can't women go to school?"

Amurtham said, "When I was young, very young, they got me married. That's the way things are. You must understand that."

Chellamma was adamant. "I don't understand! I can't understand!"

Amurtham nearly yielded to the innocent protestation, seeing so much of herself in this lovely child, her only daughter; but she had a duty. This was the way it had been for generations. This was the way of respect, of duty, of parental responsibility. Even the Scriptures said so. She did not look at Chellamma as she turned to leave. "We have decided. You must listen to us. It's for your own good." And the matter was closed.

Chellamma was devastated and Chin outraged, but there was nothing he could do about it. To Chin she was still a girl, an intelligent, delightful girl who reminded him so much of his father – the same expansive attitude to life. She was always smiling, always so full of the effulgence of life. There was something else that struck him about her. She seemed to have a sixth sense. Everyone knew how she'd sensed the disaster before her brother Loga had drowned. And the night before Karupanna died, she had cried uncontrollably and got up screaming. She had dreamt that strangers were taking her father away from her. Her father had put up a fight, but the men were too strong.

"Unna, the dream was so … so real," she'd told Chin between sobs as he comforted her in his arms. "Uppa was so weak, he couldn't fight … he couldn't stop them."

Chin gently massaged her head as he held her to his chest and whispered, "It was just a bad dream, don't be afraid. Come see, Uppa is sleeping soundly in his room."

Even when he'd gone blind, Karupanna had never lapsed into the detached resignation of the dying and the elderly. His moods were still effusive and ebullient. His sudden passing took all of them, except Chellamma, by surprise. For many a long month, all of them felt the huge emptiness his final departure had caused; but his was a presence that somehow would always be there.

The Friday cocktail hour at Baijnath's Book-keepers now had a new member: Mr Baijnath's latest client, the wealthy tobacconist Mr Gopal Puckree. Mr Puckree was, as he put it, " a good drinker". He was also an excellent businessman. His parents had only been able to afford to educate him up to standard three. He was not a bright student, but he was most resourceful when it came to making money. As a teenager without a penny to his name but with much determination, he'd approached wholesaling firms. He'd been turned down by several until he met Mr Ismail Haffeejee, who at first had chuckled to himself that such a greenhorn was actually asking to do business with his firm. But there was something about the youngster that reminded him of his own youth, when he'd started off in similar circumstances. He not only agreed to do business with him but gave him thirty days' credit. To Ismail, who lived by the Koran, this was real charity. His wife said that he was mad.

Gopal Puckree started selling candles, cigarettes, matches, sweets and cool drinks house to house. It was heavy work, lugging the items around on a discarded wheelbarrow converted into a cart and ingeniously fitted with compartments. He also set up a little makeshift stall just outside the Mayville Football Grounds on Sundays – much to the consternation of the officials, who had their own tuck shop inside the grounds. The officials chased him away, until he complained to Mr Sooboo Rajah, the chairman of the Mayville Sports Grounds Association, who was a friend of his father. Mr Rajah said, in his usual bombastic fashion, "The area outside is not within our jurisdiction." Young Puckree liked the big words Mr Rajah used, and promised himself that one day he would use the same; but first he would become a rich man. After that he did a roaring trade, especially when arch-rivals Cato Stars and Mayville clashed.

By his thirties, Puckree had saved enough money to graduate to wholesaling tobacco, cigarettes, snuff and pipes from a small warehouse in Prince Edward Street, called "Puckree's Tobacco House."

Puckree took an instant liking to Chin, who went around every week to the wholesalers to deliver the books or collect statements and receipts. This service was reserved for the big clients. One day, Chin had to take the books to Mr Puckree's posh house in Stratford Road because Mr Puckree was in bed with flu.

Two palm trees stood sentinel on either side of the jarrah-wood gate. There were neat rows of hydrangeas along the edges of the manicured lawns, which flanked the cement pathway to the heavy, hand-carved mahogany door. The doorbell ostentatiously chimed "Jingle Bells" – and it certainly was Christmas for Chin when the door was opened by an attractive young lady with a much younger clone in tow, probably her sister. He stood there staring into the shimmering pools of her eyes.

"Yes?"

"Is your dad, I mean, Mr Puckree home?"

She was also staring at him, but he didn't notice. Nor did he notice the glint of mischief that danced in her eyes. "Why do you want to know?"

He realised that he was making a fool of himself with his lack of composure. "Oh! I'm sorry … I've brought the account books from Baijnath's Book-keepers …"

"Please come inside."

This was the daughter of a wealthy man, one of the wealthiest in Durban. She was way above his station, and must surely already be spoken for. The shy smile that crept over her high-cheekboned, olive-complexioned face when she noticed his discomfiture enhanced her good looks even more. She seemed far more self-assured than other girls he'd met. Perhaps one day he would marry someone like that – so beautiful, so cultured, so much in control of herself.

When Chin left to get on his bicycle, Rani peeped surreptitiously through the curtains. The young man was tall and good looking. He'd stared at her but hadn't said much beyond asking for her father. Perhaps he was already married. What a pity. Maybe not, though – he'd stared at her in a way that married men did not or should not stare at unmarried girls.

She couldn't put him out of her mind, although she was well aware that it would be unthinkable in the Puckree household to fraternise with someone who was working for her father. Her mother would have a fit. To Mrs Puckree, class and caste were the same. She would say, "You can't mix pigs with lions. God made us all different! We are not meant to mix with people like that. They must marry their own kind. Even the government says so."

That night, Rani dreamt that he was in a forest with her. He was leading the way, dancing and singing a love song to her like a hero in a Tamil film. No real-life hero had ever sung and danced so beautifully … Suddenly, in their way were thorn-laden plants and tall, dark trees that blocked the sunlight. She was not afraid because he was with her, holding her, protecting her. The dream ended abruptly. She sat up in bed for a long time, letting her thoughts wander on forbidden but titillating terrain. Ah, perhaps one day he would be rich and worthy of asking for her hand in marriage …

Impossible, impossible! Ways of life were fixed, especially for young, marriageable girls. She got up from bed without disturbing her little sister Mogie, who was sleeping soundly beside her. It was hot and stuffy and she was sweating. She tip-toed to the window, pushed aside the heavy drapes and opened it. The cool night air wafted in and she took in a deep breath.

When Chin returned, he remarked casually to Baijnath that Puckree had a very attractive daughter.

There was a strange ambivalence in Baijnath's feelings towards Chin. This was the son he didn't have. Chin was endearing in so many ways, and Baijnath looked forward every morning to his arrival. He was an excellent worker and much praise for him had come from clients. Yet it didn't occur to Baijnath that he was not giving Chin what he was really worth in wages. Still, there was a nice easy rapport between them. He believed that Chin had a great future and he didn't want anything to stand in the way of that. At this stage in the youngster's life, an emotional entanglement with no future could be a serious setback.

As "a man of the world" – as he described himself to Mr Peters and Gopal Puckree during their mutually back-slapping cocktail sessions – Baijnath looked back on his own life and how vulnerable he himself had been in similar circumstances. There remained a lingering wistfulness about not having been able to marry the young lady of his dreams. He would never forget the stolen, fleeting glances, which had evoked such deep passion within him. He'd been depressed for months after her forced marriage to someone who, at the time, was much more worthy of her station. If it hadn't been for the very practical way his parents had taken control of his life, he might have ended up very badly. He was, as he was later to recall, "in a dwaal" when his parents sought out the daughter of a reasonably well-off family in Clare Estate. He was thankful that his arranged marriage had not only worked out quite well, but had afforded him a sense of security. Knowing this, he wasn't going to let Chin destroy his life.

He called him into his office and told him bluntly, "Forget it right now. Right now. That young lady is going to get married soon. I believe the young man comes from a very wealthy family."

Chin felt uncomfortable. This man was like his father. You did not talk about your intimate feelings to your father. He didn't even know her, but he could not deny that she was the first girl to have made such a strong impression on him. He said, "I wasn't thinking of marriage at all."

Baijnath was pleased. He was right. The young man had strength of character, and a set purpose in life from which he would not be so easily swayed.

Had either Chin and Baijnath taken the trouble to find out what the girl's feelings were and what, indeed, was Mr Puckree's opinion, things might have taken a completely different turn. The young lady was very much opposed to fixed marriages, although she loved her parents too much to go against what she perceived as their wishes. She was hoping that the proposal they had recently received would not be given serious consideration.

As far as Puckree was concerned, all they had done was accord hospitality to the parents of the prospective groom. Rani, as an obedient daughter, could not show her resentment directly to her parents, so she'd sulked in her bedroom, coming out reluctantly, keeping her head down and not looking at the young man. Puckree had noticed this. Nothing had yet been agreed upon. Mrs Puckree, however, was thrilled that a family so wealthy and high-up in society was showing an interest in her daughter.

But Rani's thoughts dwelt constantly on Chin. In that exciting moment of their first encounter, Chin had aroused feelings in her that she had not known before.

Mr Puckree had taken to Chin, appreciating his commitment to his work and seeing great potential in him. Indeed, he'd told himself that this was the kind of son-in-law he would like to have, even if he had to go completely against his wife's wishes.

Chin struggled to get the girl out of his mind. At work, he applied himself even more rigorously in an effort to distract himself. Even fishing failed to divert his thoughts. He devoted a lot of time to choosing the right tackle, and soon had an excellent collection of fishing rods, reels, sinkers, hooks and varying strengths of fishing line. He spent hours cleaning and storing his equipment – a laborious and time-consuming task. He studied the tides, the different types of fish, their habitat and the type of bait that would lure them. Whenever he had the time, he went into the recently opened non-white reference section of the Durban Municipal Library and pored over the many books on fishing. The librarian, a kindly, matronly woman, was most helpful. Not many people used this section of the library, and she did all she could to encourage him. Soon he was quite an expert, and fishing was to become a lifelong passion. However, not even fishing enabled him to forget Rani completely.

It was not long before he received a lavish wedding invitation. The ornately designed card read, "Mr and Mrs Nayanaraj Guruswami of 29 Clare Road, Clare Estate (Guruswami's Transport Company) and Mr and Mrs Gopal Puckree of 46 Stratford Road, Durban (Puckree's Tobacconists) take pleasure in inviting you and your family to the marriage of Balakrishna (eldest son of Mr and Mrs N Guruswami) and Devikarani (eldest daughter of Mr and

Mrs GM Puckree) at Umbilo Temple at 12 noon on Sunday 25th November. Lunch will be served."

Baijnath insisted that a reluctant Chin attend the wedding. Chin would much rather have spent the Sunday fishing. "This is our best client. We cannot afford to upset him, so please be ready on Sunday. I will pick you up."

Chin hesitated for a moment and then, feeling a little unsure of himself, replied,"Okay, can I bring my mother please?"

"Of course you can. What a stupid question. I'd be delighted."

In the days that followed, Chin pondered what he was going to wear to the wedding. He liked clothes, and what little he had in his wardrobe reflected good taste, but until now, he'd never had any need for formal clothing. Now, however, it was something he couldn't avoid. He had to get a suit. And there was not enough money for such luxuries. Jack had his own family to care for. His other brothers, Marnie and Mike, who were working as shop assistants, didn't earn much. The rest of the children were at school. Chin's earnings went directly into the joint family coffers, leaving very little to spend on himself.

He approached his brother Jack. "Unna, I need to make a suit."

"Make a suit! You know what that costs? What for?"

"I need to go to a wedding."

"A wedding? You have enough clothes."

"Mr Puckree's daughter is getting married …"

"So?"

"Mr Puckree is one of our biggest clients. My boss insists I go to this wedding."

Jack grunted, but clearly this was something Chin was duty-bound to do and he relented – provided Chin could find a tailor who would make the suit on easy terms.

Lalla's Tailor Shop was at the bottom end of Victoria Street, squeezed between the Indian Market and the Marchenie or African Beer Hall. He went there on a busy Friday evening. The tiny shop was still unofficially open. In terms of the municipal trading bylaws, Lalla had to close his shop at five; but on Fridays, he let his special customers come in through the back door until seven.

Lalla was a slim, short man who talked a lot, laughing loudly at his own jokes. Still, he made you feel very much at ease. After he closed the front door he would provide tea and bhaja made from pea flour, spinach, curry powder or green chillies. He also kept a bottle of cane spirits, which he would occasionally share with special customers and friends.

"What style would you like, man? American Rudolf Valentino, or English Bond Street, straight from Saville Row?" Lalla showed him some different styles he had recently cut, which were waiting to be collected by customers. Chin settled on a dark-blue pinstripe with wide lapels, the type Humphrey Bogart wore in his films. The suit was cut to perfection. Lalla wasn't a tailor, he was an artist.

Early on Sunday, Chin polished his black shoes until they shone in the sun. He put on a white shirt with a button-down collar and a plain blue tie. He had imitation gold cufflinks and a tiepin with a tiny little chain. He put on his coat and looked into the mirror. Yes, Lalla was an artist.

Amurtham was excited. She was thrilled to meet Mr Baijnath eventually, and was soon in animated conversation in Hindi with Mrs Baijnath, who was virtually smothered in her heavily sequinned blue and yellow sarie and tons of gold jewellery.

Chin was fascinated by the odd bits of conversation between Mr and Mrs Baijnath.

"The girl is so pretty. I hope the boy too is pretty."

To which Baijnath said irritably, "What's pretty got to do with it? He is rich and he comes from a well-known family."

Mrs Baijanth was just as irritable. "Never mind well-known family and all." Turning to Amurtham, she said, "If girl is pretty then boy must also be pretty, isn't it, Auntie?" Amurtham just smiled, not wanting to offend either party.

The wedding took place in a tent, which didn't help in the hot, humid conditions. The groom wore a beige suit and a white turban with gold trimmings. He was full of himself, the very picture of smug contentment. Balakrishna remembered his grandfather, a tall, strikingly handsome man, telling his father, "People got no respect for a poor man. Money is first, then you can talk about life hereafter and all that. Yes, you must take the Kavadi, do the prayers and all that, but if you don't have money, there's no place in heaven for you." His grandfather had laughed heartily and laughed a lot. He'd burped and farted as he laughed, a big bear of a man with a throaty laugh.

This was Balakrishna's moment and everybody was looking at him and his beautiful wife. His grandfather would have been proud of him. He would have said, "Three things wife must have – rich family, must be good cook and must have good thighs." Rani satisfied all three requirements and more – she was very beautiful and hard-working. Yes, his grandfather would laughed, burped and farted: "Rombo! Rombo! Plenty, plenty!"

It didn't occur to Balakrishna that his bride was not as happy as he was. She wore a cream Benares sarie with a delicate gold and white floral motif. She kept her head down most of the time.

Chin was sitting in the fifth row. He tried to be as inconspicuous as possible and sat in a position where she could not detect him easily, but when he saw her he found it difficult to control his feelings. His face was hot and flushed. Astonishingly, the only time she lifted her head, her eyes immediately found his in the throng. She looked straight at him with a strange look – a mixture of deep sadness and betrayal.

He was lost in his thoughts when a booming, bombastic voice brought him back to reality. "Ladies and Gentlemen, on this auspicious occasion, it is my great pleasure and indeed very great honour to talk on behalf of the bridegroom. I have known Balakrishna from the time he was born, a most obedient son, an erudite scholar whose achievements would have been unsurpassed in the annals of academic history had he not cut short his studies to dedicate himself, with unswerving loyalty and amazing enterprise, to his father's magnificent initiative. His parents, who have scaled the heights of economic success, have every right to be proud of their wonderful son, who follows so diligently in their footsteps …"

As the pompous voice sonorously droned on, Chin caught another fleeting glance. She looked directly at him. Her eyes were moist. The look seemed to say, *All that you see now – the pundal, the expensive clothes and jewellery, the vows before the blazing havan – mean nothing. Only you and I are real, only you and I are true …*

Mr Baijnath shook him by the shoulder. "Come along, it's time for us to eat."

Chapter Four

CHELLAMMA HAD COME of age. People who met her for the first time found it hard to believe that she was barely thirteen – she looked closer to sixteen. Of course, that's when she was not in a playful mood, which was seldom. Life was fun – why spoil it by going around looking as if the cares of the world rested on your shoulders?

There had to be a special ceremony to indicate that she was now of marriageable age. A manjal neer was performed. Behind the house, a kolum or a series of patterns were drawn with coloured flour in a square of levelled ground hardened with cow dung. On this were placed the koothu velkoo and the kamatchi velkoo, brass lamps that had been brought by Karupanna's parents from India. The koothu velkoo was long-stemmed and had several wicks dipped in oil, while the kamatchi velkoo was much smaller, with a single wick dedicated to the Goddess Kamatchieammal, who, as the female aspect of God, brought light into the household. Chellamma sat on a manakatte or wooden stool at one end of the square, and oblations were made. A variety of fruit and sweetmeats – chilli bites, sweet rice and fried chick-peas (kudle) – were offered. A coconut was broken and an aalum, a container of water reddened by koongo, was turned three times around the girl to ward off destructive vibrations, which are believed to emanate from the third eye of intensely jealous or envious people.

Chin had begun to earn extra money by selling some of the fish he caught. His entire wage-packet was handed over to Jack. That was a strict rule. The only way to survive was to pool a family's resources. In a way, the traditional belief that the wealth of a family was measured by the number of sons was vindicated by this system. In "respectable" families, women were not allowed to seek paid work, and were a liability. If one person in an extended family of ten or twelve people got a job, the whole family celebrated. Now there would be something to eat and the kids could go to school.

Along with Marnie and Mike, Chin dutifully left his pay packet on the table for Jack to collect, to see to the needs of the family. But what he earned from his fishing, he kept to himself. He bought Chellamma a pair of black court shoes, her first ever pair of formal shoes. Hitherto she had worn slippers or sapath. From the family budget, Jack bought her a pair of gold bangles.

Chellamma seldom walked. She skipped through the house, ran through the yard, ran to school and was quite often out of breath. Smiles played around her almond-shaped eyes and her high cheekbones, and laughter danced around her perfectly shaped teeth.

At five o'clock every day, Chellamma would pretend to be feeding the chickens with grain, when in fact she was waiting to catch a glimpse of a dark stranger passing by. The young man was quite a bit older than she was – about twenty. Unfamiliar feelings assailed Chellamma when she saw him, feelings that bathed her in a warm glow and at the same time confused her and, for some unknown reason, made her feel guilty. Thus her studied focus on feeding the chickens was excruciatingly self-conscious.

Jack Dorasamy Govender, known as Dorrie, whose family lived about a quarter mile down the road, had to pass Chellamma's house to get to the bus stop. About a month before, Dorrie had seen her hanging up the washing. He hadn't noticed her before that. It was a bright Saturday morning and he couldn't take his eyes off her. She's too young for you, he told himself, but he couldn't resist staring.

From the corner of her eye, Chellamma became aware of someone staring at her as she hung up the clothes. She was hurrying to finish her chores so that she could join her friends in a game of hopscotch. She turned to face him and he smiled. Chellamma gaped. He winked. She blushed and ran into the house.

She felt drawn to the young man. His hair was cut short but it was still wavy, and his eyes seemed to light up when he smiled. All the neighbours, including his parents, had been invited to the Manjal Neer and knew of Chellamma's coming of age. This meant she would soon be married. While Dorrie told himself that she was far too young, he also told himself that they would marry her off anyway. There was something about this shy, smiling little girl … no, she wasn't a girl; she was a young lady. He saw himself as one of the heroes in the English films he loved to watch, saving this beautiful young woman from the clutches of some idiot. No, he would marry her. She came from a good family and it was time he got himself a wife.

He first had to find out how she felt about him. There was no way he could get to talk to her. So he wrote a little note, and one day, while she was taking the clothes off the line, he dropped it over the fence. She blushed and blushed and wanted to run into the house. When he disappeared down the road, she looked around and walked quickly to the fence. The letter read, "I like you very much. Wave your hand if you like me." She tucked the letter into her blouse and ran into the house.

There would be big trouble if the letter were found. Her brothers were all very possessive and very strong. The young man would get into lots of trouble. She didn't want that, but she had to speak to someone. The only person she felt would listen was Chin. She crept into his room that evening and shyly showed him the letter.

Chin's first reaction was, "He's got a bloody cheek!"

Sudden alarm clouded her face. He gently made her sit on the bed and asked her whether she liked the young man. She nodded shyly.

Chin smiled and said, "Then wave your hand but don't talk to him. I'll do that."

Chin didn't tell her in so many words that he didn't like what the young man had done. If he could be so forward, how could he be trusted? He decided that he would go to see him on Sunday.

The next day, Dorrie lingered alongside the fence. Chellamma smiled, waved her hand shyly and scooted off into the house.

On Sunday, Dorrie was caught off-guard when Chin suddenly confronted him. He hadn't expected Chellamma to have given the letter to anyone. Chin got straight to the point: "What's your game? Who gave you the right to write to my sister? She's still a baby."

Dorrie was going to apologise, but he stood his ground. He was not easily intimidated. He had honourable intentions, and he didn't like bullies. "I wrote to her because I like her. They say she's grown up now. All I wanted to know was whether she liked me. You can't marry someone who doesn't like you."

He wanted to marry her. That, for Chin, changed things somewhat. Chin didn't like it, but it was common practice for girls to be married off while they were very young. Besides, Chin knew Dorrie's family. They were of the same caste. He decided to put his sister's interests above his own feelings. They parted on an amicable note, provided there was no more hanky-panky. If Dorrie was really interested, he would send his parents.

Dorrie was the eldest son of Veeraswami Govender. Veeraswami's wife, Yanambal, had died when Dorrie was only ten years old and his sister Umavathi was eight. It was not long before Veeraswami remarried. Veeraswami's second wife, Meenatchi, was not too keen on the prospect of Dorrie getting married so soon. The family had grown to seven and his wages were needed to supplement the little money Veeraswami made from his market garden. She had a long chat with her husband. They were tying up little bunches of dhania with the strips cut from dried banana stalks when she said in a matter-of-fact way, "A new wife costs money."

Veeraswami tried to make light of her concerns. "Don't tell me!"

She was not be diverted by his dry humour. "Dorrie will now not be able to carry on giving us money. It will be very hard."

Veeraswami was anxious that the conversation not continue alone these lines. He said simply, "You're right."

She was persistent. "So what are you going to do about it?"

He was caught in the middle, but his wife had a point. A daughter-in-law would be an added financial burden. Much of Dorrie's wages would now go towards his own family. This would have serious consequences for the extended family's already strained budget. As it was, there was never enough money to see to things. He heartily agreed when Madramuthoo said his sister was far too young; if Dorrie was serious he could wait another two years. First, there had to be an engagement or nelengoo.

Meenatchi wasn't pleased. She had misgivings about whether Chellamma would fit in to her scheme of things. The girl appeared to have been very well taken care of – so well taken care of that she might be spoilt. A spoilt girl would need money for her vanities. She was to remain very cool towards the young girl.

There had never been enough money from Veeraswami's market garden, and Dorrie had had to leave school to go to work. His first job was as a conductor for the bus-owner, Naicker. He'd made friends with Naicker's son, Thunga, who could drive his father's car. A Chevrolet, it was the only car in the neighbourhood. It was two-tone, light brown with an avocado-green top, with white-walled tyres. Always kept in mint condition, it amply reflected the proud, extravagant tastes of its rich owner. It never failed to draw attention, especially when Naicker drove up at weddings and other ceremonies with his flashily dressed wife sporting her necklace of genuine gold sovereigns and his stuffily dressed children.

Dorrie seemed to have a natural affinity for cars, and was soon proficient as a driver. Naicker also had a garage to which cars from the neighbourhood and even as far afield as Clairwood would be brought for repairs. After work and on weekends, Dorrie would hang around the garage with Thunga. He listened to the mechanics with the kind of awe reserved for miracle men, saints and gods. Everything sank in – ball joints, pistons, bearing knocks, transmission oil, ignition … such words were poetry to Dorrie: the poetry of immediacy, real poetry. And he became more than a poet, he became a car doctor with an uncanny knack of being able to diagnose a problem just by listening to the engine.

He knew all the road signs and was a very good driver, but obtaining a licence was a different matter. The licensing inspector, a burly Englishman, acted as if he were God incarnate. His fat jowls, beady eyes and pug nose were contorted into a permanent scowl, enough to intimidate the most confident. It was whispered that one didn't have to take the test – all one had to do was to leave a chicken in the boot. Dorrie was not going to bribe anyone. He would get his licence on merit. Initially, the Englishman's provocative barking unsettled him. Dorrie had a quick temper but managed to keep it in check. He passed and was asked to come back in two weeks' time to collect his licence.

The licence was his passport to greater independence. He got himself a job as a taxi driver, and with the extra money he earned was able to improve his father's wood and iron building. A tidy structure, it was plonked in the middle of the market garden which stretched from Montille Road all the way down to a little stream at the bottom of Ashwell Road, a sloping plot of just under an acre. Only the main bedroom had wooden floors. The rest of the floors were hardened cow-dung. He bought some good second-hand corrugated iron and timber and, working on Sundays with his father and brothers, built three more bedrooms, a kitchen, a dining area-cum-lounge and a small prayer room, all with wooden floors. The cement floor of the new verandah was stained red and polished rigorously and regularly with Sunbeam floor polish. The corrugated-iron walls and roof were painted green, and the neat little cottage blended in with the mango, avocado and jackfruit trees alongside and behind it. In the front of the house stood the garden, fronted by the stream. There were rows of lettuce, chillies, beetroot, cabbages and turnip, or whatever other vegetables were in season. From frames constructed of reeds hung clusters of podlenka or snake gourds. There were also thriving pumpkin and cucumber vines beyond the rows of vegetables. On the fences along the sides of the garden hung heavily laden vines of double beans and granadilla.

Veeraswami was proud of his son's efforts. He was especially proud of his little prayer room, to which he retired for long hours to meditate. Over the years he had acquired a reputation for being a faith healer, but he was also a mantrakaran, one who could wield a mantra for good or bad. It was said that strange things happened to you if you got on his wrong side.

Occasionally, Dorrie would drive past the Govender homestead. This home was partially made of brick, although most of it was wood and iron. There was a long cemented pathway from the road up the small hill on which the house was built. A flamboyant tree spread its branches over the house. Amurtham's little temple stood beneath the spreading bows of a syringa tree. A well-trimmed bougainvillea hedge, covered with perennial sprays of mauve flowers, separated the house from the road.

Even after his parents had relented and he was formally engaged to Chellamma, Dorrie was not allowed to be alone with her, and their chief means of communication were long, lingering looks over Marie Biscuits or woorende and tea. It was obvious that both were very much in love. Dorrie grew to be firm friends with Chin, who came to respect his frankness. Dorrie taught Chin to drive, and it was during one of these lessons that Chin was given a small taste of Dorrie's whiplash temper. He had forgotten to depress the clutch while changing gear, and Dorrie exploded, "For God's sake, you'll fuck up the gear box!" Dorrie was normally mild mannered and there was always a hint of a smile on his face, but when he did get angry or upset, the expletives flowed forth liberally. Nonetheless, Chin's anxieties about his sister's future with this man soon abated.

Chapter Five

ARCHEE WAS EXPECTING her fourth child, and was becoming increasingly irritable. She felt oppressed by Amurtham's presence. The old lady never used a harsh or angry word against her, but it seemed as if she kept constant vigil over almost every aspect of the younger woman's life. Her continuous advice about everything got on Archee's nerves. When was she going to have a life of her own, her own home where she could rear her children as she wished?

Jack was a good husband, but it was time he realised that he had a family of his own. She wanted a good education for her children, especially for her eldest, Sathasivan, who was consistently top of his class. But at the rate they were going, it was not likely that the children would finish their schooling. She urged Jack to think of moving out. She didn't want to tear him completely away from his other family responsibilities, but if it came right down to it, if a choice had to be made, it had to be in favour of the children he had fathered.

Slowly, a sourness crept in. Human relations are delicately balanced: one small slip and sourness can turn to bitterness, often irrevocably. Archee found herself saying things she didn't really intend, and then being forced into a position of defending those things.

Jack hadn't expected things to turn out this way. He was caught between his obligations to his mother, brothers and sister and his love for his wife and his family. He had been the South African Champion for three years, but the gloss was wearing off in the face of his taxing, high-pressure schedule – made worse by his wife's growing irritability.

He took out his frustration on the punch bag, but was not able to focus on his boxing. In the ring you were your own master. You were alone. And you needed to be totally alert. One mistake and you paid the price. Jack found this out when fighting someone he could easily have accounted for just a year ago. A sucker punch caught him high up on the cheek – the first time he'd failed to avoid a punch to the head. His trainer was angry. "The punch was telegraphed. You should have seen it a mile away. You've never taken a sucker punch in your life. What's happening with you?"

The punch shook him but he refused to go down. He saw out the rest of the fight on sheer instinct and narrowly won on points, thanks to a big lead in the earlier rounds. He was wise enough to see that if he didn't quit soon he'd end up badly hurt. And so, as much as he loved the sport, he retired – undefeated.

But you can't retire from life. You're stuck with it, for better or for worse. Jack was caught in the middle, and somebody was bound to be upset; he dearly wished that it wasn't his wife. Archee became increasingly sullen. She did not throw tantrums, but just withdrew, drawing a veil of silence around her. Even her lovemaking became a distant, automatic act, as if she were discharging a compulsory duty. Sometimes he almost felt as if he were raping her. He tried to cheer her up with gifts – which merely evoked a patronising smile. Until one day, for the first time in their marriage, he lost his temper. "What the hell do you want, dammit?"

She didn't say anything, continuing with her work, her anger evident in the hard, swift strokes of the broom as she swept the passage. She didn't see Chin as he walked straight into a vigorous sweep.

Chin joked, "Hey Unnee, don't sweep me away too!"

Jack wanted to say, "Why the hell don't you do the

sweeping yourself?" Instead he walked out of the house, borrowed Chin's bike without asking and headed for the Indian Bar at the Mayville Hotel.

The huge hotel, set amidst rolling gardens, stood atop Mayville Hill, about a mile away. Although he'd retired from the ring, Jack was still the toast of the town. He hadn't drunk while he was a boxer, and although it was only a few months since he'd become a casual imbiber, everybody knew him at the hotel. The barman, Billy, knew Jack's drink, and the moment he walked in, a double cane and a pint of stout were thrust into his hands. The builder, Mahadeo, shouted, "That one is on me! Hey Kid, come here, sit with me."

Jack obliged, taking a seat at the enamel kitchen table, a standard item of furniture in the makeshift Indian bars. A crowd gathered around him, and in the convivial atmosphere, eased by the liberal flow of cane spirits, he felt warm and welcome.

"Kid, why don't you make a comeback?" Mahadeo pleaded. "Nobody can beat you. The fighters are no good these days. You'll wallop the lot."

The conversation turned to more serious business. "You must join our school building committee. Our children need more schools with higher standards."

"We are paying our rates and taxes," Jack said. "The government must build schools for our children, like they do for the whites."

Perumal, the truck driver, chipped in, "Huh! You think they worried? They not worried!"

Mahadeo said, "Yah, you know what these people are like. If we wait for them, our children won't get education. Look how our fathers somehow built Stella Hill School, AYS School ... the other day, I was talking to John, you know that Christian feller, he said his church – what they call his church?"

"Methodist church!"

"Yah, same church – he said if we get together and all of us collect some money, they will then help us to build a school."

That same evening, Jack became the chairman of the Cato Manor Indian Education Society.

Jack held his drink well. No matter how many drinks he'd had, he was never unsteady. Instead, he became expansive and sang a lot. He'd convinced himself that he sang well, although those listening to him didn't agree. He sang all the way as he pedalled his way home through the darkness.

An anxious Archee was standing outside, waiting for him. The moment he got off and placed the bicycle against the wall of the verandah, she embraced him, whispering softly in his ear, "I'm sorry, I'm sorry."

He held on to her tightly, and resolved to make every effort to move out of his father's house into his own home, although he really could not afford to do so. He'd heard that in the farming village of Merebank, land was cheap. A few months later, he paid the deposit, two pounds, on a third of an acre of ground.

Here he began to build a solid brick and tile four-bedroom house, with a big room in front which would become Govender's Butchery. As the months went by, building over weekends, Jack was hard put to meet the costs of construction. Eventually, he dug into the combined earnings of his brothers without their knowing. He promised himself that one day he would repay what he considered to be a loan. In any event, he consoled himself, he'd spent much of his own money on them in the past.

His fourth child, Sarojini, was ready for school and the family budget was taking strain. Jack worked overtime, even over weekends. By the time he got home he was exhausted, and although she never complained, he could see that his wife was on edge. As much as he tried to cope, he found that his own nerves were increasingly frayed.

Amurtham sensed that all was not right. She spent more time in her garden, planting large beds of dhania, mustard, brinjals, sour herbs, bush herbs and chillies. The watercress, which she planted around a shallow little pond, continuously yielded a lush crop. Chellamma and her younger brothers Iyathoray, Saminathan and Chidambaram, who was named after his late eldest brother, helped her after school. There was a growing tendency for young people to take English names. So Nadasen had become "Mike" and Manickum had shortened his name to "Marnie"; Iyathoray turned into "Freddie", Saminathan became "Steve" and Chidambaram was "Sonny". Amurtham refused to call them by their English names. "Your names come from the Panjagum. They sound so nice and have rich meanings. I don't know why people want to be like white people. It's all very stupid!"

They supplied their crops of seasonal vegetables, together with jars of mango, chilli and lemon pickles, to CN Rana's shop. Rana's Gujerati-speaking parents had been so-called "passenger Indians" – the mostly Gujerati and Muslim traders who had followed the Tamil- and Hindi-speaking indentured labourers to South Africa. With the passage of time, Rana had replaced their small general dealer's shop with a new building on the corner of Bellair and Jan Smuts. The impressive shop was bigger and posher than the other small corner shops in the district. It retailed almost everything: furniture, pots and pans, clothing and groceries. Mrs Rana was in charge of the fresh-produce section, which stood on the verandah and consisted of a few wooden racks and boxes laden with produce purchased from market gardeners. A stout, surly woman who was constantly chewing betel, Mrs Rana drove a hard bargain. She had a lot of respect for

Amurtham's religiosity. Indeed, she regarded Amurtham as a faith healer. It was only after prayers by Amurtham in her little temple that the Ranas' daughter, Shanti, was able to have a baby after four years of waiting. Mrs Rana looked forward to Amurtham's visits and paid her a little more than she did the other market gardeners.

Amurtham spent much time in her temple, engaging in elaborate rituals. There were several major festivals, which were meticulously observed: the Kavadi and Mariammen festivals, Deepavali, Pongal and Purtassi. Although both the North and South Indian communities celebrated Deepavali as their main festival, there was much debate as to its actual significance. The mythology behind the festival was the return of Lord Rama after the conquest of Ravanna and the rescue of his wife Sita, whom Ravanna had kidnapped. Rama was said to be the reincarnation of the God Vishnu and Ravanna a demon. But Amurtham had once heard a Tamil scholar, Mathiemugam, explain: "Ravanna was a heroic Dravidian king who had successfully defended his kingdom against the conquering Aryans, until another South Indian king, Hanuman, sided with Rama."

Amurtham had been aghast. How could this man talk about the Gods Rama and Hanuman like that?

Mathiemugam had continued, "You see, these things were written by people … God didn't say these things."

When somebody had objected, saying that the Ramayana was a holy book and the man had no business to talk like that, he'd smiled. "What makes a book holy?" He'd gone on to say that the highly advanced Dravidian civilization had existed over five thousand years BC. He'd said that Tamil was the oldest living language in the world while Shaivism, the worship of Siva, was the oldest living religion and a precursor to Hinduism.

This had been too much for Amurtham and the

other people listening. They'd dismissed the man for his blasphemous talk.

She'd been upset when Karupanna had agreed with the scholar. They'd had long arguments. Karupanna, never a religious man, had said, "Who can really say that God said this and God said that? Who can prove that?"

She'd scolded him that night. "God said this, God said that! God only said one thing – the truth."

A few drinks down, and Karupanna's smile had widened. "Did you hear God say the truth to you?"

"Now you see, when you drink, you talk all this nonsense. The holy books were written by man, what?"

"Then who wrote them?"

And he'd kept badgering her in his good-natured way until she'd given up. She'd gently tapped her cheeks with her crossed palms, a gesture pleading forgiveness from the Gods for her wayward husband, lifted up her arms to heaven and said, "Thapoo, thapoo!"

To Amurtham's annoyance, Karupanna had said the same things when he was dead sober, with that same irritating, patronising smile. Yet he'd happily go through with the abstinence, the oil baths and the festivities.

Karupanna had been satisfied with the explanation that Mathiemugam had given. He'd said that the mythology was unimportant; that Deepavali, like its corollary, Karthigai Deepam, which meant "a row of lights", signified the conquest of the forces of darkness or evil by the forces of light or virtue. It was meant to be a time to focus on personal regeneration. A time to re-examine one's life and recommit oneself to self-purification in order to attain moksha or liberation. "All we do is eat a lot of sweets, show off with new clothes and set off crackers. They terrify the poor dogs and cats. That's not what Deepavali means. We are supposed to think about our souls – to cleanse our souls."

Deep religiosity pervaded all aspects of their lives. When Chellamma's son, Guru, was five years old, he took a hearty swig from a bottle of paraffin, thinking it was lemonade. He turned blue and limp. They didn't have transport to get him to a doctor, whom they couldn't afford anyway. Amurtham placed him before the altar, naming him Mariemuthu, which means Jewel of Marieammen, dedicating him to the Goddess Marieammen. While everyone around her panicked, she steadfastly chanted the mantras. He slowly recovered, and from then on she would always call him by that name.

Every one of the children had to observe the Kavadi festival, a punishing ritual of penance undertaken more to propitiate the Gods than to achieve its original aim, which was to induce a sense of spirituality in order to achieve liberation from the cycle of birth and death. After the flag-hoisting ceremony at the Cato Manor Temple, the weeks of fasting before the festival were strictly observed. During the festival, hungry and tired in the heat, devotees carried wooden, flower- and lime-bedecked Kavadis on their shoulders. The heavier the Kavadi, the more devout you were. Some of the devotees had needles stuck through their tongues and cheeks, and lime was hung on hooks sunk into their chests and shoulders. The voice of Ramani Ammal singing Kavadi songs came over the loudspeakers, competing with the sounds of conches and the ringing of bells. Many devotees broke into trance. One very devout man had large hooks sunk into his back, attached to a chariot which he pulled for quite a distance. He'd been doing it for years, and not once did the hooks tear out of his flesh. It was a daunting sight for the youngsters – the hypnotic, trance-like states of the devotees, tongues sticking out, eyeballs bulging, with the high-pitched music blaring.

Like his father and his brother Jack, Chin was not particularly religious. He stopped taking Kavadi when he started work, but never failed to attend the festival. For a hard-working community who had little time for pleasure, it was also a social occasion. The district's young men and women had an opportunity at least to eye one another, if not to meet. Many a marriage began in this way.

In the full flush of manhood, Chin cut a striking figure. Over the past two years, he had filled out considerably. Every evening he did his exercises in the back yard with his brothers, on occasion even daring to spar with Jack, and his sharply defined biceps gave a hint of his well-proportioned musculature. That day, he wore a short-sleeved, cream golf shirt and pleated beige pants. He was admiring the peacocks which roamed the temple's expansive grounds when he noticed someone looking intently at him. It was Rani, holding a child in her arms. He stared, recovered himself, smiled and said a soft hello before walking off into the throng. There was no one in the crowd remotely like her.

Her secret thoughts about him were exactly the same.

His days at Baijnath's were very busy, but he enjoyed his work. Amurtham was proud of her son; on the occasions when she met the Baijnaths, she listened with deep pride as they sang Chin's praises.

"Auntie, it's time you got Chin married," Mrs Baijnath said. "Our next-door peoples are good Tamil peoples. They got two pretty girls just right for Chin. You want I must talk to them?"

Mr Baijnath, for once, agreed with his wife. "Yes Auntie, Mr Naidoo is a very wealthy man. They have a fish stall in the market and his daughters are beautiful. They have been brought up properly."

Amurtham thanked them for their interest and agreed to take the matter up with Chin. Thank God for such a good son.

At the break of dawn, beneath the custard-apple tree in the front of her home, Amurtham lifted up her arms in prayer to Suriyan, the Sun God, and gave thanks that her children were all healthy and were growing up so nicely. She gave thanks that Jack had filled the shoes of her husband so well, never mind Archee's sulking; that her two younger sons at least had jobs; that Chellamma had reached puberty and was spoken for; and that Chin had such a nice job and was such a well-behaved, obedient son.

One Friday morning, Chin, who was always punctual, got up late and rushed to work, forgetting the lunch which his mother packed every morning. He only realised this during lunch hour, when his empty stomach growled. He'd not had a proper breakfast, just gulping down a cup of tea before rushing off on his bicycle.

With his pay packet in his pocket, Chin walked into the non-white section of the café next door. It was Baijnath's practice to hand out wages to his staff at mid-morning tea. It gave him much pleasure and indeed a sense of power to see their faces light up when they received their envelopes. Today, Chin had torn open the packet, the first time he'd ever done so. There was a very strict rule that the only person allowed to open the pay packets in the Govender household was Jack. Chin didn't have any objections, but he felt that on this occasion his brother would understand. All he was taking out was a shilling to buy a duff cake and a pint of milk, which he gulped down hungrily.

That evening he left his pay packet together with those of his brothers on the dining-room table as usual. It was a large mahogany table, which Karupanna had bought at a bargain price from a second-hand dealer who was a friend of his. The table, covered with a large doily tablecloth which was replaced with a linen tablecloth during meals, was in the middle of the large room which served as both dining room and lounge. Ornate mahogany chairs with wicker seats and ball-and-claw legs were pushed close to the table to make room for the aging settee and easy chairs. A large paraffin lantern hung from the supporting beam in the ceiling of the corrugated-iron roof. On the wall was a large painted portrait of Karupanna, with his handlebar moustache, looking sternly at the artist. It was completely out of character – Karupanna had seldom been without a smile on his face. On the opposite wall was a sepia photograph of Karupanna seated and Amurtham standing next to him, and next to that a photograph of the entire family taken a year or so before he died. In these pictures, he had his trademark smile. Overall, the unmistakable impression one got when entering the room was that Karupanna was watching you.

The table was a symbol of the family's unity. Around it, over meals, major decisions were taken and important issues discussed. On this very table, Chellamma's proposal had been sealed over cups of tea, freshly fried vade and goolgoolahs. Within the consciousness of the Govenders there resided a firm commitment to what the table stood for: they were a family, and all other considerations took second place.

Jack emerged from his bedroom, towelling his hair after a hot sponge bath in the outside bathroom. It was a daily ritual for Archee: at about four o'clock she would chop the wood, light an outdoor fire next to the bathroom and start boiling the water in a huge paraffin tin. When Jack arrived, he'd bring the hot water into the bathroom, as well as a tin of cold water and a third, empty container in which to mix the two. Occasionally, he'd throw in some leaves from the notchie shrubs next to the bathroom. This, together with pine leaves, was used especially after women had given birth to refresh and heal stretched skin. The notchie leaves were soothing and gave the water a pleasant aroma, not unlike the heady smell of freshly cut grass.

Jack picked up the three pay-packets. One of them had been opened, the first time this had happened without his permission. Jack seldom raised his voice. He called for Chin in a matter-of-fact way, giving no indication of his feelings. "This is your packet, isn't it?"

"Yes, Unnah."

"It's open. Who did that?"

"I did."

"Why?"

"I was hungry – I forgot to take my lunch."

It was so swift, Chin didn't see it coming. The palm of the former South African champion's right hand smashed into the side of his face, staggering him. As he steadied himself, he gripped the back of the chair. In an instinctive reaction, he was about to lift the chair and hurl it against his brother. He struggled mightily to keep the chair down, saying to himself, "This is my brother, my elder brother, I can't do that." Instead, he stared at Jack for a full minute. It was a moment mixed with malevolence and regret. Amurtham and Archee screamed and ran between them.

Chin walked back to his bedroom, foregoing his evening meal. He locked the door, not responding to the entreaties of Amurtham, Archee or even Chellamma.

The next morning, as usual, Amurtham and Archee got up to make the lunches. Jack and the others took their lunch parcels and went to work, but there was no sign of Chin. An hour later he was still not up. Amurtham and Archee went to his room. They forced open the door. He was not there. Something was wrong, something was wrong. Amurtham couldn't stop the keening sound that emerged from deep within her as she hurried to her temple to light the lamp.

He would come back, he would certainly come back. He had so much going for him. Such things happened all the time. A family quarrel. Anger. A little violence. These things happened. They happened all the time. God knows, life was a struggle. You were lucky to be alive, to be well fed, to have a roof over your head. He was doing so well at his work. Mr Baijnath had said that he was going to make him a partner in the business. Surely he wouldn't throw all that away.

That night, the family talked and talked into the early hours of the morning, seeking comfort in such easy rationale, trying to quell the gnawing doubts. No, no, he would come back, he would come back …

He didn't come back. Not the next day nor the next. They went to the police. There was absolutely no sign of him. Someone whispered the unmentionable: could he have committed suicide? Suicides were not uncommon in Cato Manor.

Jack went to the Mayville Police Station. The station lay to the west of Westridge, the crest of the Berea, where the palatial homes in park-like gardens on the gentle eastern slopes were bordered by the uniformly soulless suburban homes of lower-middle-class whites running down into the valley to the west. Even the warbling of the huge variety of birds that frequented these parts failed to lessen the intimidatory nature of the station – evident in its sharply rectilinear architecture and the permanent scowls of its police force. Conversation flowed easily in the main hallway and reception area, reserved for whites, with the odd guffaw. As you passed by on your way to the small non-white section, you felt immediately like a trespasser, and unconsciously hurried to remove your alien presence without attracting too much attention.

Jack was of a different cloth. He didn't hurry. He walked into the little non-white charge office at the back. Behind a large counter sat two policemen, one white and the other Indian. Both seemed preoccupied. After a while Jack cleared his throat. The Indian constable got up and approached the counter. He recognised Jack and his face broke into a smile. "Hello Kid, what happened?" At the word "Kid", the white cop looked up. "Sir, this man is a champion boxer," the Indian cop said.

The white man was impressed. "Really? You must be a different kind of coolie. Champion, eh?"

Jack said quietly, "Not any more." And before the conversation could continue on those lines, he added quickly, "Have you heard anything about my brother?"

"What's happened to your brother?" the white cop asked.

"He's missing from home."

The Indian constable took out the station record-book and began paging through it. The white cop smiled, "Ag man, you people worry too much. How long has he been gone?"

The Indian constable looked at his book again. "You reported him missing Sunday the tenth."

Jack became impatient. "That's two weeks, and you people have done nothing."

The white cop stood up, "Now listen here, just because you's a boxer, you don't talk like that!"

Jack knew he was wasting his time. He was tempted to invite this bully outside, but he turned and walked off.

As he walked back home in the gathering darkness, he was assailed by feelings of guilt. He had been too hasty. Chin was a good brother. He'd worked hard and till that moment had brought his wages home intact. That was the first time he'd stepped out of line. Jack argued with himself: he'd had a job to do. There were so many things to be seen to, so many expenses to be met ... for the first time, he was angry with his father. Such a big family and so little money. What was he to do? The guilt stayed. What if his brother had committed suicide? He would never be able to forgive himself. For the first time in his life, he prayed: "Please God, let him be alive." But suicide was a very real possibility.

Amurtham wouldn't entertain any such thought. Neither would Chellamma, whose pillow was wet with weeping. Every moment of her waking life, Amurtham prayed silently: He's alive, please Muruga, he's alive, my son is alive …

Chapter Six

For the weeks and months to follow, in the first self-conscious bungalows slowly replacing the pioneering, rude lean-tos of corrugated iron, in temples, mosques and churches, in CN Rana's Bazaar, at the Cato Manor Sports Grounds, at the Mayville and Berea Hotels and even in the Cato Manor Cemetery, there was whispered and not-so-whispered speculation. How could a man disappear into thin air just like that? Had Chin taken his own life? Had he jumped into Durban Bay, or into the still, dark waters of BM Singh's abandoned bluestone quarry? This lay in the wooded valley below the huge BM Singh Mansion, now deserted because of the evil spirits which were said to roam its impressive halls at midnight. The legend – and Cato Manor was full of legends – was that a suicide's body never surfaced once it hit the water of the fathomless quarry.

"I heard his bro bust up his face – he lost two front teeth. Hell man, that Jack can hit. You don't fool with him."

"He must have jumped in the bay …"

"Nah, Chin is not like that!"

"What you know? When somebody does that to you, you'll like it, what?"

"Not to take my life, hell!"

"It never happened to you, that's why you're talking like that. You remember that chap, Butchna? He didn't think twice about his small son and daughter and his poor wife. He jumped in the bay when his brother gave it to him, remember? It took so long to get the body."

"Yeah, but Chin's not like that. He's strong."

"Then where's he? Tell me, where's he? So long now he's gone …"

"Yah, they must do the funeral prayers, otherwise his spirit will be going all over the place."

Chellamma heard the whispers. She gritted her teeth. Chin was not dead! Never! She shook her head as if to shake away the dreaded thought, but it wouldn't go away. When Dorrie tried to comfort her, she read his unspoken thoughts and almost resented him for thinking that way.

Her brother was not dead. He couldn't be dead. Yet if he was alive, why had he not even written a letter to them? It was simply not like him. He'd been so considerate all his life. She treasured those court shoes – the best present anybody had ever given her.

The spring in her step was no longer there. Her friends had to drag her into games of hopscotch, three-tins or five-stones. Even then, she didn't seem to care whether she won or lost. This was a girl who in the past had not been above cheating to win.

One Friday, weeks later, Amurtham told her to wash the lamps.

"Amma, we're not going to do those prayers, huh?" Chellamma said.

"What prayers?"

"For the dead …"

"Hush child, he's not dead, he's not dead … I told you, you must use the lemon – no need to squeeze, just rub the lemon on the lamp …" And Amurtham turned away to hide the tears that welled up instantly in her eyes.

Then, after wiping her eyes, she held Chellamma tightly to her bosom – the way, long, long ago in Thanjaoor in faraway India, her own mother had held her when she'd had to let Amurtham go away with Karupanna to this strange land. It seemed so long ago, so long ago when she'd run through those paddy fields with frogs hopping out of her way and little fish frantically swimming away in the pools around the rows of rice plants. She would help to catch the fish to make nethli, dried fish, which came in handy whenever drought came over the land … yes, it had been hard, but home was home and she'd dreaded going away with Karupanna, for she was still a child and this strong, strange man was taking her away from her mother, from her home, from the paddy fields and the coconut palms which her brothers had climbed with such triumph, waving their hands as they reached the top to pluck the ripened coconuts. Still she would often hear echoes of her father's strong voice leading the family in songs in praise of Siva and Muruga, the old man's strong hands caressing the keys of the harmonium as her eldest brother's nimble fingers and sure palms wrought a pattern of beats on the thubla, while she kept in tune with her tiny cymbals. Their small temple, shrouded in the heady scents of the special incense that they couldn't get in South Africa, had rung with those stirring songs – now just nostalgic echoes serving to bring some balm to her troubled spirit, trying so hard to take root in this hostile land of so much sorrow, so much grief … *Muruga, my son is safe somewhere, Muruga watch over him, keep him …*

In that confusion of dreadful thoughts and meditative prayer she worried, too, about Chellamma. Did this child, who was to marry soon, have the strength that Amurtham had been blessed with, to bear the wretchedness that was life? Yes, yes … It was not all pain, she chided herself, lest she upset the deities with her ingratitude. She'd had such a wonderful family back home in India, and her husband had turned out to be so strong, yet so caring. She cherished those times of love, when his abiding humour was like a staff to lead them through life's many vicissitudes. On the steam boat, which took weeks to get to Durban, the women had been separated from the men, even their husbands. She remembered the night when Karupanna smuggled her into the lifeboat and his strong member entered her loins as the boat rocked gently on the dark ocean …

Chellamma was so … childlike. Indeed, she was hardly a woman, although all the physical signs were there. A woman needed to be strong, God knows, to raise a family. She worried that Chellamma didn't seem to have that strength. Yet who would have said, all those years ago, that Amurtham would discover such strength within herself? When the time came, one acted. There was nothing else to it. You faced your moments of sorrow and your few precious moments of happiness and you got on with life. You had no choice. That's the stuff that Chin was made of. He would never commit suicide, not Chin, not her son. Never.

They had just emerged from the temple, Amurtham carrying the pot of sweetened rice sprinkled with diced almonds, raisins and cinnamon, Chellamma with the kudle and the fruit, when they came running to her. A body answering to Chin's description had been found, hanging from the Hanging Tree in Umhlahli. Amurtham dropped the pot and the still-steaming rice fell heavily, the lumps of mushy grain scattering on the ground.

Even as awful thoughts assailed her, she clung to the hope that this was yet another false alarm. There had been three such alarms, and each time they'd visited the mortuary, there'd been huge relief when they found that the body was not Chin's. But it had to be done; they had to get to Stanger. They heard that the dead man looked very much like Chin, tall and sturdy with curly black hair.

Jack had taken much time off from work these past few weeks, following up leads. Wally Davis, his boss, was always sympathetic and understanding, but not so Wally's partner

Ian Barrow. Ian was a hard-working man and he expected the same from his workers. He often argued with Wally for being soft on them. "How many times has that chap been off lately?"

"He's looking for his brother ..."

"That's his business. Not on our time."

"He's feeling very guilty about it ..."

"I've heard that story a thousand times. You're too soft on that coolie."

Wally had to agree that Jack's absence had been affecting the business. Orders were too often delayed and that cost money. As much as he felt for Jack, this couldn't go on indefinitely. Wally called him aside. "Look, I'm sorry, but your constant leave-taking is not good for the business."

Jack waited for the weekend – just a day more. On Sunday they took the train to Stanger. Amurtham had insisted on coming. When Jack objected, she said, "I'll pay my own fare." It was said, Jack felt, in an obliquely accusing way. It was useless to protest. How could he convince his mother that his actions were in the interests of the family, when he couldn't convince himself? The guilt tore into his conscience. Sleepless nights were plagued by terrifying thoughts. He once woke from a nightmare in which Chin was screaming as he hung on a rope from the ceiling of their house.

Amurtham had packed some lunch. As the train clattered through the rolling hills of the lush Natal coast, not even the bright sunshine or the miles of sugar cane, fresh green leaves wafting gently in the balmy breeze, could take their minds off the grim task ahead of them.

At the mortuary, the surly Indian policeman, accompanied by an equally surly Indian orderly, resentful that they had to work on a Sunday, didn't say much. Jack was upset by their attitude but he kept his feelings to himself.

The body lay on a metal table covered by a dirty white cloth with large blood stains on it. The feet stuck out from under the cloth. Amurtham gasped – but she knew immediately that those were not her son's feet. When they lifted the cloth to expose the unfortunate stranger's face, the relief on Jack's face was apparent.

They ate their lunch at the Stanger station. On the way back, although they were silent, they could take in the vast sweep of rolling hills of sugar cane, interspersed with occasional clumps of trees, as the train wound its way home.

Chapter Seven

HE WALKED ALONG the highway to Pietermaritzburg. It was seven in the morning, and the chill of early winter was just setting in. Unlike the perennial green of the coast, there was a dryness in the Midlands, a clear delineation of the seasons. Malnourished cattle munched forlornly on rat-patch tufts of dry grass, tended by equally malnourished, barefoot herdsmen clothed in ragged hessian. The aridity of the landscape heightened his growing feelings of despair.

Chin did not have a penny in his pocket. All he had were the clothes he was wearing – the long-sleeved white shirt, grey pants, black socks and black lace-up shoes that he'd worn to work the day before. He hadn't slept, so he hadn't changed. He'd sat silently in his room all night, not responding to the knocks on his door, pondering his next move. All he'd wanted to do was to get away – to where he did not know.

He'd made his move when he was convinced everyone was fast asleep. He'd left the small change he had in his pocket on the dressing table. Even in the heaviness of his heart, the fleeting thought had crossed his mind that Chellamma could use it to buy herself some liquorice, her favourite sweet. For a moment before he opened the door, his thoughts had dwelt on Chellamma's face, her effervescent smile, her teasing, giggling naughtiness. Chin had struggled to rid himself of the images that swarmed through his mind. He'd gripped the knob firmly and turned it as carefully as he could – it tended to creak. He'd always intended to oil the lock but had never got down to it. Thankfully, this time it had turned with hardly a sound. Hearing the somnolent sounds of his sleeping household, he'd closed the door behind him, stepping out into the night.

Some distance before Maritzburg, an off-ramp read "Richmond". Aimlessly, he branched off. As dawn broke, it warmed up somewhat. His legs began to ache and he felt tired. He stopped and sat at the side of the road. A truck was coming past. He stepped in front of it and the truck braked sharply. The driver, a middle-aged white man, got out angrily. "You got a nerve, coolie! You could have got yourself killed."

Chin stiffened, but he quickly took control of himself and looked sufficiently apologetic. He said, "I'm sorry sir. I need a lift." It was the first time since leaving school that he'd called anybody "sir", and it grated, but he needed a lift badly.

"For shit's sake, you could have got me killed too!"

Chin again apologised. The white man was looking at him intently. This was no vagrant. "Where you going?"

He had no idea. He mentioned the first place that came into his head: "East London."

As it turned out, the truck was going to East London and the driver was actually grateful for the company. On the seat between them, Chin saw some oranges. He couldn't stop looking at them. The driver noticed. "Go ahead, help yourself."

He voraciously downed two oranges.

"Visiting someone?"

Chin needed to talk to somebody. What the hell, this was a stranger. He told him the full story.

The driver came from a different world. "You mean to say that your brother was in charge of the money you were earning? I've never heard anything like that." But he also said, "You seem to have been a very close family. Your mother must be worried to death."

Chin agreed. "I want to get a job, and then I'll contact her."

When he'd closed the door behind him on that fateful day, there'd been just one thought in his mind. He would only contact his family again or return home when he was his own boss, completely independent. Nobody, not even his own brother, would ever push him around again.

Was his sole mission in life now to even the score? For the resolute, for those whose pride will not entertain any other thought, retribution is a waiting game. The hurt lies dormant, apparently dead, deep within the psyche, at once a strength and a weakness. But sooner or later it will have to show its head, whatever the toll, whatever the pain. His mother was right: stubbornness was second nature to him. Chin had been humiliated and deeply hurt. He needed to vindicate himself before his family. It didn't occur to him that he might hurt many people in the process. He just could not see, or perhaps didn't want to see, the sorrow and pain he was bringing to the people he loved, especially Chellamma and Amurtham. He was going to save all his money and eventually own his own business, even if it took many years. Just what sort of business he wanted to own, he didn't have a clue. Opportunities were few and far between and there were very few jobs around. That was of little concern. He was on his own and on his own he would make it.

The driver said, "You're one helluva stubborn coolie! I suppose that's not surprising, considering your brother's a boxer. First time I've heard of a coolie boxer. I thought all you people were mad about religion, like that troublemaker, what's his name? … Gandhi!" The driver had decided he liked this Indian. "Look, I don't know what job you're looking for, but I know the owner of a hotel in East London. I'm sure he'll be able to help. They say coolies make good workers. The hotnots are no good, they drink too much."

Chin didn't like those words, "coolie" and "hotnot", but he was in no position to argue.

The Royal Hotel was close to the beach. It was a modest ten-bedroomed hotel built in the Tudor style, a piece of Olde England, built to keep out the cold. It also kept out the sunlight. Chin had been given a position as a wine steward.

His first day on the job was a disaster. Saloon doors divided the lounge-cum-dining-room from the private bar. He was serving four people in the lounge, and diligently wrote down their order: two Castle Lagers, a double gin and tonic and a double brandy and coke with lots of ice and a slice of lemon. Chin read out the order smartly to the barman, placed the drinks on the metal tray and confidently strode towards the swing doors, the tray balanced on one hand and the other poised to push open one of the doors. The high-ceilinged bar was lit by a dim sixty-watt bulb and visibility was poor. He didn't notice that the carpet had worn through, so that the edge stuck up unevenly … Chin tripped, the tray went flying and he catapulted through the swing doors. It took a great deal of control to avoid colliding into his customers who, after an initial jolt, broke into guffaws as he landed on the floor.

The hotel owner, David Fulham, ushered him back into the bar, livid. He bellowed, "That was fucking stupid!"

Chin was quick to apologise, "I'm sorry, I didn't see the torn carpet, I'm sorry …"

David didn't let up. "When you carry drinks, you've got to watch your step, not the fucking ceiling. That's simple common sense!"

Chin practically got down on his knees. David was not a hard man, and relented. However, Chin did not receive his first week's wages. It went towards defraying the cost of broken glasses and spilled drinks. He swore that he would not make another mistake.

Before long, he'd settled into a comfortable routine. The job was a piece of cake. Within a few months he'd graduated from wine steward to waiter. His gracious smile was always at the ready. His quick, efficient service and his intelligent remarks about the food, the weather or the latest news made him popular. The regulars asked for him by name. One of the perks was that breakfast and lunch were provided; he ate in the kitchen with the other members of staff.

Chin walked barefoot to work, holding his shoes and socks in his hands. When he got to the hotel, he went round the back, washed his feet and put on his shoes and socks. They were his only pairs and they had to last a long time. He saved every penny he earned, hardly spending money on himself except for packets of Needlepoint Tens cigarettes, which lasted him a week. Every now and then he bought second-hand Western novels, especially the ones by Zane Grey. For two weeks he slept on a park bench, newspapers his only protection against the biting cold.

The fat, jolly coloured cook, Wilhelmina, took to him. She laughed at everything and he could not help laughing back, feeling completely at home in this stranger's presence. She was aghast to learn that he was sleeping out in the open.

One evening, Wilhelmina took him to visit her sister Mary, whose house was about a mile away. It was a pleasant walk, with Wilhelmina passing him many compliments – how nice and wavy his black hair was, how good looking he was and what a nice man he seemed to be. His ego swelled, but he felt somewhat overwhelmed by her gushing compliments; all he could say in response was that she was not bad looking herself, although it was not quite the truth. There was a charming innocence about the way she lapped up the compliment.

They were soon out of the well-ordered white residential area. For a moment, as they took a sandy path through the bush in the darkness with Wilhelmina's torch showing the way, he suddenly felt lonely and homesick, wondering what Chellamma was up to. Of all people, he missed Baijnath.

Some dim lights emerged out of the darkness and he could make out the outlines of several neat cottages. They were in a residential area. He wondered whether he'd fit into this strange environment and whether the people would accept him.

The Johnsons were a religious family; Mr Johnson was a lay preacher. Mary welcomed him warmly and they sat in the kitchen around the coal fire. She quickly made some coffee and brought out the homemade biscuits. The Johnsons had seen a few Indians before, but this was the first time they were actually talking to one. They politely plied Chin with questions, frequently punctuating his tales of life back home with expressions of amazement. "You mean the sardines actually jump onto the shore?"

Chin grinned. "Hundreds of them!" He did not tell them why he'd left home.

The Johnsons accepted him as a boarder into their modest but neatly kept home. He stayed in an outside room, with its own kitchen and bathroom, which had been standing empty for some time.

He did not eat beef or pork in deference to Amurtham's beliefs, although Jack and his other brothers had no such inhibitions. On Sundays, the only time he ate at home, Mary made succulent roast lamb. Mary Johnson was in her early thirties and, like her sister, full of fun; unlike Wilhelmina, she was quite pretty. Slightly plump, she had a far more shapely physique. Chin suspected that she was not half as religious as her husband, Peter, a hardworking, God-fearing man whose speech was littered with quotations from the Bible.

Peter didn't quite like it when he heard that Chin was not a Christian, but kept his feelings to himself. Right now, the few extra pounds in rent were a big help. He felt drawn to Chin and soon became quite fond of him. One day he would bring this lost soul home to the Lord Jesus.

When they'd grown more familiar, Peter wondered why Chin, such an intelligent man, was doing such a lowly job, "You should be a teacher or something."

Chin said that in Durban there had been no schools to further his education. He had to start somewhere, Chin said; he didn't tell them about his previous job and why he'd left so suddenly.

At work, he was always ready to serve, a hint of a smile playing on his face. Patrons' requests were greeted with "With pleasure" or "Certainly!" He was the epitome of courtesy, but despite the odd forced smile he was not a subservient, grinning idiot like many of his fellow waiters. His pleasant, obliging manner won over the patrons, even the most difficult. Soon the tips from satisfied customers amounted to more than his salary. One patron, a crusty, seventy-year-old businessman from England, told Fulham, "That Indian of yours is marvellous! He goes beyond the call of duty."

Another patron, a hotel owner from Port Elizabeth, gave him a huge tip of one pound. She told him, "If you ever come to Port Elizabeth, I might have a job for you." Unusually for a white lady, she'd hugged him. The smell of her perfume lingered in his nostrils long into the night, and as he sank into grateful slumber he wondered what it would be like to sleep with a woman like that.

One evening, when he'd just gone to bed, he heard a light tap at his window. Parting the curtains, he saw Mary motioning him to open his door. She darted inside. Awkwardly holding his hands, she said, "Peter is away at a church meeting. I thought I'd spend some time with you alone. You don't mind, do you?"

Behind her obvious self-consciousness, there was no mistaking her intentions. It was the first time a woman had held him like that. It was an awkward moment for both of them. He tried to control his shaking hands as he offered her a cigarette. Wordlessly they lit up. She sat on his bed. He stood over her, holding out the ashtray. She gently took it away and placed it on the chair next to the bed, where he kept his Zane Grey and his reading candle. At the same time, she took his hand and pulled him down next to her. She was breathing heavily as they awkwardly clasped each other. She held him to her fulsome breasts and then pulled him down as she sank back on the bed. Speech was difficult. He tried to think of something to say.

"What about Peter?"

"Don't worry ..." She didn't seem to know what to say either. She eventually got out the words, almost unintelligibly: "I'm tired of this ... I've tried to be a good wife, but it's hard, it's hard – and you're so good-looking." Before he could reply, her lips were on his, hungry, her sensuous, probing tongue searching the recesses of his mouth. All restraint left him. The self-consciousness and awkwardness gave way to uninhibited fondling. He found his hand wandering beneath her flimsy evening gown. She was not wearing any underwear.

Chin tried to look normal when Peter greeted him the next day. Alone in his room, he was swamped by feelings of guilt and anxiety, which receded the moment Mary entered. Her cheerful presence was infectious and made it seem all so normal.

Once a week, Peter would be away at his church meetings, and Mary made a habit of coming into Chin's room. One day, Peter had forgotten to take his church files and he rushed back. Fortunately, they had not yet begun their love-making – Chin had grown blasé enough to finish his cigarette first. Peter found Mary standing in front of Chin's doorway, Chin leaning against the wall, smoking.

It didn't strike Peter that there was anything wrong. She'd probably taken him some tea or something. Yes, that must be it … but he was troubled by the startled look on his wife's face … Peter tried to put the uncomfortable feelings out of his mind.

Chin needed what Mary gave him. There was much more to it than the sex, although Mary was a sexually attractive woman. She was just as extrovert as Wilhelmina and just as ready to laugh, but underneath that often simple facade lay a compassionate and understanding nature. He hadn't mentioned why he'd left home, but she seemed to sense his loss, his emptiness, his loneliness. Their encounters did much more for him than satiate a physical need. His self-respect had taken a battering that night when his brother had slapped him, and he was still in a state of shock and confusion.

He grew to be very fond of Mary, but their relationship was fraught with danger. Chin did not want to be caught in a dead-end relationship. This was his first really close liaison with a woman and he felt it was getting too intense. He thought of her most of the day. He also thought of Peter and her children. It just wasn't right. One day, while he was having his lunch, Wilhelmina said, "My sister likes you very much, you know." Perhaps he was imagining it, but it seemed she knew what was going on.

Then Peter began to notice things he hadn't noticed before. The special look on Mary's face whenever Chin was around; the extra attention she paid to him. One evening, he turned back after setting out for his regular church meeting. Mary wasn't home. He tiptoed to the outhouse and peeped through the window.

The next day Peter visited his brother Andrew, whom he hadn't seen for ages. Andrew was a huge, burly man who ran a shebeen. Peter thoroughly disapproved, and the brothers had parted many years ago. Andrew was taken aback at the visit. He respected his brother's views, but he'd had to make his own way in a tough world. Now he listened with growing anger.

The next evening, when Chin answered a knock at the door, a fist almost as big as his face slammed into his jaw from out of the darkness. As he lay semi-conscious on the floor, a boot thudded into his ribs, again and again. Then everything blacked out.

When Chin regained consciousness, he found himself in a hospital ward with a broken jaw and three broken ribs. It would take several months for his wounds to heal completely. In the weeks he spent in hospital, Chin only had two visitors, Wilhelmina and his boss. It was Wilhelmina who told him the news: Mary had accused him of rape. She planned to lay charges.

Chin's trusting nature had again led him into a mess. Could he have foreseen such an eventuality? He should have known that people will go to great lengths to save their own skins. He should have read the signs when, after their intimacy had been firmly cemented, Mary had joked about Peter's sexual inadequacies, saying that Chin was so much more of a man. While he had to admit that he'd felt pretty good about that, he hadn't been comfortable with the way she discussed her husband. Didn't she have a tinge of guilt? Even so, there was another side to her. She was kind, considerate and genuine in so many respects. He tried to convince himself that she had not turned against him on her own. Despite his shattered emotions, he felt he should give her the benefit of the doubt. It was likely that she'd been heavily pressurised.

In his bed, alone, deserted and comfortless, Chin stared into the darkness. Rape was a serious crime. He could land in jail for a long time. Instead of becoming wealthy and making a name for himself, he was suddenly facing ruin and disgrace. It would kill Amurtham if she ever got to hear of it. He cursed himself for being so stupid. Everything had suddenly become hopeless. He was, as Zane Grey would put it, staring down a barrel – except this was not fiction. He could not afford a lawyer. For the first time in his life, he turned to prayer, albeit with wavering intensity. Was God listening to him? Was there a God, anyway? Was it wrong to entertain such thoughts? Surely, if there was a God, he couldn't be so small-minded. The sequence of discordant, contradictory thoughts was absurd, but still, he endeavoured to pray. He wished so much that he had his mother's absolute belief. If nothing else, it would serve to bring some comfort to his troubled mind.

In the end, Mary did not press charges. Perhaps she felt guilty. Chin wished he could talk to her, at least to say how much he felt for her and how grateful he was for all she'd done for him. But it was best to stay far away. She was a sad, pitiful figure. Her marriage was in tatters, and the small village they lived in had become a hell-hole of biting gossip from which there was no escape.

But the Johnson family would not let him get off easily – it was a matter of family honour. After the beating, before he lost consciousness, his attacker had threatened him: "That hiding was nothing. When I finish with you, you'll wish you were never born!"

In the depths of his despair, despite his wavering faith in the divine, Chin had still been able to summon a familiar resolve. For some time now, he'd been thinking of moving elsewhere to get a better job – East London was a small town and there were not many opportunities. He had to get out quickly. Perhaps that nice lady who'd given him a one-pound tip would give him a job in Port Elizabeth.

David Fulham was disappointed, but he understood. He said with a wry smile, "If you want to get on in life, stay away from married women!" He readily gave him a splendid letter of reference. Chin left by train over the weekend.

Chapter Eight

AT THE RAILWAY station, Chin asked the porters if he could leave his luggage in their storage rooms. The black porters looked puzzled. No black man had used this facility before – it was normally for whites. He went to the station manager but was rudely told that there was no place. Chin was at his servile best: "Sir, I know how difficult your job is, and I'm prepared to pay."

"You damned right it is, especially putting up with you people …"

Chin placed a ten-shilling note on the desk.

The man bellowed, "It costs one pound for a week!"

Chin was ever so polite. "Oh no, sir, that's for you. I'll gladly pay the one pound also."

The man's scowl disappeared. This smartly dressed and well-mannered Indian had money.

For three days, Chin wandered around, looking in vain for a place to stay. There were no hotels or boarding houses for "non-whites". He shaved and washed at the station and slept in its shabby non-white waiting room, but he had no place to bathe. The smell of stale sweat rose faintly through his suit as the days progressed, and he felt mightily uncomfortable. At night he lay awake in contemplation. The future looked bleak, and he cursed himself for being so reckless. He wished he were back home.

Then someone told him, "Why don't you go to South End, where the Indians stay?"

As he entered South End, for the first time since his arrival he began to encounter a few Indians, and immediately his feelings of loneliness left him. Most of PE's small Indian population lived in South End. Except for a few Gujerati and Muslim traders, the rest of the Indians, mostly Tamils, were either waiters or barmen or in the fruit- and vegetable-hawking business.

Chin went house to house, lugging the suitcase containing all his worldly belongings. Without exception, the people were warm and friendly. They seldom had visitors from Durban, and offered him whatever hospitality they could. The Rungasamy family insisted he stay for lunch, but they did not have room for a boarder. It was Monday, the day of Shiva, when Tamils abstained from meat, alcohol and sex, and the dinner consisted of veggies – in this case, potato, herb and sugar-bean curries with dhall and rice. Chin had been eating pies and sandwiches, and the hot meal was most welcome to his curry-addicted palate. Over lunch, Mrs Rungasamy insisted that he spend the night with them, if he didn't mind sleeping on the floor in the lounge. Chin expressed his gratitude.

Mr Rungasamy said, "I know some people two streets from here who may be in a position to accommodate you. They are a very nice couple in their fifties. They have a big house and I'm sure they'd welcome you. We'll take you there tomorrow evening, when they are home from work."

The next evening, the Reddys welcomed this tall, striking figure from Durban into their home. They warmed to him immediately and listened with utmost politeness. They were generous people, especially Mrs Reddy, and were prepared to put him up for nothing. Mrs Reddy said, "Ayo thumbi, you are one of us. How can we turn you away or take money from you? We got plenty place and you can eat what we eat."

Mr Govindappa Reddy didn't seem entirely happy with this, but didn't object. The Reddys had no children of their own and the entry of this young man into their household was most welcome.

Mrs Reddy sold fruit and vegetables from a stand near the harbour, while Mr Reddy worked as a senior counterhand and clerk in a busy Portuguese restaurant. Mrs Reddy employed a young Xhosa girl, Mabel, to assist her both in the home and in her business. Mabel, who had been with them from childhood and could speak Tamil fluently, was regarded as a daughter. The Reddys also spoke Afrikaans with many of their customers. It was a strange experience, listening to an elderly Indian woman in a sarie, wearing the traditional botu on her forehead, speaking fluent Afrikaans, complete with guttural sounds – a total contrast to the pebble smoothness of Tamil.

Chin soon decided that he would have to learn to speak Afrikaans too. Throughout the Cape Province, the language was used more frequently than English. His facility with Zulu, which he'd learnt from Jack and from the kids in Cato Manor with whom he'd played football, enabled him to pick up a smattering of Xhosa from Mabel. He was fascinated with the click sounds and soon mastered them. He would click away at Mabel and she would click right back, in between hysterical bouts of laughter.

Chin put on his best suit, a readymade one almost like the hand-tailored one he'd worn to Rani's wedding. He'd bought it from Stuttafords in East London. As he dressed in front of the mirror, his mind wandered, dreaming of what life might have been had Rani not been forced into marriage, had his brother not laid a hand on him. He would not have done that to a younger brother.

Yes, life was hard and every penny counted. The family was large and the demands were several. Food, clothes, school books … a million and one things and they all cost money, and there was so little of that around. You had to be very careful with how you spent your money, or you could end up like some families in Cato Manor, destitute and in pitiful need of charity, easy victims of disease or, in the case of a desperate few, swallowed up in dissolute lives. Still, that was no excuse to hit anybody, to rob them of their dignity. He shook off the swarming feelings of self-pity and anger and brusquely wiped his moist eyes, angry with himself at his momentary weakness. No, he was going to do it. Damn it, he was going to make it even if it killed him.

The bus service was much better than in East London, and the bus stop was only a few yards away from where the Reddys lived. Chin boarded the bus into town. Asking around, he eventually located the Hotel Cologne, which was some six miles out of Port Elizabeth, in a posh residential area with splendid views of the sea. The beams from the lighthouse at the entrance to the harbour flashed regularly on its whitewashed walls, ghostly in the silence broken only by waves lapping the nearby shore.

It took seconds for Mrs Schmeling to recognise him, and she flashed him a surprised smile. "David must be an idiot to let you go. There aren't enough trained people around."

Trained people. He smiled. Nobody had "trained" him. What he knew, he'd learnt on the job. It wasn't a difficult job, except for the long hours, and he had plenty of time on his hands. Of course there was a job for him. He could begin immediately as a barman in the ladies' bar.

Chin didn't count the hours or the sweat. One regular imbiber called him "Speedy Gonzales". Another said that he was much faster than the previous barman. "He was always so slow. The kind of guy who'd be late for his own funeral."

Chin winked. "He's a wise guy. Actually, I'd like to be about a hundred years late for mine!"

Oh sure, he was aware that many of the patrons regarded

him as something of a freak, a charming one but a freak nonetheless – Gandhi, Satyagraha, snake charmers and all that, and here he was serving drinks. Alcohol! Gandhi and alcohol, smirk, smirk!

Chin knew that, apart from giving the world the concept of nought, his forebears had also been among the first to brew alcohol. Mathiemugam and his father, during their many drunken soliloquies on the glories of the Dravidian civilisation, didn't separate the two. The discovery of the process of fermentation as one of the gifts of nature, his father would have said in choicest Tamil, was every bit as illuminating and rewarding as the numbers system which seemed to underpin life in its entirety.

Although sensitive enough to constantly resent the stereotype, and proud as he was of his heritage, Chin never allowed himself to be carried away by the romance of his ancestry. He'd learnt and learnt fast that life had a habit of bringing you down to earth. On two occasions, he felt his hackles rise at racial innuendoes and blatant insults from the odd surly customer – whom he would have chastened with his fists, if he'd had his way. Rather, he learnt to deflect them harmlessly. In any other situation, he would have reacted as his father or Jack would have done. Once, when the non-white section of the trolleybus to Mayville, four rows of back seats, was full, Jack had led him to the next empty row, which was reserved for whites. The white conductor had been livid. "Get back to your section, coolie!" Jack had knocked him unconscious and pressed the buzzer. They'd got off at the next stop without the driver knowing what had happened. It had become a family point of honour – you just didn't "take crap from a white man".

But now it was a question of survival. Chin had learnt that there was no alternative, if he was to make it in life, but to stick it out, no matter how galling the remark. He responded with as much dignity and civility as possible. He did his job, but shit if he was going to call another man "sir". He called his customers by their names, and did it with a disarming smile, which had shed its earlier hints of being forced. It now began with his eyes, the epicentre of the genuine smile. It was genuine not because of any special qualities of the customer, but because that's the way he'd become used to smiling; it came easily here, in what he sensed was a much more secure and stable situation.

It took a while for the regulars to get used to a "man of colour" not addressing them as "sir". One of them, "Budgie" Steenkamp, so named because he looked so birdlike, complained to Mrs Schmeling: "That coolie thinks he's Lord Muck. He doesn't know the word 'sir'. Teach him."

She just smiled. Some months later, Greta Schmeling recalled Budgie's remarks with a laugh: "My first reaction was to tweek his beak!" As it turned out, "Budgie" grew to like Chin so much that they got to be on first-name terms.

Even when Chin got into a brief exchange of blows with a particularly nasty customer, Mrs Schmeling said nothing. The enraged man had lost his temper after Chin had refused to wipe the counter when the man had "accidentally" spilt his drink. Chin was prepared to take a lot, but this was too much. He said quietly, "Do it yourself." The big man leant over the counter and grabbed him by his shirt. Chin pulled himself free and ran from behind the counter. They went at each other until the customers pulled them apart.

The other customers, surprisingly, sided with Chin, some even applauding him for standing up to "that bully". Despite a resulting black eye, Chin felt good that he hadn't backed down. Greta Schmeling pretended that she didn't know of the fight.

He saved most of his pay, making enough from tips for his day-to-day requirements. Although the Reddys objected, he regularly bought meat and groceries and did odd things around the house, like fixing the plumbing and repainting the interior. In his spare time, he went fishing. The fishing was excellent all along the PE shoreline and in the nearby Fish River, with plenty of shad – called elf in these parts. Mrs Reddy was always thrilled at his catches, especially the large crabs, which were plentiful at the river mouth. She made a nice crab curry. Tucking into the hot food, he felt a twinge of nostalgia. As good a cook as Mrs Reddy was, she could never match his mother's cooking.

He wondered about his sister Chellamma and prayed that Dorrie hadn't got up to any mischief. The contradiction bothered him. Was it okay for him to have got up to mischief with Mary, but not okay for Dorrie to get up to mischief with his sister? Most people wouldn't give a damn about such contradictions, and he was angry with himself for being so "sensitive". It was something his mother had once said to him. It had stuck in his mind, making him uneasy in such situations.

The rituals Amurtham regularly performed hadn't meant much to Chin. Neither had the festivals and ceremonies, which bored him and seemed meaningless. He'd taken part in them largely out of consideration for his mother's feelings. He was not, however, untouched by the spiritual atmosphere these observances induced. He had a sense that something was hovering over him, ready to put him in his place if he did something wrong, although he couldn't really picture it; but there was more to it than that. Once, his mother had said in her matter-of-fact way, "You can bluff everybody else but you can't bluff yourself. That is what God is." Those words had puzzled him at first, but the more he'd thought about them the more he'd realised that his mother had a more instinctively profound grasp of spirituality than her steadfast observance of meaningless rituals would suggest.

At times his "sensitivity" was a hindrance, and he was irritated with himself for not being more like many of the people he encountered. Most people did things that suited them, things that were of immediate benefit to them. It was not a question of being deliberately dishonest or anything like that, but if you wanted to get on in life you couldn't be a saint. You had to deal with the world on its terms. Yet the thought was always there – "You can bluff everybody else, but you can't bluff yourself." That, perhaps, had helped to carry him through his ordeal with Mary.

Even so, he swore to himself that if Dorrie didn't play the game with his sister, he would have to answer to him. If anything would bring him straight back to Durban, it was that. But the thought was absurd. He had no way of knowing what was going on back home, given that he'd cut ties with his family. He consoled himself that Dorrie had made a firm commitment and seemed a decent chap, if just that little bit arrogant.

One day he would be back with his family, but there were things he had to do first. He knew what he wanted. He'd steeled himself against failure, and he had no illusions. The odds were against him, but life was a gamble anyway. If it didn't work out, he didn't have much to lose. He would simply return, quite sure that old Baijnath would welcome him back. That would be the very last option, one that would further humiliate him but that was available nevertheless.

All over the country, there was far too much competition for jobs in the factories and hotels, and the few white-collar jobs which "non-whites" were allowed to take on. The faceless majority were unskilled, and labour was cheap.

But Chin had been told that, in the Cape, the rewards for someone like him were much better, and you could work half as hard as you did in Durban.

It seemed to Chin that although people in the Cape were poorer, they were a lot happier. They didn't seem as bothered about who you were and what your race was. In Durban, the English, the Indians, the Zulus and the coloureds kept to themselves. This wanting to be together as a group, this feeling of being more comfortable with "your own kind", was perhaps helped along by the English conservatism of the province, and was evident in the racial exclusivity of the Indians and the ethnic pride of the Zulus. Chin felt uneasy when he encountered attitudes of racial superiority from any quarter, and there'd been many times he'd wanted to say, especially to his own people, "You can't speak to people like that!" Why hadn't he? He couldn't really say.

Back home, people didn't smile so easily; they seemed to wear their cares on their faces and on their shoulders. Life was a dead-serious business. The "non-whites" in the Cape seemed, on the surface anyway, a lot more easy-going, not so hung up about their backgrounds. People just mixed, and this had been going on for generations. As Chin saw it, they fell in love, let the juices flow and what the hell! The general bonhomie appealed to him. This was the way he wanted to live his life: just letting things be, enjoying things from day to day – but that would come later. For the time being, it was work, work, work. He put almost every cent he earned into his savings.

One day, before he could open the bar, he was called to the office. Greta Schmeling was sitting behind her desk. She was dressed to go out; her tasteful pink chiffon blouse was slightly revealing. A subtle, expensive French perfume touched the air. The natural curls of her auburn hair hung free around her longish neck. Although the widow was smiling, Chin was a little apprehensive. He hoped that he hadn't got himself into any trouble. He couldn't remember having done anything wrong. Perhaps the hotel was having some problems. It couldn't be financial – the occupancy rate was always high, the bars were busy and the kitchen wasn't doing badly. It might not have been as busy as the Royal Hotel, but it was making money. At some stage, he would speak to her about how David Fulham organised his kitchen. Besides the excellent menus, David had full control – there was very little loss or wastage.

She asked him to sit. "Are you always so serious?" she asked, smiling. The slight lilt in her voice made him feel somewhat relieved, but he didn't know how to answer the question.

"No," he ventured.

"I called you in to tell you how much I appreciate your work. The ladies' bar takings have increased since you took over. Either the other barmen were doing a bit of pinching, or they were just bad barmen. You're very good."

"Thanks, Madam."

"Don't call me Madam. My name is Greta," she said with an odd smile. "For God's sake, you make me feel like some old … like some old bossy type."

Chin didn't know what to say.

She continued, "I'm not that old, you know. Do I look old?"

"No, no you don't look old at all," he said quickly. "You look, you look very … nice, very pretty." He was not being entirely honest. She was not pretty in the conventional sense, but also not unattractive; although her squarish jaw gave her a touch of masculinity, she had a shapely figure.

A faint blush rose to her cheeks, and she was smiling even

more now. "Thank you, Chin, you're a real gentleman – a good-looking one too."

Chin felt buoyed, but all he could say was, "Thank you, Madam."

"You call me that one more time and I'll fire you," she giggled.

He felt much more at ease, and laughed also. "Okay … Mrs Schmeling."

"I said my name is Greta …" She came over to where he was sitting, putting her arm on his shoulder. "You're so … so nice."

He got up with another "Thank you". She stood where she was, close to his chair, so that as he rose, his face almost touched hers. He could smell her subtle perfume. The effect was arresting. She looked directly at him, smiling, her deep blue eyes fixed on his. His pulse quickened. Struggling to steady himself, he stepped back. As he moved towards the door, again saying, "Thank you", she took him by the hand.

"I also called you in to tell you that from the end of the month, your job as a barman is over."

He would have gone into shock, but for the way she held his hand. Still, this must be pretty serious for him to be called in the middle of work.

Her smile was like her touch, reassuring. "From the end of the month, I am making you manager of the hotel." She explained that she'd fired the previous manager, who'd been stealing her blind. "I will spend a month with you in this office, taking you through the routine and all the things you have to do. Your salary will be two hundred pounds a month."

Chin stared. Greta laughed, "Don't I even get a thank-you kiss?"

He leaned forward nervously and kissed her on her

cheek. She held his face in her palms and placed her lips on his, her tongue gently probing his mouth. Despite himself, he found his hand wandering to her thigh. She whispered into his ear, "Not now … later."

She asked Chin to move into the hotel into the previous manager's suite, rent free.

Chapter Nine

THE REDDYS WERE clearly upset that he was moving. He tried to reassure them that he would visit them at every opportunity, and they could do the same. They were family. Of course, they were very pleased at his success, and told everybody in their neighbourhood. For an Indian to be given such a position was honour indeed. Mr Reddy said, "You must be the first Indian manager of a white hotel. It's a feather in the cap for our people. We are very proud of you, my son."

There was great excitement in the hotel the day he moved in. The black staff were elated – for a "non-white" to get such a position was quite something. Michael Mbele, the doorman, greeted him heartily in the morning, but with a touch of irony: "Mr Chin, now you're a big man – now I must call you baas!"

The irony was not lost on Chin, who was a little bit defensive. "Thanks, Michael, but I'm not your baas. See my skin, it's the same as yours. Don't you ever call me baas."

That first night in his en-suite bedroom, he luxuriated in the private bath for a long while. When he came out of the bathroom with only a towel around his waist, she was there waiting for him, sitting on the edge of the bed. She wore a pink silk gown with a feathery collar, and her perfume wafted through the room.

Chin was annoyed with himself for feeling nervous. He ventured an embarrassed "Sorry!" and turned his back to her as he reached for his briefs. He started putting them on underneath the towel, but before they reached his knees, she was holding him gently from behind. She untied the towel and as it fell to the floor she let slip her gown. She wore nothing underneath. She pushed down the briefs with her slender leg, and he caught a glimpse of her slightly curved thigh between his hairy legs. Holding him gently under the arm with one hand, she caressed his groin with the other. He could feel her plump, firm breasts against his back. Her breath was hot against his neck. He turned around and, holding her around the waist, buried his head in her breasts, his tongue working its hungry way up to her eager mouth. Locked in each other's arms, they fell on the bed. He tightened his grip around her in answer to her soft entreaties, "Hold me … hold me … hold me." He was ready but she held back, gently whispering, "In a little while … just kiss me, my darling, just kiss me." Then slowly her legs parted. His hand could feel the warm wetness …

Chin retained his easy informality with the staff, but they soon came to realise that he would not tolerate slackers. Some of the staff who'd been in cahoots with the previous manager had been having it easy. He soon put an end to that. Proper controls were adopted, and this raised the ire of Sam, the unofficial food and beverages stock clerk. "Are you trying to tell me that I haven't been doing my job all these years?"

"No, I'm not saying that. But we are changing the old system."

Sam couldn't change his old ways. He was caught out when two blocks of butter were not accounted for, and was asked to collect his final pay packet.

Michael Mbele approached Chin. "Mr Chin, Sam has been working here all his life. He has a big family. This will be very bad for them. Give him another chance."

It sounded more like a demand than a request, and Chin didn't like his tone. "You know, Michael, I also come from a big family. We were also very poor, but we did not steal. If I give him a chance, it will be bad for the hotel."

Michael's tone hardened a little more, breaking through the practised veneer of servility – this was an important issue for him. "When people are poor, when they have families to feed, they sometimes do things that they wouldn't otherwise do. You can't condemn a man for that."

Chin had known that kind of poverty, and Michael made sense. He replied, "I tell you what, I'll give him another chance, but he won't be doing the same job. If he can drive, I'll give him a job as a driver."

As it turned out, Sam could drive. Michael was satisfied. "Mr Chin, you're not a bad man. One day we must sit down and have a long talk." He said this in a measured way, as if what was to be talked about was of great import, beyond mere personal concerns.

"Yes, we must do that, Michael – but now I need a food and beverages manager. You're really too clever to be a doorman. I'm making you the manager. I've spoken to Mrs Schmeling and we'll teach you everything you need to know. You will also receive a much better wage."

That night, when Michael went home, he told his wife, "Soon we'll move out of this house into a better one."

He'd expected Naomi's cynical laugh. "Where are we going to go? Everybody knows you as a native. You act like a native. I don't know why. You're a coloured like me, but you insist on being a native, on keeping your mother's name … my sisters laugh at me."

Past taking offence at an oft-repeated jibe, Michael smiled in his disarming way. "Don't you love me?"

Naomi had been through it countless times and she knew it was pointless, but she still said, "Natives cannot own land. We cannot own a house."

"I got a promotion," Michael said. "We can afford to rent a nice place. This place is not good for our children. The area is bad – no water, no lights and the people are always drunk and fighting."

Naomi was going to say that he'd cut his own cloth and now he had to wear the suit, but she stopped herself. Although she often didn't agree with his politics, she loved him. And even if she couldn't fully understand some of the things he did, she would, despite her nagging, stand by him to the death.

Sadly, Michael had to admit to himself that there was little he could do to change Naomi's fixed ideas. But the children were responding: one day they would take their place alongside the other cadres. No need to rush them. Imbued with socialist ideas, Michael often had to stop himself from lecturing his family in the manner in which he lectured young cadres in the movement. He knew he had to talk to his children in a different way. They were still far too young. He tried to point the way, lovingly, allowing them to absorb often lofty ideas. Their time would come.

The changes at the hotel had the desired effect, and for the first time the kitchen began to show a tidy profit. There was no set time for stocktaking – Chin would walk in at random intervals and do a stocktake. That way, the barmen could not bring in their own stock to sell. Michael was quick to learn, and the losses that the bar had been showing for years came to an end. However, Michael reasoned with Chin, "These chaps are bringing in their own stock because their wages are low. How about giving them incentives?" It was a good idea.

Soon there were two signatures on the hotel's cheques, Greta's and his. Once he'd signed, she signed without checking. Greta was a realist. She knew the temptation was great – a couple of pounds here and there would not be noticed. Surely only a saint could resist? As long as Chin wasn't overdoing things. After all, it was largely through his efforts that they were showing such nice profits. Nonetheless, despite this freedom, Chin fought the temptation.

The feeling of being wanted, of being loved, perhaps for the first time in her life, had given Greta a new lease on life. She left everything in Chin's hands, including important tasks such as the annual renewal of the liquor licence and the banking. One of the sweeping changes he made was to increase the wages of the staff, particularly the unskilled workers. Greta didn't object; indeed, she went further, raising Chin's wages by fifty pounds. Their profits had increased substantially since the new measures had been introduced, and the raises hardly made a difference. As was to be expected, the staff responded with enthusiasm.

She visited his suite every night, not always to make love. "I just love cuddling up to you," she said. They made every effort to keep their relationship a secret. While their rooms were not next to each other, they were not far away – a brisk walk down the passage and she was there. She kept the hotel's duplicate key and would enter his room late at night, leaving very early in the morning when there was no one around. It was the perfect arrangement – but love is not easily hidden. Soon little things were noticed: a stolen glance, a tender word, a special look, Greta's anxiety when Chin was away longer than expected. The gossip began, as it always does, with a word planted quietly in one ear and then not so quietly in the next. It was still mere gossip and speculation. Their behaviour in public, for the most part, was very proper. Both were conscious of the "abnormality" of their relationship – firstly, she was white; secondly, she was older; and thirdly, they were not married. Amurtham would be aghast.

He wondered how his family were doing, and felt tempted to write to them. He said to himself, "No, no, not now – only when I'm ready. Only when I can stand up in front of my brother and tell him: 'You want money, here's money – don't hit people for money, don't rob people of their self-respect for money' … only then will they know that I'm alive, very much alive."

His reading habits had undergone a sea change. He read almost everything he could get his hands on. Zane Grey had become predictable and boring, and he discovered HG Wells, Somerset Maugham, Charles Dickens and even Thackeray in a stack of old books in the hotel. He developed a voracious appetite for the works of the Romantic poets. His spirits soared when he read such lines as, "Full many a flower is born to blush unseen and waste its fragrance on the desert air …"

He seldom worked on Sundays, spending time with the Reddys, or fishing – trying his hand at his own poetry while waiting for a bite. His rhymes were laced with sentimentality and nostalgia.

He used the hotel's bakkie to move around, although Greta insisted he use her car when she was not using it. He was a good driver, thanks to Dorrie, who had shown a great deal of patience in teaching him. He bought several rods and had a wide range of fishing tackle. There weren't as many fishermen here as there were in Durban. He sought out those places that were hardly fished and made some impressive catches, which he shared with the Reddys. The hotel's refrigeration facilities were very handy. He soon discovered a small Gujerati shop which sold spices from Durban. He introduced Greta to fish curry, which he made himself. Starting off mild, it was not long before she was enjoying it quite hot.

One of his regular customers was a Mr Richard Turnbull,

a divorcee who lived alone not far from the hotel. He would walk to the hotel every evening for his favourite tipple, Scotch on the rocks. With his rosy cheeks, he looked as if he had walked out of a whisky advert. His limit was usually three doubles, although over weekends it would be four or five. Chin suspected that the old man, full of good humour, was not really keen on returning to his lonely home. His wife had left him long ago for someone else and his only son had died in the war. He'd never remarried. When the old man had had one too many and was in no condition to walk home, Chin would drive him. Turnbull was very grateful and a bond developed between them. Once, when quite inebriated, he muttered, "It's funny, never thought a coolie would be my friend … my good friend."

One day, after a few drinks, he said to Chin, "I have a smallholding in Sandflats. I bought it for my son." Sandflats was about thirty miles out of PE and was what its name implied, flat and sandy. "It's a poultry farm, and there's a small income from the cottage. It has five bedrooms – a solidly built farmhouse. I want to get rid of it. I'm saying this to you because you're young and you can't beat investing in property. Let me know if you're interested."

Chin hadn't considered investing in property, but the old man had awakened an interest in him. He discussed it with Greta. She thought it a good idea. The next day, he asked Turnbull what the price was. He said, "I just want to get it off my hands. It cost me six hundred pounds about twenty years ago. I'm sure it's worth much more now. I'll let it go for eight hundred – to you, not anybody else."

Chin drove out to the farm with Turnbull and fell in love with the place immediately. He'd done some investigating, and from all accounts it was a bargain. A few evenings later, after the old man had had his drinks, Chin asked, "Do you want cash for the farm?"

The old man was in an expansive mood. "Look, my boy, I really don't need the money. I have enough. I just want to get it off my hands. You can pay me as you want."

Chin couldn't believe his luck. He paid Turnbull a deposit of two hundred pounds, and thereafter instalments of twenty-five pounds a month.

Chin immediately put the rent up. It seemed to him that the tenants were making good money and that the rent was far too low. Naturally, the tenants weren't happy. They couldn't understand how Mr Turnbull could have sold the land to an Indian instead of giving them the first option. Turnbull felt that they hadn't been good tenants, quite often making him wait for his money, and he suspected that they'd been living very well off the farm. Chin was polite but also firm: they had no choice but to pay the increased rent. If he had to, he could easily get other tenants. This way, he was not only able to pay the installments without touching his own wages, but also to make a small profit.

Turnbull got to visiting Chin in his office, where the waiter would serve his drinks when Chin was not busy. Turnbull was never pushy and always polite; he just liked Chin's company. He would knock at the door and invariably say, "Just throw me out if I'm a nuisance or if I'm disturbing you."

One day he didn't knock. The door was open and he walked in and sat without even greeting Chin. When Chin greeted him he just nodded his head. Chin called the wine steward, who brought Turnbull his drink. Turnbull stayed unusually quiet. Eventually, after a few drinks, he said, "I don't mean to pry, but what's this talk about you having an affair with Greta?"

The directness of the question unsettled Chin. His flustered reaction was, "Who told you that?"

"Never mind who told me, is it true?"

Chin had no choice. It was a straightforward matter: if he told the truth over this relatively innocuous matter, two lives, at least, would be thrown into turmoil. He tried to sound convincing: "No, definitely not."

"You're not lying, are you? It's not good, this mixing of the races. You know I like you a lot, but I'm sure you wouldn't want your sister to marry out of your race. Like marrying an African, for instance. You Indians are good, hard-working people. You have your own customs and I have nothing but the greatest admiration for your people. That's why you are my friend. That's why I practically gave you the farm."

Chin was in no mood to argue with the old man, but this put a different complexion on their relationship. It became harder to laugh at Turnbull's lame jokes. He told Greta one day, "That old man's jokes are as bland as the food you Germans cook!"

A few weeks later, he heard Turnbull tell a fellow customer, "I'm voting for the Nats in the next election. They won't win, but you mark my words, they'll win the next one. The Boer War is over, we English must accept that. This country needs taming. The soft approach is no good. The Afrikaners have the right attitude – they are a strong people. No nonsense with them. The blacks are uncivilised, they're not our equals. There must be laws to keep them in their place."

The English, soft? Chin laughed inwardly. He recalled something that Michael had said. It was one of those rare moments when Michael, with his easy disposition, talked with a measure of seriousness. He was usually given to laughing and joking. Michael had said that the United Party hid its iron fist in a velvet glove. Michael's whole visage had changed to a sudden, transient steeliness when he recalled that Africans had been deprived of their land through the Native Land Act of 1913. They could not own land outside their demarcated reserves, which amounted to a mere thirteen percent of the land mass of the Union of South Africa.

It was a fleeting moment, revealing a side to Michael's character that Chin hadn't seen before. He had never before encountered an African who could talk with such knowledge. Chin had not known that the land of the natives had actually been taken from them through law. The way Michael put it, Africans had been robbed. Chin hadn't seen it that way before. He'd always had the greatest respect for wealthy white businessmen, industrialists and farmers. If someone worked hard, surely they were entitled to the rewards? Still, it was a political issue and he was no politician.

That night, he told Greta about what Turnbull had said. She exploded, "That pig! This is my hotel, this is my life. It's got nothing to do with him! I have a good mind to ban him. The right of admission to this hotel is reserved."

"You do that and we're in trouble. We've just got to be careful."

"These people don't own our lives!"

But Greta knew she could not ignore the threat, and soon agreed with Chin that they had to be more cautious.

As usual, the weekend was busy. Michael had not reported for work on Friday. When he didn't arrive the next day, Chin got worried. It was simply not like Michael – he'd never stayed away from work for a single day. Chin waited until Monday. There was still no sign of Michael. Something must be wrong. Chin found out where he lived and drove there with the bakkie.

Chin was surprised to find a run-down cottage. Although valiant attempts had been made to make the house as presentable as its neighbours, Chin somehow just could not picture the suave, well-dressed Michael in such conditions. Michael's wife, Naomi, politely asked him to sit in their neat front room, which was a bedsitter. Chin looked around. On the wall there was a photograph of man, with a caption that read, "Sol Plaatje, First General Secretary of the South African Native National Congress". On a table were a few books, one of which was called *Das Kapital*. Michael had never given any indication that he read such important-looking books.

Naomi was alarmed. When Michael hadn't arrived home, she'd taken it for granted that he'd slept over at the hotel, as he sometimes did. Chin drove to the police station. They had received no reports. He drove to the mortuary. Yes, they had a body that answered to that description.

Michael's body lay on a slab. He'd been stabbed to death. It was a mystery as to who stabbed him and why. Chin went back to the police station. He told the African constable in the non-white section, "They told me at the mortuary that you were the people who brought his body there, and yet you told me that you had no idea."

The constable looked through his book and said in a uninterested way, "There was an unidentified man who was stabbed on Thursday night."

Chin was angry. "Why didn't you people tell me that before, and why haven't you notified his family?"

The constable raised his voice. "I said it was unidentified."

It was useless. Chin drove back to break the terrible news to Naomi.

Michael's death drove home to Chin that the lives of his fellow countrymen were shrouded in deliberate anonymity through a single-minded political will. Michael had lived in this run-down cottage in a poor coloured area because Africans were not allowed to own property in the developed areas. Chin did not know that he'd lived in even worse conditions before his promotion. He also did not know that Michael was, officially, a coloured, but had chosen to affirm his African roots, despite the great cost of such defiant action.

Greta agreed to pay for the funeral expenses. At the funeral, a representative of the Communist Party made a speech in which he praised Michael for being a staunch member. He had done much work in organising a branch in his area. Chin had no idea that Michael had such strong political affiliations and beliefs.

Greta didn't like communism, but went out of her way to see to the needs of Michael's family. There was no insurance of any sort, but she promised to help pay the fees of his two sons and daughter who were still at school. Chin was pleased that she was such a caring person, and later that evening told her so. They gave the boys part-time jobs at the hotel. The girl, Grace, was still a child, but Chin told Naomi that she was welcome to do work at the hotel when she grew up.

It took some time for the death of her father to sink in. The first time Grace had experienced death was when she was three years old. She had vague memories of the funeral of her eldest brother, Welcome, who'd died during the ceremony to initiate him into manhood. His wound had turned septic after the circumcision. Until that moment, Naomi, who was also of mixed parentage, had gone along with Michael's wishes that they adhere to traditional African beliefs. When Welcome died, Naomi had returned to Christianity with a vengeance. She didn't want the same thing to happen to her remaining two sons. Naomi often spoke of her eldest born. He was a sturdy child who had been doing well at school.

With his work and other commitments, Michael had spent little time with Grace. He'd always been working or attending meetings. The only time they'd been together was on Sundays, when Naomi would nag him to take them to church. Sometimes, on weekdays, when he got home early in the evenings, he would take Grace on his lap, with her brothers sitting at his feet, and tell them stories in the candlelight until they fell asleep. A story that Grace particularly remembered was the one about Nongquause – the Xhosa princess who'd been told in a dream that her people should burn their crops and bury their cattle, and that the ancestors would rise to drive the white man into the sea. Her father said that the cunning settlers had exploited the superstition of the Xhosas by planting and spreading the story, thus breaking the back of the strong Xhosa resistance. "Before this treacherous act, our people had been fighting back, although they only had spears and a few guns."

Grace remembered how her mother would scold her father. "That kind of talk is no good. The children must worry about their education, not politics. They must read the Bible. You must stop putting these ideas into their heads."

Michael never got angry. He'd just smile and say, "Even your Christ said we must fight against injustice."

Grace's brother, Peter, would agree loudly, "Yes, we must fight against the mulungus. They have taken our land!"

"You see what you have done to the child!" she'd say angrily.

Michael would just hug Peter proudly, smiling at Naomi.

It had been a big day for them when they'd moved into a better house next to Indian and coloured families.

The coloured owner was not prepared to spend money on renovations, and could not get Indian or coloured tenants. When Michael came along, the owner had been only too pleased to lease it to him. The house had two bedrooms, a lounge, a kitchen, a bathroom and an outside toilet. Michael had spruced up the interior, fixing the plumbing and painting the walls. He'd just begun attending to the exterior when he was killed.

Before they moved in, Grace had never been inside a real bathroom. She loved it so much that when it was her turn, she took her time, making the others in the family angry. She loved to scrub herself thoroughly and soak in the bath.

That first evening, Naomi had said, "That boss of yours is a good man."

"Yes he is. He said I must not call him 'baas'."

"He is a different kind of Indian."

Michael had grinned, "What do you mean?"

"Well, he's not mean … he doesn't have a beard and he isn't rich."

Michael had laughed mightily. "Not all Indians wear beards and not all of them are mean. We should not judge people by their race. That is the way we are being judged …" Grace knew he'd been about to get on his soap-box again, but had stopped himself.

Grace had met this "different kind of Indian" when her father had once taken her to the hotel. He and the white lady had been very kind to her. They'd given her ice cream and a half-crown. She'd showed off the coin to her brothers. Peter had chased her around the table for it and accidentally pulled down the doily tablecloth, upsetting the vase of flowers. Naomi had made him stand in the corner right through dinner time.

Three weeks after the funeral, the house had returned to some kind of normality. During the ceremonies, there had been many people around and lots of activity. Grace sat alone in her bedroom. It was suddenly very quiet. It was then that the full realisation of death crept into her consciousness. She would never ever see her father again. She would never again hear his booming voice, his hearty laughter. Never ever. She wept softly.

Chapter Ten

It was Friday. Amurtham began the morning as she always did: first, a hot bath before the sun rose. With her long wet hair tied with a towel into a bun, she put the dhall, which she'd cleaned the day before, into a pot of water and placed it over the fire. It would take some time to boil. Next, she said a prayer to Suriyan. Then, together with Mike's daughter, four-year-old Mama-girl, following her, she placed grains of sugar at all the ant holes in the grounds around the house. All life was sacred. Then she prepared some sweet rice, after which she swept the dung-hardened yard around her small temple.

The temple was behind the house, on a higher level. A small stairway of loosely packed bricks led up from the back door of the house. The temple itself was a tiny room of brick and cement and could only house one person at a time. A huge syringa tree towered above it, and all around grew a profusion of sacred tholsi and wild rose. In front of the temple was a raised mound of earth which served as an altar. The pathway around the temple was daubed daily with cow dung, which dried quickly in the hot sun. It was autumn and the huge syringa tree was shedding its yellowed leaves and dried berries, some of which clung stubbornly to the twigs.

Amurtham's midday prayer to Muruga lasted an hour. With sambrani and incense smoke swirling around the temple, she chanted her mantras, ringing the small bell. Then she stood silently in meditative prayer, her mind focussed on her son, Chin. She had not lost hope. She prayed he was still alive, and vigorously pushed down the frightening thoughts that rose up. *Please, Muruga, help him, wherever he is.*

Jack had moved out to his new house in Merebank. Once more there was a vacuum in her life. Again the household would never be the same. And once more Amurtham turned to prayer. She also tilled the soil with a vengeance – as much vengeance as her increasingly arthritic limbs would allow.

Her third son, Marnie, was doing something else with a vengeance. He was saving every penny he could, scrimping but not scrounging – he was too proud to do that. But pride is seldom accompanied by compassion. All he saw when Amurtham knelt over her lush watercress was more money from Mrs Rana. He didn't notice the jabs of arthritic pain that shot through her limbs and made her straighten up every so often. When one is preoccupied with getting on with one's life, one seldom notices the pain of others, even loved ones.

Soon Marnie aimed to pay the deposit on the "goodwill" – the business rights – for a small tearoom in Bellair Road. It was a big risk, because as well as installments on the goodwill, he still had to pay the rent.

Much to Amurtham's disappointment, Marnie had made a young girl, Chinma, pregnant. Chinma had come from Clairwood to work for them. Her father had lost his job as a municipal worker and Amurtham had taken pity on the struggling family. She'd agreed to take on Chinma as a helper, although she really didn't need help. Amurtham made sure she ate well and had given her some of her old clothes. She even paid her a few shillings whenever she could. And now Marnie had gone and done this. Chinma was the same caste as them, but a working girl was a working girl. There was no way out but marriage – something for the neighbours and certain members of the family to gloat over. Marnie was over the moon – he loved Chinma. Amurtham bore this indignity with her usual stoicism.

Marnie kept his day job as a shop assistant, while Chinma tended their own shop until he got home in the afternoon. They worked long hours, with barely time for the one meal a day they allowed themselves. It was tough going, but they were prepared to scrimp. Chinma was even more vigilant in watching every penny. As Archee sarcastically remarked, it was the first time Chinma had seen so much money and she wanted to hoard it all. Late into the evening, she'd count and recount the money. The sound of jingling coins in the biscuit tin was music to her ears. Within a year, they'd paid a deposit on the small property on which the shop was situated and had moved into the two rooms and kitchen behind the shop. The rental from the remaining room helped them pay the bond.

Jack continued contributing his share to Amurtham – more than the contributions of the others. Archee said, "Your brother now has a shop. Surely he should be giving more and giving you a break. He only has one child. You have done your share."

Had he done his share? Jack was the eldest. It was expected of him to carry the reins in the absence of his father and his older brother. Was he doing that? He'd tried to, and look what had happened. Chin had disappeared.

Had he killed himself? Chin wouldn't have done that. He was a strong lad, proud and strong willed. Jack remembered the moment when Chin's hand had moved in a reflexive reaction to grab the chair. In that moment, when his open palm connected with Chin's face, Jack's boxer's instinct had alerted him to Chin's reaction. He'd seen the hands move. He'd readied himself. There was not much room, but there was enough to bend low, out of the way of the swinging chair. Instead, Chin had let go of the chair. Why? Respect? Fear? Love? Late that night, as he'd lain awake, unable to sleep, Jack had told himself it was love, because genuine respect is founded on love, pure and unconditional. He'd realised then that he'd made a huge mistake. Was it too late now to put that mistake right? He would do anything to do that.

Archee sensed the pain Jack was going through. Right was right. She told Amurtham that Marnie should make a bigger contribution so Jack could reduce his. When the matter was put to Marnie, Chinma threw a fit, threatening to cut ties completely with the family. The matter was left as it was.

Mike had found himself a better job with Baijnath as a clerk, and had married a pretty but very frail girl. It was not long before she fell ill and, emaciated by tuberculosis, died during childbirth. It had fallen to Amurtham to raise her daughter, Mama-girl. The fun-loving Mike did not like his job, but bided his time. He told Jack, who had a soft spot for him, "Unnah, I have never seen such a miser – apart from Chinma, of course."

"But he was very good to Chin."

"Yes, but I think that old age has changed him. You know, when people get older, they hoard things."

The younger brothers had all left school before high school. Freddie was full of mischief, always getting himself into trouble. Amurtham had warned him not to associate with Niney Chittigadu, whose poor, dissolute family lived in a derelict home down the road. Niney's father owned the only shebeen in Cato Manor. Chittigadu sold itshwala or "kaffir beer", brewed from sorghum, to the African "kitchen boys" who worked over the hill on the Berea. Freddie and Niney were the same age and, in spite of Amurtham's disapproval, had become firm friends. Niney's idea of fun often went beyond ordinary mischief. Niney told Freddie that their tenants, a man and his girlfriend, made love during the day. When their door was closed,

Niney could hear loud, frenzied sounds of pain and pleasure coming through the flimsy walls. Niney gave him graphic descriptions. Freddie didn't have a clue what love-making was all about. His curiosity was now aroused. Niney told him that he'd let him peep through the keyhole as soon as the sounds began. Freddie saw the naked man on top of the naked woman and giggled at the ridiculous sight. Both the man and woman were quite fat. The woman had folds on her tummy while the man's belly sagged. The man panted and grunted while the woman, her legs up in the air, groaned. Freddie didn't realise that the man had heard them laughing. The man got up. For some time, all Freddie could see was the naked woman on the bed. Meanwhile, the man crept along the side of the wall, unseen by Freddie, with a straightened wire coat-hanger in his hand. Suddenly Freddie felt something pierce his eye. He sprang back, holding his eye in pain and terror.

Amurtham held her son in her arms. She said in anguish, "Why did you go to those people's house? I told you not to!"

They could not afford a doctor, but they just had to get one. It was a long time before the white doctor came. The family shuffled about helplessly as Freddie's screams rent the air. Eventually he arrived, making his way through the throng that had gathered outside the house. He waved his small torch around and said, "I'm afraid he's lost the sight of his right eye."

The scriptures say that the cycle of birth and death is a karmic chain. The only way to achieve moksha or liberation is through detachment. One eventually has to give up all worldly ties, including one's family. The soul or Jeevatman then merges with the Paramatman or Godhood. Amurtham had tried, God knows she had tried. It was hard, but if people did not live by the scriptures, what else could they live by? She'd lived through the deaths of her husband and her two sons. She'd slaved her heart out when her husband died, doing midwifery and selling the greens from her garden and the pickles she made to Mrs Rana. It had been an almighty struggle to feed her children and give them an education, and now she had to take care of the infant Mama-girl. The little girl was such a bundle of joy, but Amurtham was not getting any younger. The scriptures said moksha or liberation could be attained through service without reward and the giving up of all material attachments. This was the only way to realise the God within. The only way to escape great pain was to give up pleasure. It was hard, it was hard. How could she not be attached to her children, to the lovely little Mama-girl? When Freddie lost his eye, she tried not to cry in his presence. She sought comfort in her little temple, where the sobs convulsed her body. She turned more and more to prayer.

Chapter Eleven

THE TWO LARGE front rooms of Jack's farm-style cottage facing Beach Road had been converted into a butchery. There were two more rooms and a large lounge at the back, which were sufficient for the family. Beach Road was tarred where it branched off from the main South Coast road, but tapered off into a sandy path as it moved eastwards through lush market gardens. Eventually it reached a crest, thick with sub-tropical growth, that sloped sharply down to the white sands of the beach. Deadly green mambas nestled among the long leaves of the sisal plants which pushed their way through the undergrowth.

Archee oversaw the butchery while Jack was at work, and the children pitched in after school. What with the housework and seeing to the children, it was a taxing routine for Archee, but she didn't mind. It was her own house and this was their own business. One day it would make enough money for Jack to stop working at Davies and Barrow.

Jack's former sparring partner, Paulus Ngcobo, was their block-man. Paulus had an easy rapport with the customers, taking an interest in every one of them. Instead of upsetting the customers, his often deeply personal questions somehow endeared him to them. He had a fatherly attitude, freely proferring advice as he went about cutting and weighing the meat and doing a thousand and one other things at the same time. He liked to sing – even the latest Tamil film songs. He was helped by Jack's younger brothers, Freddie, Steve and Sonny. Sonny was in his late teens, a tough, wiry youngster who wanted to be a boxer like his brother Jack. Paulus trained him after work in their backyard with a heavy sawdust punch-bag, which was hung from a low branch of a mango tree.

Paulus went along to the abattoir, choosing the meat himself. At first, the abattoir had simply disposed of sheep's heads and trotters, and Paulus had loaded as much as he could into the small, battered van – trotters, tripe and sheep's heads made excellent curries, and offal, cheaper than mutton, was one of the butchery's most profitable lines. It was not long before the abattoir cottoned on and started selling them the cheap meat, but the prices were nominal.

The people in the small district of Merebank looked up to Jack. When World War II broke out, he was elected chairman of the Merebank Civic Association, which held mock evacuations and exercises on what to do in the event of an actual bombing. No one dared challenge his authority. Meetings began on time and the business at hand was always concluded efficiently. He was later made chairman of the Merebank School Building Committee. He was also in charge of the Merebank contingent of passive resisters who occupied Albert Park, a white park, in defiance of the colour bar. Together with hundreds of other Indians, he willingly went to jail. When white hooligans attacked them, it took immense self-control for him not to react. Gandhi had warned that they must not meet violence with violence, no matter what the provocation.

For Jack, the issues were simple. You had to fight for your rights. In his life, he'd got into fights with bullies of all colours, most of them bigger and heavier than him, and had nearly always come out the better. Like his father, he had not at first agreed with Gandhi, and had been suspicious of the young lawyer from India who'd been brought out by some Muslim businessmen. Tamils in the Transvaal did not have kind words for Gandhi, who was seen to have worked in the interests of the extremely caste-conscious Gujerati community, who had come as "passenger" Indians and regarded themselves as superior to the descendants of indentured labourers. But Jack had always had great respect for the activist Thumbi Naidoo, who had the courage to speak his mind despite constantly being thrown into jail. And when Thumbi joined Gandhi, rousing the Indian community into mass defiance of unjust laws, Jack was one of those who threw in their lot with him.

For Dorrie and Chellamma, the two years of their engagement had dragged on, until eventually the big day arrived. As was the practice, relatives and neighbours didn't need an invitation – they arrived in numbers and pitched in, helping to clean and cut the vegetables and doing a hundred-and-one other things. The wedding was a simple ceremony, held in a tent on the slightly sloping Cato Manor Temple grounds. Four hundred people attended.

In accordance with custom, the couple had to spend the first two weeks at the bride's home. At the end of this period, it was time for the young wife to enter a new residence, a new family and a new life. Time to say goodbye. Chellamma was both a woman and a child, and the child surfaced in a flood of tears. She held her mother tightly, lost between two worlds. Amurtham tried to gently prise her arms loose, but the grip was unyielding. Amurtham held her breath, praying softly, "Aum Naamasivaya, Aum Naamasivaya." To herself and to God, she said, "She is now a wife. She has her own life. Help her to be strong. Help me to be strong." And she held back the tears. Slowly, she succeeded in gently disengaging herself from the child's grip.

Dorrie wanted to go to Chellamma, to hold her, but there was much self-consciousness about such outward shows of affection. Mike stepped forward and put his arms around Chellamma. "Hey Dorrie, what's the matter with you?

You shell-shocked or something? Look at him, he's actually blushing!" Holding Chellamma's hand, Mike grabbed Dorrie's and brought them together.

The couple shyly disengaged their hands and walked towards the car, festooned with balloons and streamers, that was waiting to take them to Dorrie's house.

The bride entered her new home at the auspicious hour. Veerasamy and his wife Meenatchi "turned the camphor", moving the tray in a circle before them, and broke the coconut. Dorrie's stepbrothers and stepsisters crowded around. Two of them, Bommie and Daddy, were smiling. The others just looked on. Bommie offered Chellamma some tea and sweetmeats, but she shyly said that she was not hungry. The conversation was punctuated by long pauses until Daddy, the youngest brother, said loudly, "It's their wedding night, leave them alone."

Chellamma blushed and Dorrie didn't know what to say. Soon they were left alone to retire to their bedroom.

On the first morning at her new home, Chellamma got up early, ready to play her part as the dutiful daughter-in-law. The household was still stirring when she lit the fire in the fireplace and placed the pot of water over it to boil. She watched the flames dance between the coals, which slowly turned a blazing red. She found the tea leaves in a tin in the cupboard and placed two teaspoonfuls into the kettle. She poured the boiling water into the kettle, singing while she did so.

Meenatchi entered. She said, without smiling, "Why so much noise so early in the morning?"

Chellamma stopped singing. She never sang again in the kitchen or, for that matter, anywhere else in the household. In the days and weeks following, it was made very clear in a thousand different ways that she was not a fully-fledged member of the family. Her station was just a notch above that of a servant. No matter how hard she tried, she failed to establish a comfortable rapport with the old lady.

Chellamma was well schooled in the culinary arts and in religious ritual, and had looked forward to performing these duties. On the first Monday, she was up early as usual, sweeping the house and the yard. Monday was the day of Shiva, the day of abstinence from meat and pleasures. She washed and cut the vegetables. Her favourite was dhall and "drumsticks", which grew in profusion in Veerasamy's market garden. She was about to boil the dhall when Meenatchi entered. "That's enough," she said – as if Chellamma were an intruder.

Chellamma stepped back. The point had been made. She could only enter upon Meenatchi's sufferance. The kitchen was Meenatchi's domain. There was a lot to do in the garden and the household, and Meenatchi did need assistance; but not the assistance of an equal. That had to be clearly understood. It was a privilege to have the opportunity to help, to enter the inner sanctum.

She was not even allowed to enter Veerasamy's prayer room. Instead, she was told to clean the house, wash the floors, polish the verandah, do the laundry, clean and prepare the vegetables, help in the market garden and perform sundry other menial tasks, even chopping the firewood.

The animosity she encountered was strange to her, but Chellamma was determined to hide her confusion and unhappiness from Dorrie. Mindful of the burden of his responsibilities as a breadwinner, she didn't want to make things any more difficult. At first she didn't have to try very hard. When he arrived home from work, all her sorrows were forgotten, and they bathed in the glow of young love. But the punishing routine and Meenatchi's imperious demeanour made it increasingly difficult for Chellamma to be her usual happy self. Dorrie's presence did much to lighten the load, but it was hard work putting on a brave face.

Dorrie was pretty pleased with himself. He had a good job. He'd rebuilt the house and made sure that his family – even though they were his stepfamily – had all the necessities, unlike others in the neighbourhood. And to top it all, he had an attractive young wife who was not afraid of hard work.

One day, he'd just taken off his coat and tie in the bedroom when he heard Meenatchi speaking in the adjacent room. "I have taught my daughters how to sew. Didn't your mother teach you?" she said sharply. There was no response from Chellamma.

A few minutes later, Chellamma entered the bedroom with his cup of tea. "What was that all about?" he asked, looking at her keenly.

The smile on her face was strained. "What?"

He picked up her chin gently. "Something about sewing."

She hadn't realised he'd heard and didn't know what to say. The smile grew even more strained.

Chellamma had always been very good at making sweetmeats, especially polee and woorende. Dorrie wondered why she hadn't made any since moving into his household. One Sunday afternoon, they were all out on the porch for a late tea. It was one of the few occasions that all the elders in the family were together. It had been hot that day and the family were resting after tending the market garden, watering the vegetables and doing the weeding. Dorrie had just come back from the Mayville Sports Grounds, where his team Cato Stars had won their league game against the log leaders, Manning Rangers. Cato Stars were lying fourth on the log and, with the season still young, the team was within reach of the Subrayen League Cup. Dorrie had once played for the team and had remained its vice-president.

Veerasamy had always kept a certain distance from his

children. Where he came from – the little village of Poolivoor in Vellore, India – male elders were treated like veritable gods by the younger generation. He tried his best to keep up the tradition: no small talk, no friendly banter; but of late, now that he was in his seventies, Veerasamy seemed to have thawed a bit. New to the skills of intimacy, he struggled to make conversation and nearly always felt embarrassed at his bumbling efforts.

Dorrie understood that undue familiarity could be regarded as disrespect. He was aware, however, that the old man was trying to introduce a friendlier rapport. "Cato Stars won today," he offered.

"Oh … they won, huh?"

"Yes. Madurai scored a terrific goal."

"Madurai …?"

"You know Madurai – Bida's son, Bida that blacksmith feller."

"Oh Bida, Mummy's brother-in-law? How many sons he got?"

"Four sons he got. All good players, but Madurai is the best."

"Yes, huh?"

"Yes, he scored a terrific goal."

The sun was setting. On the far horizon, the sky had changed from orange to red, and in the resulting coolness the family felt a cosy togetherness. "Why didn't you make some woorende for tea?" Dorrie asked Chellamma. "You make them very nice." Dorrie, who had sensed some tension between the two women, intended the words for Meenatchi's benefit.

Chellamma averted her eyes and shifted awkwardly. If she said that she wasn't allowed to cook, it would more than dampen the prevailing good mood.

"Naina, do you want some woorende?" Meenatchi said.

"I can make it for you."

Dorrie was quick to say, "No, no, you mustn't trouble yourself. You have a brand new daughter-in-law and she is very good at making woorende."

Meenatchi wasn't smiling now. With deadly aim, she spat the red juice from the betel leaf and nut she'd been chewing into her spittoon. "You mean all this time, from when you was a baby, you didn't like my cooking?"

Dorrie could sense his father watching him, although Veerasamy was not looking at him directly. The bourgeoning camaraderie which he yearned for had been so easily derailed. He attempted to get it back on track with profuse apologies. Meenatchi just stared at him. Dorrie turned away with a stifled sigh as another bullet of betel-leaf juice hit the chombu with an angry *thwup*.

That evening, he said he wanted to go for a walk down Montille Road, and asked Chellamma to accompany him. There were no street lights but it was a cool, moonlit night. In the eerie stillness, broken only by the chirping of crickets, Chellamma lapped up the comfort of his closeness. Holding her hand, he talked with pride about his team, demonstrating how the goal was scored – but slipped on the grass verge, much to Chellamma's amusement. She gave him a hand and he pulled her down.

"Don't be so naughty. Just now the people will see."

Dorrie laughed. "Let them see. We married, hell!" He hugged her and they sat down together, despite her apprehension about snakes. With a stick in his hands, Dorrie the hero reassured her that he'd take care of her. Then he held her at arm's length, scrutinising her face closely. He said gently, "Something is wrong at home. I know something is wrong. How are you getting on with my stepmother?"

She was silent for some time. "It's hard … I try my best … I try my best … and I don't like angry words …" The tears welled up in her eyes and she found it difficult to continue.

He wiped her moist eyes, put his fingers on her lips and hugged her. He made up his mind then that he would do everything he could to let them move out on their own. It was a big step. The closeness he'd yearned for, which was his only remembrance of his late mother and which lingered in his tenuous relationship with his father, was difficult to turn his back on.

Turn his back on. Words of finality. It didn't have to be that way, if there was just some give and some take.

Dorrie never cried. When his mother died, he'd just stood there looking at her in the coffin. He hadn't cried. The shock and grief deep within had dried up the tears. But that night in bed, he fought hard to hold back the tears. He succeeded, but could not mask his sighs. He sunk his head into his pillow. Chellamma heard a croaking sound and sat up, shaking him. He held her hand in reassurance. He wanted to tell her that in life there was very little giving. Instead there was much taking, even among those who had been blessed with all the things they needed. People just took and took. He got up, walked to the outside toilet built over a soak-pit, and for the first time in his life he cried.

Cato Manor was slowly changing. The land had first been apportioned to the sugar baron, George Cato, Mayor of Durban, in return for land in the Point area that Cato had donated to the municipality. The land lay beyond the lush ridge known as the Berea. He'd cut up the land and sold it to labourers like Veerasamy after they gained their freedom from indenture. They had somehow saved some money from the pittance they were paid to put down deposits for pieces of ground, which they sought to develop into market gardens, despite much of it being covered by shale. Veerasamy, like the others, had had no choice but to commit himself to a lifelong mortgage bond when he "signed" the papers with a cross. Indeed, they were effectively working for Cato, who took a sizeable portion of the money they made from their fresh produce. The virus of slavery had taken on another, more civilised guise.

The market garden produce was taken by horse-cart to the Indian Market in town or sold to the rich residents of the Berea. Those who could not afford horse-carts trudged all the way over the Berea to the wealthy suburbs to sell their wares from heavily laden baskets. Poverty took a huge toll, but a strong sense of family and community gave the people a bedrock on which to rebuild their impoverished lives. Their makeshift houses were gradually improved upon as the years went by. With large families pooling their resources, they were able to replace the simple structures with solid, well-built wood and iron buildings and some brick houses, mostly using their own labour. Rapid urbanisation and low returns from the small quantities of fresh produce forced coming generations either to wean themselves off the land or to buy bigger farms in the outlying areas. Labour was cheap; large numbers of the African dispossessed, desperate to escape the clutches of poverty, took whatever work they could. Menials. Outcasts. This calculated social differentiation took on a life of its own.

Jobs for Indians were still scarce. The first generation born in South Africa had started up businesses of their own. A few became teachers, accountants, salesmen and factory workers.

The first indentured labourers had brought with them seeds and seedlings, which they managed to keep alive despite the long, taxing journeys on rickety sailing vessels and, later, steamships. Given the conditions, this was a minor miracle. Among the plants and seeds they brought were tamarind, peepul, mango, jackfruit, coconut, avocado, guava, china guava, different types of gourd, curry leaf, mustard, dhania, chillies and brinjals. Their homes were surrounded by mango, avocado, jack fruit, banana and custard-apple trees, curry-leaf bushes, hedges of granadilla and double-bean vines, and neatly ordered front gardens of snapdragons, marigolds, carnations, dahlias, roses and pride-of-Indias. With some exceptions, regularly whitewashed exterior walls and gloss-painted interiors – often somewhat garish, in bright primary colours – reflected an abiding pride in one's home.

Dorrie soon had enough money for a deposit on a piece of land on a hill in Trimborne Road, which was above the shale-infested area and therefore full of trees and dense subtropical vegetation. The land sloped gently to the west, and to the east, beyond Cato Manor Road, was the wealthy white area of the Berea.

Within three years, after the birth of their second child, Dorrie and Chellamma were able to move into their own home. When the van came to take away their few possessions, Veerasamy shut himself off in his prayer room. Meenatchi sat with arms folded on the porch, vigorously chewing betel leaf and nut and spitting with venom into her chombu. She never forgave Chellamma for tearing Dorrie away from his father's home. The parting was bitter and acrimonious, and father and son were not to speak to each other for years.

Dorrie had changed jobs and was now earning more as a salesman-cum-delivery man for White's Bakeries. Chellamma should have been very happy, but she was plagued by thoughts of Veerasamy's reputed power with the mantra.

Chapter Twelve

HER YEARS IN the catering industry had left Greta with a fondness for fine wines. She had a cellar full of expensive, vintage wines, both local and imported. A glass or two and her mind, which she'd firmly kept in check ever since she could remember, wandered. How nice if life could always be as it seemed after maybe four glasses of wine. Dreams were okay when the wine was your steward, taking you over azure seas into bright, sunny realms.

But Greta had learnt very young that life was not all smooth sailing, and you had to play your cards carefully. She'd always been in control of her life; she been prepared to make sacrifices, and was now a wealthy woman – but there was a sense of unfulfillment. She could have had a different life … but there was so little time. The catering industry was all-consuming. She sighed. Above all, you were in the public eye and you had to be careful. Perhaps she had been too careful. Thank God Chin had happened along. He'd helped her touch that long-held dream a little.

Yet she knew she was clinging to a dream that couldn't last. He was younger than she and had dreams of his own. She tried to shut out the nagging thought that somehow Chin was too immersed in himself. He was single-minded and worked hard – reminding her of herself when she'd been cast out into an uncaring world to fend for herself.

On the odd occasion, she'd tried to persuade Chin to share a glass of wine with her before supper, but he wouldn't touch the stuff. Unlike Jack, he had a strong aversion to alcohol, which sprang from his memories of the very visible abuse of alcohol in Cato Manor when he was a youth. While most of the citizenry were sober and upright, there were a handful whose drunken sorties made them the butt of ridicule. One such was Soobremoney Pandayan who, every evening, would lurch along Trimborne Road in the gathering darkness, when other sober citizens had long since reached home. Because Indians were not allowed to buy liquor to consume at their homes at their leisure, Soobree would invariably rush to a bar straight after work and gulp down as much as he could before getting on the bus to Trimborne Road. By the time he alighted at the bus stop, he was completely inebriated, falling down every few steps. Some sympathetic soul would help him to his house, much to the embarrassment of his household.

One Saturday evening, there was a doctors' function, sponsored by a British pharmaceutical company, in the hotel's posh ballroom. A five-course dinner was laid on and a dance band was hired for the occasion. The mayor was the guest of honour; speeches were made and bouquets presented. The wine flowed, and so did the Scotch, the brandy, the gin and the vodka – cane spirits hadn't found its way into the Cape yet. The well-heeled guests took to the floor under glittering chandeliers.

Greta walked around as unobtrusively as possible to check that everything was in order, while behind the scenes Chin maintained hands-on supervision. Almost everybody knew Greta, and she stopped to exchange friendly banter. When she reached the table of her dentist, Trevor Smythe, he insisted that she join them for a moment or two. She sat politely for a while, but when she tried to get up, her hand was seized in a firm grip under the table by Smythe. She had no option but to remain seated. Smythe, whose wife sat opposite him, fancied himself as a Casanova. He had long had his eye on Greta and now, his inhibitions gone after four Scotches, he was determined to have the next dance with her. It was a delicate moment. Trevor's wife, Linda, had her suspicions, although Greta had given no cause for them. A glass of wine was thrust into her hands and she just had to drink it.

The band played "The Blue Danube", her favourite waltz, which she'd rather have been dancing with Chin. Someday she would teach him how to dance. Before she knew it, however, she was on the floor with Trevor.

Trevor was a good dancer and he whirled her around the ballroom. He whispered his admiration and affection – and she coolly deflected the conversation, as she always did. Then he said, "There's a rumour going the rounds about you and that smart-looking Indian working for you."

Greta caught her breath, but she danced on. She bit her lip as Trevor put the boot in: "Aha, an exotic love affair!"

She reacted, despite herself. "It's none of your business!"

Trevor continued dancing, but pulled back his head to look at her with a whimsical smile. "So you don't deny it."

Greta was angry. "I don't need to."

She realised that she'd put her foot in it even further. The dance over, she didn't sit at the table, but took her leave with a forced smile. "I've got to check on my stewards, they seem to be a bit slow. Please excuse me."

She rushed out of the room, went to her cellar and picked the first bottle she could lay her hands on, a 1929 Chardonnay. She took a wine glass from the bar and went directly up to Chin's room. By the time the function was over and Chin had come up to the room, she'd finished the bottle and taken a shower. She towelled her hair as she sat naked on the easy chair.

Chin could see that she'd had a little too much wine. He

smiled. "What's the occasion?"

"No occasion. In fact, just plain shit!"

"Yeah?

"Yeah!"

"What happened?"

"Seems the whole town's talking."

Chin shook his head. "I've heard some things too."

"It's none of their damn business …"

"We can't ignore them, you know that."

"I really don't give a damn. It's my life!"

"You know what we're up against …"

"What can they do? Tell me, what can they do? Call me a whore, a coolie lover? So what?"

Chin sat down on the easy chair opposite her, looking at the empty bottle.

"Okay, I've had a drink or two …"

"A drink or two!"

"I know, I know … and I'll tell you the same thing tomorrow, completely sober. Tomorrow we're going to take a drive to the beach and you're going to buy me an ice cream and we're going for a walk on the promenade."

"I don't think that's wise."

"Don't you love me?"

He had never been sure. He liked her a lot and he enjoyed sex with her. She was wonderful company and an excellent boss. He told himself that he wasn't exactly lying when he said, "You know that."

She pursued it. "Know what?"

This time he had to lie. "That I love you, of course."

She got up, straddling her legs across his lap. "Say it again."

"I love you …"

"Again."

"I love you."

And she pulled off his clothes in a frenzy, as if it were the first time they were making love.

On Sundays, you could only have an alcoholic drink if a meal was ordered. Sunday drinking somehow had to be made respectable in the eyes of the ruling elite. They couldn't ban it completely – the livelihood of many in that elite depended on the wine farms and the distilleries (and of course there were those who were closet alcoholics). The Christian National ethos, the fear of a puritanical God, however, was traded on by astute politicians, and was to have some very serious consequences for the country in the years to come.

Chin had cashed up after the first lunch session, taken a shower and was hoping to have a rest before the next lunch session when Greta entered.

"Put something nice on."

"Why?"

"We've got a date, remember?"

He remembered. "Come on, Greta!"

"I wasn't that drunk, you know."

"Okay, okay, you've made your point – but this is dangerous."

"Nonsense. What's the worst that can happen?"

He wanted to tell her, "It's all very well for you to talk like that. From where I'm standing, that's a very stupid question." Instead he said, "We've got a good thing going. Why risk it? You love me, don't you?"

"That's a silly question. I'll see you downstairs in five minutes."

It was a warm, sunny afternoon and, unusually for Port Elizabeth, there was hardly a breeze. The city had some fine beaches, but for most of the year the strong winds spoilt the fun. Greta bought some ice cream and they walked along the promenade. When they passed through the area reserved for whites, people began to stare. Greta put her arm through his.

This was an entirely new experience for Chin. He'd never really questioned the separation of the races – he'd had no cause to do so. He'd been born into it, and it had seemed natural, so ordained.

Then they bumped into Turnbull. He was sitting on a deckchair, enjoying the sun. Recognition dawned slowly. Turnbull squinted against the glare, then pulled himself up with some effort to take another look. His face turned the colour of beetroot. He stared in disbelief and he screamed at Chin, "You lied! You lied!" The old man was hysterical. "I'm cancelling the sale! I shall instruct my attorneys tomorrow."

They walked on. It was an unnerving experience. Chin said with a nervous chuckle, "He's mad. I have a signed agreement of sale and receipts for my payments ..."

Greta cut in, "How much do you owe him?"

"Oh, about three hundred pounds."

"I'm giving you a cheque tomorrow. Pay the bastard."

Chin protested, but Greta didn't want to hear of it.

It was not difficult to handle the old man. But, as Chin had instinctively feared, there were more powerful, unseen forces to contend with. His relationship with Greta was a threat to the way of life of this insular English community – a community that, ironically, in the past had achieved much through its daring and readiness to take chances.

A week later, Greta and Chin were in bed when a stone crashed through their window. It had a note tied to it. "Your days are numbered, coolie."

For the first time, Chin shouted at her. "I told you! I told you!"

Greta didn't say anything as she walked out of the room.

Chin's first-floor suite windows opened out to the courtyard – the only place from which the stone could have been thrown. Security was stepped up, but Chin could sense it was futile. He had warned her, he had warned her!

For Chin, the love-making had become almost automatic. Greta could sense his growing disaffection.

"I've never really told you about myself, have I?"

His look seemed to indicate that it didn't matter one way or the other.

"My marriage was a disaster." She sighed heavily. Her husband had been much older than her. "When I was young, my father lost his job. There were five hungry mouths to feed. Jobs were hard to come by, but I was lucky. I got a job at a hotel owned by this man who was to become my husband." She continued with a wan smile, "Déjà vu, huh? He had a large hotel in Cologne. Long before the war began, things got very tough. You want to know about poverty? We knew what it was. Somehow, we scraped a living …" She paused, looking out of the window, and said in a distant way, "My boss was a clever man, but he was Jewish. He could see what was coming. He decided to emigrate, sold up. He asked me if I wanted to join him. I jumped at the chance to get away. He bought a hotel in Windhoek. Even there, it wasn't safe if you were a Jew. My husband looked German and spoke German better than most. He could easily pass for a gentile. He changed his name and his religion." She took a long sip from her glass of wine. "One night, he proposed to me. There I was in this strange land, lonely and poor, and still sending whatever money I could to my folks back home. I didn't want to lose my job. So I married him. A few years later, he had a heart attack."

She sighed heavily and continued, "I am not cruel, but I felt like a slave set free. I sold up the hotel and came to South Africa."

In the texture of her words, in the manner of her speaking, was a plea. She was saying it had never been easy – in the pained reliving of a distant life, she was saying, *Like you and your people, I've known hurt, but unlike you I've never known love. You have given me something, please don't take it away.*

Life's ironies intrude unexpectedly. Even in the virtuous resides the grossness of self-interest. Everything else is subsumed. Once more, Chin shut out the little voice his mother had said was the voice of God. Here was this woman, once so strong, who had given him so much, now pleading with him. How should he respond? His first impulse was to gather her in his arms and probably even marry her. He could imagine what an impression that would make in Cato Manor – an older white woman, and one so well-off. But he wanted something more. His whole life had changed in that moment when his brother slapped him. He was going to do something, get somewhere. He was going to make something of himself. Nothing would deter him from achieving ultimate self-respect. And that meant he had to move on – there was no other way.

Life had snaked along for him. His childhood had been heavily anchored in the certitude of kharmic destiny. What would be, would be. And there were the wondrous things his mother seemed to have achieved through faith and prayer. But you couldn't get a job just by praying. He watched poor people spend money observing the many rituals. They stayed poor. The contradiction lay at the back of his mind, but he'd always shied away from such weighty questions. Now, however, he couldn't shake them off so easily. The questions plagued him. He had to accept that there were no certainties, no absolutes.

Strangely, in his late teens, it had been Mr Baijnath who'd opened the door to other possibilities – ever so slightly. "Life is what you make of it," he'd said. Given the optimism and vigour of youth, this had been very appealing. What was clear was that if you let things drift and hoped for something good to happen, you were wasting your time. You had to take control. Never mind if jobs were hard to come by, never mind if things were tough for people like him. He'd work himself to the bone waiting for that one opportunity, and if it didn't come he would make his own opportunities, even if he had to die doing so.

He'd known what it was to go without. It had pained him so much when he couldn't go to high school. But all these things he could cope with. Now there was a different hunger, and he would get through it the way he'd done before. So far, things had worked out for him. He had long ago decided that he was going to be self-sufficient, even if it meant that he couldn't live his life exactly the way he wanted to. Everything else took second place. He didn't want another stone thrown through the window or worse – and frankly, he was tired of Greta. Besides, he'd long ago decided that if he ever married, it would be to an Indian woman.

Chin hadn't taken a single day's leave. When he told Greta that he was taking a week's leave, she didn't object. She had a sneaking suspicion that this was a prelude to something else, something she'd battled to keep out of her mind. She didn't ask where he was going. With a forced smile, she said, "You deserve a break. Enjoy yourself." She'd tried to be cheerful, but instead sounded hollow.

He wanted to be alone, but there were no hotels for blacks. When he asked the Reddys if he could stay for a week, they welcomed him enthusiastically, although Mrs Reddy felt instinctively that there was something wrong.

One evening, after a splendid supper, which Mrs Reddy had painstakingly prepared, he told them of his plans. The Reddys didn't approve, but they gave him their blessings.

Chapter Thirteen

IT WAS AROUND midnight. The derelict bus shelter, tilting badly as if it would fly off at any moment, afforded him some protection from the persistent, dust-laden Port Elizabeth wind that swirled around him. Chin had walked at least two miles – aimlessly, out of the residential areas and into the start of the open veld, trying to come to terms with the mess he'd made of things.

It was some eleven months since he'd left the hotel. At the end of his week's leave, he'd gone back to the hotel to fetch his things. Fortunately, Greta was not in. Chin had left a hurried note: "Sorry, this didn't work out. I've got to get on with my own life." He hadn't left an address.

Chin had purchased the busy shop, Sunset Café, for what seemed a bargain. This was it: the shop was on the main road, just a little removed from the city centre; it was full of customers and sold just about everything. Chin had unshakeable confidence in his business acumen, and it did not occur to him that there might be reasons for the low price.

Mr da Silva, a large, jolly man, had been all smiles as he'd showed Chin around. "As you can see, it's mostly passing trade. A lot of people walk past here, especially the workers in the morning and afternoon. We sell a lot of cigarettes, biscuits, cakes, cool drinks, boiled eggs, sausages …"

Chin had been enthusiastic. "What about fried fish?"

Mr da Silva had smiled even more broadly. "I can see you're a businessman. Fish is cheap and we have a large kitchen with all the appliances. You can make big profits."

And with that, the deal was sealed.

Chin repainted the interior and put up an awning. Outside, under the front window, he placed some potted plants. Mr Reddy commended him for his courage. Mrs Reddy was not so sure. "Why did he leave such a nice job, where he was a boss of his own, and go into such a hard business? You know yourself it's long hours, and you've got to do everything yourself."

Mr Reddy said she was being far too suspicious. Nevertheless, they again offered their hospitality to him. Mrs Reddy said, "Your room is waiting for you, Naina. Please come back. It's the right time too now, it's Purtassi."

At the mention of Purtassi, the month of abstinence from meat, alcohol and all pleasures, Chin thought of his mother. He could see her fussing over the variety of vegetable dishes and sweetmeats, the frying of the vade and kudle. He felt a pang of homesickness, but politely refused the Reddy's offer. The shop had a small room at the back which was quite sufficient for his present needs. He told them that he also wanted to keep an eye on the business.

What Mr da Silva hadn't told him was that the road was soon to be diverted, and his shop would be cut off from the huge passing trade. Within a few days of the diversion being completed, business dropped drastically. The realisation that he'd made a huge mistake came home to Chin one morning when he found his potted plants smashed and scattered. The area was not far from a poor township and the shop was now frequented by petty thieves and hooligans.

The police, who'd made their presence felt when Mr da Silva was the owner, laughed at him. "Potted plants?!"

"Yes."

"What's so special about them?"

It was a waste of time. The police made it clear that they had far more serious crimes on their hands than the vandalism of a few potted plants.

The Reddys were dismayed when they visited the shop again. Mrs Reddy got straight to the point: "Thumbi, this place is dangerous and the people here are quite poor."

Just how poor they were, he'd learned at great cost to himself. Setting up the shop had cost him half his life savings and he was rapidly eroding the other half. He'd acted impulsively. He was angry with himself for not having done his homework and for not smelling a rat. What an idiot he'd been! He ached to get back to the hotel, but his pride wouldn't let him. Fortunately, the farm in Sandflats was yielding a small profit. He considered throwing out his present tenants and taking over the farm, but he knew nothing about farming. Work was hard to come by and he would have to start again from scratch, in some poorly-paid job in catering.

And so, that night he'd shut the shop and gone for a long walk, ignoring the swirling winds until the dust in his eyes became a nuisance. He sat down at the bus stop, which gave him some shelter, but his troubled thoughts raced on. His money was dwindling fast and the prospect of being poor again loomed large. He had made a total mess of things.

Eventually, Mrs Reddy took it on herself to do something about it. Despite Mr Reddy's warning that she was meddling in other people's affairs, she approached Greta.

The sudden separation had left Greta depressed for weeks. She almost agreed to go out with Trevor Smythe once, but changed her mind at the last minute. She could not go out with a married man, even if she was desperate for company. After a while, she'd realised she was neglecting the business. Mrs Reddy's visit gave her some comfort. The old woman was frank. She told Greta that Chin had made an awful mistake and urged her to visit him at his shop. Perhaps that would make him sell up and return to the hotel.

Greta swallowed her pride. She'd left the business entirely in Chin's hands and had come to rely on him heavily; but more than that, she missed him badly.

Chin had a two-week beard. His shirt was scruffy and his hair unkempt. She had never seen him like this. Her visit caught him by surprise and he was awkward and embarrassed. She let him stew in his embarrassment. He needed help, of that there was no question.

"How's business?"

"Oh, okay," he lied.

She was almost enjoying herself. "You naughty man. You left without saying goodbye."

All he could say was, "I left a note …"

A customer sauntered in and the conversation stalled. The young man in tattered clothing asked for a loose cigarette. When he left, she said, "I didn't know people bought loose cigarettes."

He offered her a cool drink, which she accepted. Another customer came in and asked for a quarter loaf of bread. He saw her looking into the till, which was almost empty.

She got up. "Chin, I thought of advertising for someone to take your place, but truthfully, I don't think I could get anyone as good as you. If you want it, the job is still yours."

He nodded as she got up to go.

Chin put his pride in his pocket. He had to. The next day he was back at his old job.

Chapter Fourteen

His first day back at the job, Chin received a mixed reception. "Budgie" slapped him on the back. "Where the hell did you run away to, and without saying a word nogal?"

Others weren't that enthusiastic. The antagonism that had resulted in the stone-throwing had abated when it became known that he'd left the hotel. Now it resurfaced. Chin was either greeted by hostile looks or treated as if he didn't exist.

That evening, he sat in his room, deep in thought. He'd blundered badly in buying the shop. He vowed never again to venture into something he didn't know about. His strength was that he was a good hotelier, and that's what he would concentrate on in future.

Chin lit a cigarette and was looking up at the ceiling, thinking how lucky he was to have met someone like Greta, when she entered his room. For a long moment, they didn't say anything. Gently she sidled up to him, and when they touched, some of the old fire returned.

They were reasonably busy on Friday when someone shouted, "You car's on fire!" He rushed out with Greta, but there was nothing they could do. By the time the fire brigade got there, the car was reduced to a charred shell. It was obvious that the stone-thrower had stepped up a gear. The incident shook the regulars. Greta tried to behave normally, but it was clear that fear had got to her. Chin noticed and, in an ironic way, welcomed her belated grasp of reality. They just had to be careful – very, very careful.

Within a few months, takings in all the bars had plummeted, takings in the kitchen had dropped by a third and even the occupancy rate had gone down. The signs were ominous. Chin and Greta talked well into the night. It was agreed that she would leave for Cape Town to investigate the possibility of buying a hotel there. A small hotel, somewhere out of the public glare, which would yield a respectable income. In the meanwhile, they would put the Cologne up for sale.

Chin advised Greta against selling the hotel through an agent, and so they advertised in the newspapers. Chin ignored the South African respondents – they were aware of the unofficial boycott of the hotel and were offering ridiculous prices. But when Mr Croats turned up, Chin could immediately tell from his accent that he was a foreigner. He told the English visitor that his boss was not there, and that he was instructed to show prospective buyers around.

The wealthy Englishman had been in PE for just two weeks and had fallen in love with the country. Chin showed him the books, which deliberately did not reflect the downward trend of recent months. When word got around that he and Greta were no longer in the hotel, the customers would come back, so it wasn't a totally false picture.

Greta returned within two weeks. She'd found a boarding house in a garden setting near Kloof Nek. Squirrels scampered up and down three aged oak trees. The rich, undulating lawn around the house was peppered with liberal patches of fynbos, gardenias, hydrangeas, chrysanthemums and a variety of roses. The house had about twenty rooms and was conveniently situated within easy reach of the city, with good views of Table Bay, Lion's Head and Table Mountain.

Greta was happy to get a good price for the Hotel Cologne, and thanked Chin profusely. "I don't know what I'd do without you. You've become indispensable, you know that?" In the glow of their success, the old feelings were further rekindled.

The staff were devastated about Chin and Greta's move to Cape Town, and so were the Reddys. Mrs Reddy pleaded with Chin: "Thumbi, why go so far? We have saved some money. We have no children, no relatives. Uncle's family have all gone. So have mine. We are old now and you are like our son."

Chin comforted her as best he could. They had no idea about his relationship with Greta and the problems arising from it, although the old lady had her suspicions. He'd told them only that there were some very jealous people who were beginning to make trouble for him, and that he had to leave town. Tearfully, she gave him her blessings: "Don't forget us. I know it's far away, thumbi, but you must keep in touch, and you must also visit us."

They left in Greta's car, a late-model Chevrolet sedan which she'd purchased after the old car was burnt, taking with them very few possessions – they'd sold or given away most of what they had. The rest, like the store of wines, were railed. Chin drove most of the way.

The sun was up when they stopped to look at the view on Van Staden's Pass. A little tortoise crossed the path, unconcerned. Chin picked it up. Greta said, "Let's take the little bugger with us."

Chin pulled a face. "In our community, tortoises are considered bad luck."

"You don't believe that bullshit!"

Chin laughed but put the little fellow down gingerly. "I think it's a shame to take him out of his natural surroundings."

"Ah, so we have a conscience, do we? What about all those fish you catch without the slightest feeling?"

Chin laughed again, but the contradiction hadn't escaped him. He'd had long arguments with his conscience about that one. Where did one draw the line?

A couple of hours later, they were driving along the winding road through the Knysna Forest. They stopped for a lunch break at a sheltered stream, whose slightly brackish water gurgled over smooth white pebbles, among tall ferns dappled with the sunlight that streamed through the towering trees. Coming out of the main forest, they passed mountains covered in carpets of mauve and pink watsonias. Next stop was the lagoon, where they stopped outside a café called "Die Kombuis". It was a quaint, pretty little café with a frontage of singed wood, and the smell of strong coffee seeped through its front door. He was going to go into the "Nie Blankes" section when Greta held him back. She went into the "White" section and ordered coffee and buttered bread, fresh from the oven, which Chin had a craving for.

The woman serving Greta pointedly asked if Chin, whom she could see through the shop window, was her driver. She had noticed their unusual familiarity. After she'd paid the lady, Greta shot back, "No, he's not my driver, he's my lover. Wouldn't you like to have such a handsome lover?" And she stormed out.

There was a timelessness about the lagoon, as yet undeveloped, as there'd been about the forest. A few sailing craft moved lazily across the water, silhouetted against the forested hill. Centuries-old trees rose gently from the water's edge. As they sipped their coffee and ate their bread, their immediate concerns receded far from consciousness before the splendour of nature. Greta whispered, "Have you ever seen anything like this?"

"Just look at it and you forget yourself," Chin said. "You should have bought your hotel here, far away from the noise, far away from people."

At Wilderness, they decided to stop and frolic on the white sands of a secluded beach. In a hidden spot just behind the unspoilt dunes, they made love. Afterwards, Greta said, "You know, I hardly know anything about you. You know everything about me. That's not fair."

It had never occurred to him before to tell her anything about himself. But once he began, he couldn't stop. He'd never delved into such detail before. There was a distant look in his eyes and, as he told his story, they grew moist. She gently wiped them with her beach towel, and her eyes also. When he finished, he felt washed, as if his soul had taken a hot bath. Greta said, "Your poor Mother! I think you should contact her right away. From what you told me she must be old. You might not see her again."

He had never entertained any thought of his mother's passing, and he promised Greta he would write; but a few days later his promise was forgotten.

When they got to Cape Town, Greta booked into a hotel. Chin had to sleep in the special servants' quarters at the back of the hotel. It was sparse but neat and comfortable.

Chapter Fifteen

THE STEYNSRUST BOARDING house was in a quiet street at the foot of the mountain, but within easy reach of the city centre. It had all-round views of the mountain and the ocean, and ample parking. Greta had fallen in love with its special charm and marvellous gardens.

The deal was concluded and Chin and Greta moved in. Some major structural alterations were made: they added twenty more rooms, a ballroom, a dining room, a conference room seating around two hundred people, and a Cape Dutch facade. Three bars were installed – one on each of the first and second floors, and a "non-white" public bar that opened on to the street. Chin wanted the whole place carpeted, but Greta felt that the sprung-oak flooring did much for the ambience, and so it was sanded and polished. Her application for a liquor licence and hotel status was a mere formality; the licensing board passed it without a quibble.

They opened the Hotel Steynsrust for business in September, in time for the summer season. The mayor was invited to the grand opening ceremony. Chin made sure that he plied the two journalists and the photographer with plenty of free drinks, and later treated them to a sumptuous meal. One of the journalists, who'd never met an Indian before, was fascinated by the way Chin spoke English, and wanted to know which part of the Indian subcontinent he was from. Greta had hired a tuxedo for him, and later told him that a number of women had whispered to her that he looked "gorgeous". Flattered, Chin commented that the white people here seemed much easier with people of colour than their compatriots in other parts of the country.

The opening received excellent coverage, with a full page of photographs in one newspaper.

They hadn't realised the alterations would cost so much. Greta had dug into her capital, and they reckoned it would take close on to two years before they saw profits. Chin scolded her for being so reckless, especially with the expensive fittings.

"As long as we can feed ourselves in the meanwhile," Greta reasoned.

Chin introduced free chilli-bite snacks in the bars after six – the only hotel in the Peninsula to do so. The chilli-bites, or bajhia, were made of pea-flour, a touch of chilli powder and spinach, which grew in profusion in the hotel garden. He persuaded Ohlsson's Breweries in Newlands to sponsor half-price beers every evening between seven and eight, and the Stellenbosch Wine Company to provide dart-boards in both the white and non-white bars. They held weekly competitions, with prizes such as chickens and bottles of wine. The pubs soon proved to be the most popular in Cape Town.

The construction of the conference room was a stroke of genius. It was nearly always booked out, mostly for political and sporting-association meetings, from which there was always a nice spin-off in the bars and the kitchen.

In the pubs, there was always somebody selling "back-door" produce. Initially, Greta was scared to have anything to do with such stuff, but Chin was very careful whom he dealt with, and the profits in the kitchen swelled. He had "contacts" who regularly brought them crayfish, prawns and even good fresh beef. The first contact to approach Chin, Gammat Daniels, had false teeth that rattled every time he spoke. Gammat regarded himself as a "professional". He was a fisherman for a big fishing company that specialised in catching snoek, which was plentiful off the often stormy

Cape coast. The first time they met, Gammat rattled through his "falsies", "Jes' think what they make from the catch. We go in the boats, sometimes we doesn't come back alive and what they give us? What? Fokall! So I says, Gammat, you sommer show them. You don't want it? No problem. I'se got lots of customers."

There was something else about Gammat besides his rattling teeth and his thievery, something which Chin was instinctively able to relate to. They were on the "other side, ou pêl", as Gammat put it – both "darkies". He was not as stupid as he looked. Chin soon saw that his unsophisticated appearance was a camouflage, masking a sharp intellect. Chin was charmed by Gammat, and the feeling was mutual. Gammat introduced Chin to his friend, Willie, who sold fresh meat, corned beef and cold meat at well-below-market prices. It was a risky business but Chin had got used to risks. Besides, some of his best patrons were high up in the police force.

The ballroom was very popular and the bedroom occupancy rate was always over eighty percent. Incredibly, they were showing profits within eight months. That evening, when Greta popped the champagne in Chin's room, he told her that although he'd been worried about the way she'd spent her capital, he'd never had any doubts that the hotel would be a success. He hinted that they should now be extra careful in their relationship, as they had so much to lose. She muttered, "Don't lecture me," but for once the headstrong Greta didn't argue much.

The cable car on Table Mountain and the scenic drive around the breathtaking peninsula, around Cape Point and below Chapman's Peak, had just been completed. Visitors were pouring in from all over the country, as well as from Europe and America. The hotel found itself booked out for most of the summer season. Even in the cold, blustery Cape winter, they still did good business.

The Cape was full of excellent fishing spots with plenty of snoek, kabeljou, galjoen, harder, musselcracker, salmon, steenbras, stumpnose, hake and elf. Through his fishing, Chin made some good friends, two of the closest being "Stomps" Diederichs and Rooks Duvenage.

Stomps was a young policeman he'd met at Mouille Point. Stomps had never met an Indian before – there were very few living in the Western Cape then. Chin had attracted a small appreciative crowd around him, pulling in the elf – or shad, as he'd known it in Natal. Stomps was in that crowd, and it wasn't long before he'd struck up a friendship with this strange Indian fisherman who spoke both English and Afrikaans – fluently, and without that funny accent that white comedians often mocked on the radio. Chin was a successful businessman, but not the bearded, greasy sort that Stomps had always heard about.

Chin didn't fit the mould. He was always smartly dressed, even when he went fishing, with galoshes and a well-worn Stetson instead of the regulation floppy sun-hat. Stomps thought he looked a bit like Gary Cooper. (Later, when Diederichs told him this, Chin was flattered, but shot back, "I'm no cowboy!")

Stomps got his nickname from playing rugby. At school, he'd taken the usual schoolboy badgering and rough play in his stride – until a rugby player from a rival school had singled him out for some rough treatment. After a third vicious high tackle, Stomps had lost his temper. He'd felled his tormentor and stomped on him, hence the name. But it was a complete misnomer. He was not an aggressive man. He was gentle off the field and stuck to the rules in rugby, and it took a lot to upset him. A bachelor, he spent much of his spare time either fishing or playing rugby. Once or twice a week, he would spend some time in Chin's office, drinking a few pints of beer.

Rooks was a big, bluff man from the upmarket coloured area of Walmer Estate, who loved his fishing. Both Stomps and Rooks had developed a fondness for curry, the hotter the better, and didn't need a second invitation whenever Chin cooked some. The three developed a very close relationship, and it was inevitable that they would get to know of Chin's relationship with Greta. Initially, Stomps resented the fact that a white woman was in love with an Indian, but kept it to himself. As he got closer to both of them, it seemed the most natural thing in the world – even to him, a conservative Boer from the Platteland. He told himself that there was an exception to everything in life. Stomps and Rooks were good friends, and were indeed extremely protective of him and Greta.

They would go out together on picnics, with both Greta and Chin preparing hampers. On such occasions, Rooks would bring his cheerful, talkative wife, Maureen, with him. They would both break into paroxysms of raucous laughter at the slightest provocation. While it sometimes seemed a little bit forced, there was something wholesome and appealing about their readiness to laugh. Greta would dig into her stock of wines; the bottles she'd railed from Port Elizabeth had been supplemented by the excellent wines she regularly purchased from farms in the winelands. She got to know several wealthy farmers, who often drove up with their families from the sprawling wine estates of the Boland and Franschhoek to have their Sunday dinners at the Hotel Steynsrust, which was fast gaining a reputation for its excellent cuisine. Their chef was an Englishman who had worked on the *QE II* and had chosen to settle in the Cape, which he felt was the most beautiful place in the world. Chin had taught him to cook a reasonably good curry.

One heady Sunday on a big flat rock in Bakoven, overlooking the deep blue Atlantic, Greta insisted that they all have a glass of wine. Stomps said, "He's an Indian. Indian people don't drink, jong. It's in their holy book. What you call it?"

Rooks said, "The Koran."

Chin said he wasn't Muslim, to which Stomps said, "You're the first blerry Indian I met who isn't … So now you got no excuses, verstaan?" He playfully thrust the glass into his friend's hands. He wouldn't take no for an answer. "Man, don't be such a spoilsport! You're a bad policeman," Chin joked, "forcing people to drink."

Both Chin and Rooks, who were non-drinkers, overwhelmed by the bonhomie, the blue skies, the bright sunshine, the exhilarating atmosphere, dropped their defences and took up their glasses. Chin screwed up his face after the first sip, but before they knew it, they'd had a few glasses each. Chin remarked that he felt as if tiny multi-coloured bubbles were bursting around him. Suddenly everything was so much brighter and everybody he saw looked so much happier. He couldn't stop grinning.

Greta teased Stomps, "What have you got that I haven't? I've done my best, but Chin has always refused to drink with me."

Rooks took out his Kodak box camera and insisted that he take a photograph of Chin and Greta together. Chin's inhibitions had disappeared after the fourth glass of wine and he grabbed Greta's hand. She put her arms around him. A couple across from them stared.

Greta laughed. "Don't look now, but we're the centre of attention."

Stomps, who by now had finished a bottle of wine, said loudly, "It's none of their blerry business!" The couple walked off.

Chin grinned. "No more wine for you. A policeman behaving like that. Disgraceful!"

Towards evening, they piled into the car. Rooks, who was the most sober, drove. Greta sang some of her favourite songs. She did a fair job with Marlene Dietrich's "Lily Marlene" in German. Stomps and Rooks raised the roof with "Daar Kom Die Alibama" and "Vat Jou Goed en Trek, Ferreira."

Greta said, "It's your turn, Chin."

"But I can't sing any English songs."

"Sing us a song in your language," Stomps urged him.

"No. It won't sound good to you."

Rooks yelled good-naturedly, "Never mind, sing!"

His inhibitions gone, Chin sang. It was a long time since he'd sung in the presence of other people, but he let himself go with his favourite, "Muruga Tha Manam". He had a reasonably good voice. They listened politely. At the end there were a few moments of embarrassed silence.

Rooks said, "It sounds different."

Chin laughed. "Sounds strange, doesn't it? That's because your ears are attuned to Western music." He told them that Carnatic music was the oldest form of orchestrated music in the world. The ragas were pure melody, unlike the harmony of Western music, and were intended to induce such moods that would put one in tune with the rhythms of the universe.

They listened with fascination – until Greta felt they were becoming far too serious and sang "The Tennessee Waltz". Everybody, including Chin, joined in.

Where the road branched off to Constantia, there was a tea room noted for its scones. In the long embracing Cape twilight, it seemed perfectly natural to sit down together on wooden benches in the open and order scones. The waiter took one look at Chin and stiffened. He took their order but Greta was quick to notice. Out of the corner of her eye, she watched him drawing the attention of a stern-looking man to their table.

The man approached them. "We don't serve non-whites here."

He looked directly at Chin. Rooks and his wife could have passed for white, although they'd never tried to do so.

Stomps said, "Are we breaking the law?"

The man hesitated. "That's not the point. Right of admission is reserved."

Stomps got up, swaying. "We done nothing wrong. We done nothing illegal." He whipped out his badge. "I am a policeman. Watch what you do."

Chin held his friend back. In one moment, the mood had changed completely. Chin said, "Keep your scones, Mister."

With that, he walked to the car, despite Stomp's entreaties. They drove home sombrely, each one expressing indignation and vowing never to go back.

Back at the hotel, Stomps insisted on another drink. They'd never seen him this way before. Stomps seldom drank hard spirits, but now he ordered a double brandy on the rocks. No one could stop him. After his fifth brandy – that after all the wine – he put his arm around Chin. He didn't say anything. Every time he tried to speak he just sucked in his breath. A tear or two rolled down his cheeks. Rooks and Chin, their arms around his waist, guided him to the room Chin had set aside for him. As they got him onto the bed he managed to get out the words, "Jou moer! Right of admission ... jou fokin' moer!" It was the first and only time they'd seen him so drunk, and it was the first and only time they'd heard him swear. His limp fists flailed in the air as if he were lashing out at somebody.

Chin's wardrobe reflected good taste and his suits were tailor-made. He'd discovered a Malay tailor, Samsodien, who operated out of his house in the Bo-Kaap. Everyone called him Sam. Sam was never without his red fez. He reminded Chin of Lalla back home in Victoria Street – the same attention to detail, the same excellent workmanship. As Sam put it, "A suit must not scream at you. In a good suit, people must notice you more than the suit."

That's more or less what Lalla had said, and Chin couldn't agree with him more. He was so pleased with the first suit Sam made for him that he immediately ordered another. "Play it again, Sam!" he said with a wink – movie buff that he was.

He opened an account at a leading men's haberdashery, Garlicks in Adderley Street. He could afford to buy silk shirts – pure imported Cambridge silk shirts made in England. He had a passion for bow ties and plain socks, generally dark ones. He preferred plain shoes, either black or brown, to the fashionable "two-tones", and was seldom without his gold cuff-links and tie pins.

Everyone knew him at Garlicks. He would walk in and the white salesmen would jump to attention. He just loved to have them in tow and would deliberately take his time, a salesman silent but ready at his elbow. Once, when a voluble high-pressure salesman launched into the merits of a shirt he was eyeing, Chin turned to him with a cold stare and said, "Did I ask you for your advice? I'll pull the chain if I need assistance." The salesman was about to react, but Chin whirled around and snapped, "What? You want me to take my business elsewhere?"

The news quickly spread. The manager told his staff, "That man is an excellent customer. I don't care what his colour is. If any of you are rude to him, I'll fire you on the spot." They showed him a healthy respect after that.

When he'd finished looking around, he'd point to the items of clothing he'd chosen and walk off to his car.

Within minutes, the parcels would be delivered to his car, without even a signature. He was one of a few customers with unlimited credit.

Cape Town exploded in a riot of colour and pulsating music during the festive season when the "Coon Carnival" bands roamed the streets. In the preceding months, housewives and tailors would spend hours designing and sewing the colourful satin outfits. The troupes held aloft banners proclaiming fancy names such as "The Red Indians", "The Dazzlers" and "The American Wise-Guys". The more formal Malay Choirs were smartly outfitted in impeccably tailored maroon, royal-blue or black blazers, grey pants, white gloves and walking sticks, with which they would beat out a rhythm on the tarmac or the cobble-stoned pathways of District Six and the Gardens in tune with the songs they sang. As they paraded through the streets of Cape Town, they sang all the favourites – "Sonny Boy", "The Tenessee Waltz" – along with traditional Afrikaans and Malay songs, to the accompaniment of piano accordions, saxophones, banjos and tambourines. Excited crowds would pour out into the streets, joining in the infectious fun, singing, dancing and clapping. The New Year was ushered in with a competition at Green Point Common where trophies were given to the Best Dressed Band, the Best Male or Female Vocalist, and so on.

Rooks and Greta once got into an argument about the Carnival. Rooks was among a small minority who felt that it degraded coloured people. "I mean, the very word 'coon' is racist."

Greta didn't agree. "For God's sake, it's a celebration of life. We white people don't have such spontaneity. We don't know how to have fun! Many white people would love to join in, but we are too damn self-conscious!"

"What you are saying is that freaks enjoy themselves more than normal people."

"Aw come on, Rooks, you know that's bullshit!"

Stomps thought Rooks was "sommer talking kak." It was one of those arguments that nobody could win.

Chin had some empathy for Rooks' feelings, although he didn't participate in the argument. But despite his uneasy feeling that Rooks had a point, to an outsider like him, the annual Carnival seemed as natural as the great scenic beauty of the Cape Peninsula.

Chapter Sixteen

CHIN HAD KEPT in touch with the Reddys, and almost every month received a letter from them. Mr Reddy collected the rent from his Sandflats farm, immediately forwarding the money to Chin by postal order. He was very strict with the tenants. But he refused to take the commission that Chin offered him. "Don't insult me, naina. You are my son, how can I take money from you for such a small thing?"

Chin was busy doing a stock-take when he received a telegram. Mr Reddy had collapsed at work and had been rushed to hospital. Greta knew how much he was attached to the Reddys and insisted that he visit them immediately. Shortly before Chin arrived in Port Elizabeth, Mr Reddy succumbed to a second massive heart attack.

After the funeral, Mrs Reddy said to him as she sobbed quietly, "Thanks for coming, my son. You better go back now. It's not nice to stay away from your work. If you lose your job, nobody will put food on your table."

Chin was deeply moved. The Reddys had been married for over forty years. "Ma, why don't you rent your house and come and stay with me?"

Chin hadn't given his offer much thought; it just seemed perfectly natural to make it. For Mrs Reddy, long settled into a fixed way of life, it would be a life-changing unpheaval. But indeed, her life had already changed dramatically with the death of her husband.

"You are so kind, naina."

"No, I need you …"

"You have everything. An old woman like me would be a burden."

It dawned on Chin that Mrs Reddy had far too much self-respect to want to live off someone else. Although she must be dreading the impending loneliness, she had to be sure that this was not an act of charity. Chin sensed the struggle in her mind and tried to put her at ease. "You know, I don't even have a lamp at home ..."

"That is terrible! Must have kamatchi velkoo in every home."

Keeping a lamp at home was not a simple matter. Every Hindu had to have a shrine at home, usually in the bedroom. A special prayer was necessary to consecrate the portion of the house in which the shrine was installed. The shrine usually consisted of a brass lamp, chombus, incense holders and garlanded pictures of the deities. Then there was the regular washing of the lamp, which had to be done in a special way. Chin's busy schedule didn't allow time for such things. He did think about it on occasion, saying to himself that he would get around to it sometime.

"Maybe I'll come for a short while, just to place the lamp and teach you how to care for it. It's very, very important, thumbi." She could not hold out any longer. A lifeline had been thrown to her in the ocean of grief into which her husband's death had plunged her – and in such a way that she still had her dignity. This young man was indeed a son, her own son. She looked at him for a moment, and then couldn't hold back the flood of tears and the sobs that shook her body.

Naomi, Michael Mbele's widow, was thrilled to see him. She was alone in the house. She said she was indebted to Greta for having put her children through primary school. Her eldest son, Peter, had become a priest, and there was now enough every month to pay the rent and to buy the groceries. Peter and Grace were paying for the education of her younger, Welile. Chin was pleased to hear that he was studying law at Fort Hare University; but Naomi said, "He's just like his father. Politics, politics, always politics. It's no good – see what happened to my Michael."

"But how is he doing in his studies?"

Naomi was obviously concerned. "He's got through every year, but Peter had a word with him when the police came here for him."

"Police? Did he do something wrong?"

"No, he's not like that. He's a good boy … but the police were from the Special Branch. I keep telling him politics is no good."

Chin could feel for this long-suffering mother. There were lots of things that were wrong in the country, but it took an almighty struggle just to eke out an existence. The lines became blurred. One could only fight from a position of strength. Or was a lack of strength not reason enough to fight, even if that fight meant total sacrifice? There were times when he was tempted to join up with his old friend Monty Naicker. He hadn't forgotten a chat they'd once had: Monty had told him of his determination to do something about the "way our people are treated". Their conversation had been brief, although he'd wanted very much to sound out this man who was so dedicated to the struggle, who bore banning and imprisonment with such deep faith, such absolute conviction. Chin had read the small items in the English papers about some of Monty's activities as president of the Natal Indian Congress, and he admired his friend's courage. He was always being thrown into jail, but his detentions didn't seem to deter Monty. Instead, they seemed to spur him on. Yet, despite the fact that he was a doctor and a respected political figure, Monty was a fun-loving man who enjoyed a Scotch or two. Chin read that Monty had called Prime Minister Malan "a two-headed monster". He understood why Malan could be called a monster, but why two-headed? For the moment, these things were beyond him. Monty was a very clever man. He wouldn't say things that didn't mean anything. One day, Chin would have enough time to understand these things. He promised himself that, when he eventually got back home, he would make a point of talking to Monty. But right now it was work, work, work. He had to be in full control of his life. Nothing was going to get in the way.

Grace was working full-time at the Hotel Cologne. She had done well in her exams and wanted to become a teacher, but there was not enough money. Naomi said with pride, "You must see her now, such a beautiful young woman!"

Chin said, "Tell her that if she ever wants to come to Cape Town, I'll have a job for her at the hotel." He left his address.

He left PE on the understanding that he would send for Mrs Reddy the moment he'd bought himself a house in Cape Town. He'd been watching the papers for some time, and had recently just missed a bargain at an auction sale. Greta, of course, wasn't chuffed about the idea, but his mind was set on a house. Mrs Reddy would be the right person to take charge of it when he was at work, once he'd persuaded her to stay with him permanently. What he hadn't told Greta was that he intended to settle down one day and raise a family, and that she didn't figure in his long-term plans.

Mrs Reddy had evoked thoughts of his mother. Alone on the train back to Cape Town, Chin's mind wandered to the warm fireside in his father's house, his playful sister barging into his room and his mother chanting her prayers in the little temple ... what were they doing, how had they taken his disappearance? Bugger all this, bugger this pride, bugger this wanting to be someone! The wheels of the train clattered on into the darkness and hills and trees whizzed past, barely visible.

He didn't sleep well. The train approached Cape Town in the early hours of the morning. The sunlight bounced off Table Mountain, clearly visible around the Salt River bend, and his homesickness receded in the glare. As the train pulled into the station and he gathered his things together, his mind became focused on the routine of a well-ordered life. First things first – but when those first things were done, he had to find some way of telling Greta. He knew that the relationship could not continue indefinitely, and at some point she had to understand that.

He didn't have to tell her in so many words. Greta already knew. She wanted to tell him that when you hold someone you love, you *hold* them. You hold them so they can feel you, feel your heartbeat, feel your love. For her, the holding had become one-sided: she held him tightly, but she could feel the looseness of his arms around her. She had tried to ignore it.

He'd said that he loved her. He was not a dishonest man, she thought, but in such matters even the virtuous are sometimes at a loss. Yes, he clearly enjoyed sex with her. It was passionate, sensual and the high points gave way to a lingering satisfaction. But of late, the passion had receded somewhat before an increasing self-consciousness. Her marriage had taught her that no matter how alluring a sexual relationship was, it was unsteady if not founded on the bedrock of love. She didn't frequent his room as much as she once had done.

Eventually, she broached the subject. "What's happening, Chin?"

"What do you mean?"

"Look, I'm not a young girl. I've lived long enough."

Chin found it difficult to speak his mind. He looked out of the window, smoking a cigarette.

She said, with a touch of cynicism, "Look, this has got nothing to do with your job."

He reacted quickly to that. "If you think that's what it was all about … for God's sake!" He stood, walked to the ashtray on the dresser and forcefully stubbed out his cigarette. It wasn't half smoked, but he ground it down with angry movements of his hand, using so much force that the ashtray fell to the floor. He walked out, slamming the door behind him.

They kept away from each other for some time. Stomps was the first to notice. He took Greta for a drive, bringing with him a couple of bottles of wine. She hesitated at first, but she needed some comfort and there was nobody more comforting than this warm, good-natured soul. They went up to the Steenbras Dam, high up in the Hottentots Holland mountains. At the entrance to the dam, a view site and picnic area had recently been turfed and walled off. In the bright sunlight they had a panoramic view over Gordon's Bay, right across to the lighthouse on Cape Point, proudly standing guard at the tip of the peninsula. It was a breathtaking sight, enough to draw one into an uplifting communion with nature. They sat in silence, drinking in the view and the wine.

"You can talk to me, you know," said Stomps.

She squinted at him. "Life can be shit sometimes, huh?" she said, trying unconvincingly to make light of her concerns.

Stomps could see she was not really ready to talk. "Ja, ask me!" He was no stranger to the complications of love. In his gentle way, he spoke for the first time of the young lady he'd been in love with in Oudtshoorn, where he was born and grew up. She'd been his childhood sweetheart, and there'd never been any question about their eventually getting married. Then one day, without any warning, she'd run away with a married man. He had never got close to a woman after that.

When they got back in the late afternoon, they encountered Chin in the garden, apparently checking on the pruning of the poinsettias. He tried not to look at them as they got out of the car, giving the impression that he was engrossed in what he was doing, but he was too close to the driveway for any such pretence.

"I'm famished! What's for dinner?" Greta said, quickly and perhaps a little too enthusiastically.

Chin took the cue, perhaps a little too eagerly also. "The linefish specialty of the day is fresh steenbras, curried à la Madras, caught, prepared and cooked by your imported chef, Monsieur Chin Govender!"

That made all of them feel a little more at ease, and they went inside the hotel. Stomps offered Chin some wine, but he surprised them by having three double whiskies, on the rocks, in quick succession. Neither had ever seen him have so much at one time. As they all tucked into the "baie lekker curry", as Stomps put it, they were like old friends again … almost. In between the familiar cues of life's drama, the challenge of the performance lies in coping with the unexpected. If you allow yourself to be thrown, you're a lousy actor – with the added discomfiture that, unlike the stage, in life neither the bouquets nor the brickbats are reserved for the final curtain: they hit you immediately. None of the three thespians in this instance could be satisfied that theirs was a convincing performance.

Chin would have dismissed any notion that he was jealous of the very close bond that suddenly seemed to have developed between Stomps and Greta. He reasoned with himself that it suited his plans if the relationship became even closer. But life was not so clear-cut, not always reasonable. Chin and Greta had been together for some time, very close together. Why did it have to be Stomps and why did it have to happen without warning?

The sudden turn of events served to harden his resolve to become not just independent but self-sufficient beyond the ordinary notions of wealth. He was constantly casting his line into such waters as might provide him with a juicy catch. He read the classifieds assiduously and constantly talked to friends and acquaintances. Rooks, reacting to his friend's persistence, mentioned a house in Walmer Estate which was going for a song. It was situated in a quiet cul-de-sac just below the highway, and had unobstructed views of Table Bay in front and a sharply rising Devil's Peak and Table Mountain behind. A variety of Council-tended proteas formed the decorative hedge between the drive and the house. The owner had put in many tasteful fittings and fixtures. Each room had its own built-in cupboards. There were three bedrooms, a large lounge and a two-bedroomed outhouse with its own kitchen, toilet and bath. Chin immediately decided that this was the house for him. It was owned by a middle-aged carpenter who had died suddenly. His wife could not afford to pay the bond and had fallen into arrears. The building society was about to foreclose and she was desperate to sell. Chin paid the arrears, paid her four hundred pounds and took over the bond. He allowed the widow and her two children to stay in the outhouse, rent-free, for one year.

He sent for Mrs Reddy, who brought Mabel along with her. "Mabel is a very good worker, thumbi. She will not only clean and look after the house, she will also help you when you get your own business." That suited him fine, as he'd hardly be spending time at the house anyway. Mrs Reddy insisted on buying and fitting the curtains. He took her to the hotel, where she renewed acquaintances with Greta.

"Nice to see you again, Madam."

"Nice to see you too, Mrs Reddy. Please accept my sympathies."

"Thank you, but what can you do? Life's like that ... are you looking after my son here?"

Greta laughed. "Your son is very good at looking after himself."

As they drove back, Mrs Reddy, who had long ago sensed that his relationship with Greta was more than one between employer and employee, said, "Thumbi, you are running such a big hotel but you are working for someone else. Why don't you get your own place? Then you'll be working for yourself, and you can get married to a nice Indian girl."

He'd been determined to own his own business for years, and now he wondered why he hadn't got down to it yet. There wasn't a single "non-white" hotel in the country. He scoured the papers for a place that he could convert into one. Some months later, he read that a large building in Cowley Street in District Six was going under the hammer. He outbid the only other person at the auction, a Jewish estate agent. Most of the houses here were owned by Jewish families who had businesses on the fringe of the District and in Woodstock. The small shops in the District itself were owned or rented by Malay Muslims and a few Indian Muslims. Most of the people who lived there were very poor. Yet there was a vibrancy about the place. The songs and the laughter seemed to flow from an assertion of life-spirit as much as it did from desperate escapism. Hanover Street, the heart of the district, never went to sleep.

Having paid the deposit on the Cowley Street property, Chin needed to take out a mortgage bond. He talked to Mrs Reddy about it. He knew that she'd saved much of the money from her business as well as her husband's earnings.

She knew what he was hinting at. She was a good businesswoman and would immediately have stopped the conversation if it were somebody else. Instead, she said simply, "It is not easy to get such a big loan." Then she made a quick decision – a bit reckless considering her conservatism when it came to money. After a short silence which hung heavily in the air, she continued: "I have all this money, thumbi – what am I going to do with it? Instead of going to the banks I can help you."

She didn't spell out exactly how she would help. Chin was quick. "I'll tell you what – we'll treat it as a loan. You must allow me to pay you back."

Mrs Reddy nodded, hoping that she was doing the right thing. Praying silently that he would not let her down, she gave Chin the money. He never did pay her back and she never asked him. She didn't resent him for that. Instead, she was happy that he had this streak in him – it was the only way to succeed in business. What was one little fault, when he had given her and her husband so much joy since entering their lives? And she was confident that he would never abandon her.

He brought in the contractors he'd engaged at the Hotel Steynsrust, but this time he was a lot smarter. He planned the alterations himself and asked for written quotes. He managed to get them to do it over weekends, charging him well below the normal rates, and the costs were well within reach. The work took six months to complete. Emblazoned across the gleaming white facade of the hotel was the legend, "GOVENDER'S MODERN HOTEL". Chin stood across the street looking at the sign for some time. This was it! Mrs Reddy conducted a prayer and strung a garland of marigolds across the front doorway.

Mabel was given the position of receptionist-cum-housemaid – when she sat at the front desk, she seemed ready-made for it. Her facility with English, Afrikaans and Xhosa, not to mention Tamil, came in handy. There were times when a customer was difficult and Tamil was useful in discussing the problem with Mrs Reddy, sometimes in the presence of the patron. Mrs Reddy was put in charge of the kitchen, with two people helping her. Two waiters were employed and the grandly named Govender's Modern Hotel was soon open for business. This was the first hotel for blacks in Cape Town – and, for that matter, in the country. At the time, "non-whites" did not have the liquor franchise, and so the hotel was not fully licenced. But Mrs Reddy's curries, the only "Indian" curries in Cape Town, caused a stir in the District and her reputation soon spread. The kitchen did brisk business. The news got around quickly and rooms were soon occupied by visitors from places like Swellendam, Graaf-Reinet and Worcester – people who'd come to find work in Cape Town. Occasionally there were travellers from Johannesburg and Durban.

Just when everything was going along so nicely, Chin received a letter from his tenants at Sandflats, giving notice. Upset, he showed Mrs. Reddy the letter. "Don't worry, thumbi," she said. "It won't be difficult to find a tenant."

He was worried anyway. He needed to see to the farm, but he could not take leave again, not after committing himself to his hotel and to managing the Steynsrust. Although she never complained, the hotel was getting too much for Mrs Reddy to handle alone, and Chin realised he had to do something about it. He was in a position to quit his job and manage the hotel full-time. He just had to give notice to Greta. That was not easy.

He waited for what he thought was the right moment. Greta had just come back with Stomps after watching him play rugby. They sat down to some coffee in the comfort of the hotel's old-style lounge, with its large settees one could sink into. The room was bathed in sunset hues and lit by large amber table lamps. It drew one into a warm, embracing intimacy. Greta was full of praise for Stomps' rugby-playing abilities. Stomps was genuinely modest and felt somewhat embarrassed at the praise showered upon him. To change the subject, he asked Chin, "How's your hotel going?"

"It's not really a hotel. It hasn't got a liquor licence. The law doesn't allow non-whites to have liquor licences."

Stomps, who did not work for the liquor squad, was surprised. "I never knew that. Even for Indians and coloureds?"

"Yes. It's only got ten rooms but it's getting busy. We're doing a lot of take-outs and the kitchen has a nice little turnover."

Greta looked out of the window as he talked. She'd lost him as a lover, but it would be very difficult for her if he left the hotel. She'd come to rely heavily on his strong administrative abilities and his fine business sense. He practically ran the Steynsrust, leaving very little for her to do. The hotel's huge success owed much to Chin's exceptional acumen, and he was not averse to rolling up his sleeves. Indeed, his work schedule was a punishing one. Chin could read her thoughts and did not pursue the subject further. He'd made up his mind, however, not to sleep at the hotel any more, unless it was absolutely necessary. He didn't even talk to Greta about it. She knew it would be futile to object, nor did she really feel like doing so.

Chapter Seventeen

MRS REDDY HAD noticed that Mabel was growing fat. She had her suspicions; but Mabel was like a daughter to her – if anything was wrong, surely the girl would have told her?

Indeed there was something "wrong". Mabel was four months pregnant, a secret she could not camouflage, much as she battled to do so.

She had met the young man while popping into the Avalon Cinema on her day off. The Avalon Cinema, on the corner of Hanover and Chapel Streets, was one of the smartest buildings in District Six: neon lights flashed from it, and a plush red carpet greeted you in the posh foyer. Once you stepped off crowded Hanover Street into that foyer, you were in a different world.

Bugsy Mentoor was smartly dressed in his zoot suit and two-tone shoes. He had three gold slits in his teeth, and spoke with an American twang. It was phony, but Mabel found it charming. He wore his Stetson at a rakish angle, even inside the cinema – nobody dared tell him to take it off. He was high up in the feared Globe Gang.

He was the first man Mabel had gone out with, and she was soon caught in the spell of his charms. Six weeks later, when she told him that she thought she was pregnant, he didn't seemed alarmed at all. He said he would marry her, she had no need to worry. In the fourth month of her pregnancy, Bugsy disappeared.

Daisy January, the closest friend she'd made in Cape Town, took her to a woman who was "good with these things."

"Why did you leave it so long, dearie?" the woman said through badly made false teeth. "But we'll do our best, nê?" She wanted six pounds. Mabel had saved her money and she didn't mind the price.

The pain shot through her body. Mabel went straight to bed, telling Mrs Reddy that she had a bad tummy ache. Late that night, her groaning awakened the old lady. Mrs Reddy lifted the blankets. The bed was soaked in blood. Mrs Reddy gasped, "My God, Mabel!" and summoned the ambulance, which took a long time to come.

Before they could get her to the hospital, Mabel had bled to death. Mrs Reddy gave her a Hindu burial.

Chin took Mrs Reddy on long drives. The death had left her distraught. "She came to me as a child, thumbi. She was like my daughter, such a good child. If she'd only spoken to me … she did the wrong thing. We must pray for her soul."

For sixteen days, Mrs Reddy sang bajans and songs for the dead to help Mabel's soul in its migration towards eventual moksha. On the sixteenth day, she invited Mabel's friends to the final prayer. A photograph of Mabel was garlanded and placed amongst the sacred lamps. Songs and prayers were offered. After the ceremony, the guests were provided with a vegetarian supper and a variety of sweetmeats.

Mabel's sudden passing left Chin with a serious problem. A replacement was urgently needed – someone who was not only as hard-working but as trustworthy as Mabel. A lot of cash was now being handled and the temptations were great. He sent a telegram to Naomi to ask Grace to phone him. Grace was delighted at the offer and took the next train to Cape Town.

Chin went to meet Grace at the station. She wore a light-green chiffon dress that was flared at the waist, and her slightly kinky hair was severely brushed back. She wore no make-up – she didn't need any. There was a softness about her large eyes and finely sculpted facial features, and a compelling innocence in her spontaneous smile. The change in her since the last time Chin had seen her, ten years before, was dramatic. Here was a beautiful, self-assured young woman. Michael would have been proud.

She settled into her job immediately. Mrs Reddy was very pleased with her and the two got on famously.

It seemed to their friends that Chin and Greta had got over their initial awkwardness at their separation. But things are not always what they seem; such closeness does not suddenly evaporate. Greta hid her sadness as best she could, and was especially grateful for the comforting presence of Stomps. She was relieved that the break-up hadn't resulted in Chin's resignation from his position as manager. The arrangement suited Chin: Greta was paying him well, and his own hotel was in the hands of people whom he could trust and who did everything they could to maximise profits.

Late one Saturday evening, Chin stopped at his hotel after dropping off Rooks, having had a few drinks with Rooks, Stomps and Greta at Steynsrust. He walked around Govender's Modern Hotel, just having a look. On the first floor he surprised Grace, who had just come out of the bathroom next door to her bedroom. She had on a flimsy see-through negligee, and hastily crossed her hands over her breasts in embarrassment. The fresh smell of scented soap crossed Chin's nostrils. The firmness of her breasts and her slim waist held his gaze. With a quick greeting, she shyly ran to her door.

Chin's muddled feelings were disconcerting. Suddenly he wanted to hold her, to be close to her, to be with her … he pulled himself together. "You are in charge here. Why haven't you got a gown on?"

She was genuinely apologetic. "I'm sorry, sir. It won't happen again, sir."

He softened the unintentional gruffness of his voice and attempted some levity. "And I'm not your teacher. I'm not a … a *sir.* Your memory's bad – have you forgotten my name?"

He went to bed with his feelings still muddled and with the fresh smell of scented soap lingering in his nostrils. He felt he had to be with her.

During the next week, the feelings turned into a compulsion, a kind of hunger – almost like the hunger that had once led him to open his pay packet and buy a duff cake and a pint of milk. The duff cake had been made out of stale bread, sweetened and flavoured – the confectionary of the working class. It had cost a mere shilling. He was not to know that it would lead to him paying a far, far bigger price. He sensed that now, once more, his impulsiveness might bring him difficulties. Yet he knew also that he could not help himself. The scriptures, Amurtham had told him, held that into the apparent order of life there sometimes came – from the "games" played by Narada, the cosmic maker of mischief – a disruption that took you beyond maya, beyond normality, beyond the ordinariness of daily living, job, marriage, family, home. Chin felt trapped, unable to escape that ordinariness, even as he knew he could not avoid being with Grace.

The next Friday, he called her aside in the lounge, out of earshot of the staff – particularly Mrs Reddy. He put his hands in his pockets because his hands were trembling. He tried to sound normal, but there was an unintentionally authoritative tone in his voice. "You haven't taken a day off yet, have you? And you haven't seen the beautiful Cape … it's time you did."

He arranged to show her Cape Town that Sunday morning. He would pick her up when everyone was still sleeping, and they would return quite late. Grace was puzzled when he told her that she must tell no one, especially Mrs Reddy, that it was he who was going to show her around, but she obeyed him.

Mrs Reddy was pleased that she was taking the day off. "You have worked very hard, my child, but be careful – you are a stranger here."

Grace felt uncomfortable. "Don't worry, Auntie, I have made some good friends."

She slipped out of the hotel and met Chin in his car, at the appointed place around the corner from Cowley Street. She still couldn't understand the secrecy. Could it be …? No, no, Chin was a respectable man, a friend of her father's. Still …

There was an awkward silence as he drove out of District Six. At Muizenberg, he stopped to buy her a Twisty's Ice Cream. It was the first time she'd eaten one, and he showed her how to progressively unwind the thick paper wrapping – she let out squeals of delight. They drove past the imposing mansions on Boyes Drive, through hairpin bends down into Kalk Bay, then along to Simon's Town before cutting across to Kommetjie. Chin pointed out the beach where crayfish and perlemoen were to be caught in abundance.

At Cape Point, they stopped at a view site rather than get out of the car and walk to the main viewing station on the sheer cliff at the end of the peninsula. It was not likely that anybody would recognise him here, but he didn't want to take the chance. From the car, they looked down towards where the sheer mountain cliffs dipped into a churning sea. He pointed out the foam in the distance – "Where the two oceans meet." Earlier, driving through the nature reserve, they'd thrilled to the sight of brown and white antelope dashing through the grass, and he'd showed off by saying that there were over 2 200 species of plants growing here – a fact he'd read somewhere that had stuck in his mind.

She clung to him in alarm as playful baboons hopped onto the bonnet of the car, looking directly at them. He laughed. "No need to fear them as long as you don't fool with them." There was a sign which read "Please Don't Feed the Baboons". He ignored it and threw them some nuts and bananas which he'd bought on the way.

They sat there a long while, talking as twilight descended. She shyly recalled the half-crown and the ice cream Chin had given her years ago, when her father had brought her to the hotel. The coin had got her brother Peter into trouble. Chin said, laughing, "Serves him right for trying to take money off a little girl!" He told her how much he had admired her parents.

She surprised him by talking about her father's political beliefs. She believed it was this that had resulted in his murder. He asked her if she had the same beliefs, and she said, in the quiet tone which seemed so natural and which heightened her attractiveness, "Beliefs don't feed you. Look where it got my father. We struggled and we are still struggling."

"Well, you don't have to struggle any more. You are with me now."

She smiled, not knowing the full import of those words.

In the darkness they left the reserve, stopping at Kommetjie. The moon was high and they walked on the cool white sands. Then he took her hands. She gave herself readily but somewhat awkwardly. This was the first time she'd been with a man, but this was the man she had fallen in love with a long time ago in Port Elizabeth, and to her this was God's way of rewarding her patience.

Grace understood that it was a difficult relationship, and the way things were, she didn't mind that it had to be kept very secret. She loved him too much to hurt him. He in turn was so gentle, loving and caring.

Chin was vaguely aware that he was not being consistent. He hadn't made his relationship with Greta public, but he hadn't kept it a secret from his closest friends – as he was determined to do with Grace. However, he did not allow this to trouble him unduly.

Their secret rendezvous was a flat in Salt River, which he rented in her name. He spent Friday and Saturday nights there. Inevitably, she fell pregnant, and when he suggested that she have an abortion, she would not hear of it. She begged him, "Please, please let me have this child. I promise I won't trouble you at all."

He said he'd think about it. Two weeks later he said, "All right, you can have the child, but you know what it will do to me if the news gets out."

She vowed that no one would ever get to know who the father of the child was – "especially dear Auntie Reddy."

Chapter Eighteen

Mrs Reddy was concerned. It was merely a suspicion, but years of experience had given her a very keen insight into human nature. She sensed Chin's loneliness, and she cared too much for him not to do what a mother would do for her son. In her heart, she knew that no one could take the place of a real mother, but she did all she could to make him feel wanted, feel that there was someone he could turn to. She cared so much for him that she did not ask him to repay her loan, although she was aware that he was making good money. Neither was she upset that he did not do so on his own.

Mrs Reddy could see that his loneliness could drive him to do things he might regret later. She'd seen the way he looked at Grace, and she was experienced enough to see that Grace had the kind of physical presence that could easily stir the passions of young men. She felt it her duty to do something about it before it was too late. She mulled over it for some time and finally decided that, even if it soured their relations, she would have to act. Every morning when she lit her kamatchi velkoo, she prayed for his wellbeing and that he would marry a nice young Indian girl and raise a family. She prayed also for God to give her the strength to do what she was about to do.

When Grace's baby arrived, Mrs Reddy insisted on seeing the child in hospital. Chin arranged for her to be taken there. He was a big healthy boy with a flattish nose, longish, curly black hair – and Chin's eyes. Her suspicions were confirmed.

When Grace was able to get back to work, Mrs Reddy

asked Grace to bring the child to the hotel. "He is such a beautiful baby!"

Grace replied that Chin had told her that employees were not allowed to bring their children to work. When she asked Chin about it again, he remained firm; it was the first time he'd refused a request made by her.

Mrs Reddy pleaded with Chin to at least allow the naming ceremony to take place at the hotel.

"But Grace is a Christian," he said.

"Grace has said she would be very happy for the child to be named our way."

Mrs Reddy consulted the tattered Panjagam she had brought with her from PE, and named the child Deventhiran, the mightiest of the deities.

Govender's Modern Hotel was doing very nicely. People came from all parts of the country and the rooms were nearly always full. Leaders of the ANC and the trade unions often stayed at the hotel. Chin charged a reduced tariff – his contribution to "the struggle". He didn't mind doing his bit at arm's length, and it was much appreciated. The kitchen did a roaring trade and they made a healthy profit selling illegal liquor. Chin had developed an excellent relationship with the police, who turned a blind eye to liquor being kept on the premises. Chin always kept aside some bottles of whisky for senior policemen, who loved nothing better than a few drinks before tucking into curry and rice.

Chin still worked at the Steynsrust, and still spent time with his old friends. During the 1948 elections – which didn't matter one way or the other to Rooks and Chin – the hotel's bars were closed, and Rooks, Stomps and Chin sat in Chin's office, having a few beers. Rooks asked Stomps, "And who did you vote for today?"

Stomps laughed, "That's a secret – but I'll tell you

anyway. I voted for the Nationalist Party."

"People are saying that they are going to take away what few rights we blacks have."

"What you mean we blacks? Coloureds and Indians is okay – but the blacks, the kaffirs are different. They are not equal to us. Or to you."

Rooks and Chin exchanged looks. This was their friend talking. Not just any friend. This was their good friend talking.

Mrs Reddy marvelled at the way Chin befriended people. He had easily won the respect and friendship of people in the District and indeed from all over Cape Town and beyond. But to Mrs Reddy, friends could never replace family, and if you didn't have family you were lonely. Such loneliness was a terrible thing.

One evening, she asked Chin to take her for a drive. Chin was pleasantly surprised – she seldom asked him to do anything for her. They drove along De Waal Drive to Kirstenbosch Gardens, stopping at Rhodes Memorial. Perched high up on the eastern slopes of Table Mountain, the imposing memorial afforded sweeping vistas of the immediate countryside. To the east, the lights of the city gave way to the darkness of the Cape Flats, and to the north, Table Bay reflected the glittering lights of the harbour and city centre. Mrs Reddy loved the sight. She said in Tamil, "Cape Town must be the most beautiful city in the world." He readily agreed.

"Thumbi, you must go overseas. You are making enough money. You must visit India. You must go to Madras. I hear it is a big city. That's where my parents came from."

"Maybe I'll do that one day."

"But first you must get married."

"There's still time for that."

"Thumbi, I want to see you get married before I die. It will make me very happy."

"Don't talk about dying, Ma. You have a lot of life left in you."

"Everybody must die one day, my son. I am old now. I have no fear of dying. It is time now for me to go to the abode of Muruga."

He joked, "When you go there, Ma, you must ask him a lot of questions."

"Don't talk about God like that. He has been good to you. Now you must listen to me. I want you to go to Durban and pick a nice Tamil girl from a good family. You have enough money now and you are such a good-looking man. You will easily find a bride for yourself. Don't you have any family there?"

It struck him that, through all these years, he'd never told her about his family. He hesitated, but soon his tongue loosened. He was not aware of the tears until they wet his shirt. He wiped them with his bare hands. She held his hand and said softly, "It's alright, my son, it's alright."

They sat in silence for a while. He pulled out his handkerchief and blew his nose. Then she said, "Thumbi, I'm cross with you. This must have been terrible for your mother … and your whole family. This pride is a bad thing. And in the end, what does it prove? No, no – you must go to Durban right away."

"I will one day."

"No, not one day. Now! If you don't, then … then I want all my money back!"

He was startled. She sounded angry. This was the first time she had spoken harshly to him. He ventured lamely, "Ma, I can start paying you …"

"You didn't hear what I said. I said if you don't go right away, then I want my money back. All my money."

Shocked, he could not say anything.

"Your poor, poor mother. How could you be so cruel?"

"Ma, you don't understand ..."

"Your quarrel with your brother has got nothing to do with your mother. She raised you. She suffered for you, and you do this terrible thing to her. I want all my money back, if you don't go now!"

The matter was settled.

He had to tell Grace. She'd been expecting it. Despite herself, she said, "So I mean nothing to you."

It startled him. She had never argued with him or hinted at being unhappy about their "arrangement". He said, "This is something I must do."

As he drove away from her flat into the night, he was assailed by feelings of guilt. He had not made any promises to her. Not in so many words. Yet was it not implicit in the way he made love to her, and in the way she'd placed her whole life at his mercy, that he owed her much more than just material comfort and security? Was it his fault that he could do nothing more? He had other things to do than to swim against the tide. There were so many things that were against you if you tried to live your life exactly as you wanted to, exactly as the scriptures spelt out. *We are all God's creatures. Life is one.* That's not the way people lived their lives. If it were, it would consume them, leaving no time for other things – and there were indeed more important things he needed time for. He could do nothing more. Nothing more. She had her own life to lead and he had his.

Once more, he deliberately snuffed out the voice within. When he got to the hotel, he pulled out a bottle of Johnnie Walker and sat alone in the office.

She had not cried in his presence, but that night Grace's pillow was wet with her tears. That's the way things were. She remembered, long ago in church, the priest quoting Jesus Christ: "And the meek shall inherit the earth." Her father, who only attended church out of consideration for Naomi's beliefs, had said afterwards, with his booming laugh, "The meek will never inherit the earth unless they fight for it. I think that's what Christ meant. Until then, the meek shall inherit nothing but sorrow."

But for Grace, there was no way beyond the boundaries of her life. The barriers were too huge, too daunting to even contemplate stepping over. As a child, she had come to understand through painful experience that her life was mapped out in a certain way. She recoiled every time she was the butt of racial innuendo or abrasive words such as "bushman" or "kaffir". Unlike her brother Welile, who had qualified as a lawyer, she baulked before these constant challenges. Welile had always stood his ground, even to the point of being severely beaten up once by some white hooligans. Her father had made it worse by insisting that the family were Xhosa, not coloured. He'd spoken with such fierce pride about his Xhosa ancestry, almost totally denying his Irish forebears. Her parents had had endless arguments about it. Michael had been adamant to the end, and her mother had loved him too much to go against his wishes.

Like her mother, Grace had ultimate faith in God. Survival meant not just coping with harsh material realities; it meant shoring up your inner defences. Unswerving faith demanded strength and, like her mother, Grace had become a fortress within herself. The faith that had borne her through the crucible of human slander remained undimmed. It was this faith that helped assuage the anguish, the doubt. She would always love Chin, even as he prepared to marry another woman, a stranger. Her patience, nurtured through long years of silent suffering, bordered on fatalism. Fate had brought them together; she would never love another man and, she believed, Chin's heart would always be with her.

Chin had bought himself a late-model six-cylinder Hudson Terraplane. It was hardly a year old and used to belong to a textile merchant whom Chin had met during the early days of the Steynsrust. It was big, sleek and black. For "non-whites" to own cars, even old ones, was something. To own a practically brand-new one, you really had to be someone. He looked forward to the reaction of the people in Durban, especially Jack, when they saw the car.

He told Greta that he was at last going to see his family in Durban. She had anticipated it. She said, "I'm happy for your mother. But don't go getting another hotel in Durban. You are still wanted here at the Steynsrust."

Rooks was thrilled when Chin asked him to accompany him. He'd never been to Durban. It was a three-day journey on roads that were mostly untarred. There were no hotels for "non-whites" on the way, so they would have to park at garages and sometimes off the road to get some sleep. Company was essential. Stomps said that he would also liked to have gone, but was not able to get leave.

Mrs Reddy made some pulisadho, or rice prepared in tamarind, which helped to preserve the rice for longer periods – enough food to feed an army, as Rooks put it.

It had been eighteen years since Chin had been in his mother's home.

Chapter Nineteen

NO MATTER WHAT the scriptures said, Amurtham would not let go. She didn't have many years left. People, especially those who are not well off, always console themselves by saying that when you die you can't take your wealth with you. No, you can't take your wealth, but memory was a different matter, thought Amurtham. If there was any sense to life, the soul had to be a storehouse of memory. Her husband and her two dead sons were always there, deep in her soul; and right there, also, was Chin. Much, much more than a memory. When she chanted her mantras under the spreading boughs of the syringa tree beside her tiny temple, she saw his face smiling back at her – it was not the smile of the dead.

She was in her temple when Mama-girl, now in her early teens, and Krishna ran in. Mama-girl knew she would be scolded if she disturbed her grandmother's prayer, but a strange car with strange people in it had driven up …

Amurtham, despite her age, always sat with legs folded in yogic fashion. With the passing of the years, it was not as easy to get up as it once had been. There was a nagging arthritic pain in her joints as she straightened up, but nothing that she couldn't cope with. And when Mama-girl and Krishna burst in, she stood at once: she knew, she *knew*. Before she could leave the precincts of the temple, he was standing there smiling, tears flowing down his cheeks. She kept repeating, "Aum Naamasivaya, Aum Naamasivaya", as they held each other in a long, silent embrace broken only by Chin's muffled sobbing. She had never given up, never, Aum Naamasivaya – the primordial sound of nature, proclaiming: Love is God, God is Love!

The rice had to be cooked and the fowl slaughtered. Mama-girl and Krishna ran around the house until Krishna cornered a chicken in the small clump of sugar cane. Krishna, Chellamma's son, spent almost all his spare time at his granny's house – "getting up to mischief all the time," Amurtham said. She sent him to call Chellamma, who lived close by. "Hurry, my child, hurry!"

The neighbours came out in force, headed by Chellamma. Chin was dead, now he is alive! God is great, God is great! And look at his car, his clothes … It was a long time before Chellamma could speak.

Chin held her to his bosom. "Chellamma, I can't believe … Rooks, this is my sister! I can't believe … you're a woman!"

"Unnah, I'm a mother of five children. Two are at school, and Guru is working. This is Krishna, you've met him. This is Steva. Steva, say hello to Marmatchee."

"Hello Steva, I'm your uncle. Doesn't he look like me, Rooks? Doesn't he? And Dorrie?"

"Dorrie is at work. He's now a driver for White's Bakeries."

When Dorrie arrived later that afternoon, there was nobody at home and the house was locked. He walked to Amurtham's house. On the way, a neighbour told him that Chin had come back, and he broke into a run.

Chin had a huge grin on his face. "Dorrie, so now you have your own house. You're a lahnee now, huh?"

"Lahnee? What a car! Brand new, huh? So who's the lahnee?"

Chin didn't correct him. If he wanted to believe it was brand new, so what? It was practically new anyway. "It's okay. Life has been good to me."

While the women prepared the meal, Dorrie, on the pretext of taking the visitors for a drive around the district, took Chin, Rooks and Chin's brother Mike for a drink at the Mayville Hotel. There were many, many stories to tell over their drinks. Dorrie, who didn't drink, was not one for boasting, but he couldn't resist the temptation to talk about his eldest son, Gurunathan, who was showing signs of maturity beyond his years. At Sastri College, he'd caused a stir by bringing out a student newspaper, the *Nuntius*, and had been set on becoming a journalist. Although it was getting difficult to maintain the large family on his small income, Dorrie had been prepared to take on extra work so that Guru could finish school. But Guru, all on his own, had decided to leave school early, and had found work almost immediately. He had just joined the newspaper, the *Leader*, as a journalist. In many ways, Guru was different from the other kids – he had also joined the Natal Indian Youth Congress.

"And how are things with you, Mike?" Chin asked. "I'm so sorry to hear about your wife. How did she die?"

"It was TB. There's no cure for that."

"Lots of our people are dying from this disease," said Dorrie. "It's a good thing they started the Friends of the Sick Association in Newlands to help these people."

"Yeah. That's one thing about Durban – the way the people help themselves. Mike, you okay at your job?"

"If I could leave tomorrow, I would."

"It's that bad? Old man Baijnath was okay when I was there."

"He's very old now. The place is being run by his connection, Mothi, a real shit-arse."

"I must see the old man."

"You must. He's never stopped talking about you."

Back at his mother's house, in that neat wood and iron cottage, amidst the lush greenery of all shades that Rooks couldn't stop marvelling at, they sat down to a huge meal of sheep-head curry. Rooks, who like the rest of the men had built up a big appetite after the drinks, said, "Auntie, now I can see why Chin says nobody can cook like his mother. He says that to everybody in Cape Town."

They talked and talked. Mike said, "We don't have a phone, Unnah, otherwise we could have phoned Jack and Marnie. Marnie is doing very well with his business. So is his wife, that velekartchee."

"That's not a nice thing to say," said Chin – after explaining to Rooks that "velekartchee" meant "cleaning girl".

Mike replied, "She is mean – believe me, she is mean."

"Never mind, Unnah, as long as they are doing well," said Chellamma. "Other people don't even have jobs."

Amurtham said, "We must go and see all of them tomorrow."

Chin said it was not a good idea to visit his brothers, Marnie and Jack, during working hours. "We'll visit them in the afternoon. First I must pay a visit to Baijnath."

When he arrived at Baijnath's big house at the top of the hill in Wiggins Road, Chin gazed around in astonishment. The old wood and iron home had been replaced by a veritable housing estate of solid brick cottages with tiled roofs. They were painted in gaudy colours and had all the trappings of the noveau riche – decorative gables, sculpted Roman cement pillars, meticulously manicured gardens with gaudily painted statues of goblins and the heads of lions. At the bamboo jundha, the symbol of Hanuman, there was a three-foot-high, bright-blue statue of Krishna playing his flute. Children ran around, girls playing rounders or five stones and the boys playing gooli-dhunda. At the entrance stood rows of buses, in various states of repair. The Baijnath family, or rather clan, had gone into transport. The buses bore names: "Toofan Express"; "Rohini's Range Rider";

and, to Chin the most striking, "The Divine Wind". He joked with Rooks before they entered Baijnath's yard, "That bus probably has a broken exhaust and farts along."

Baijnath was sitting on his verandah on a large, comfortable wicker chair with huge cushions. His walking stick rested on the arm of the chair. Baijnath squinted at his visitors – and then recognition dawned. He struggled to get up. "Chin, my son … is it really you, Chin?" The old man wiped his eyes. He hugged Chin with trembling hands. "I knew you were alive, I knew it! You were too good to die. I'm so glad, so glad. Ram, Ram!"

Baijnath's wife was equally thrilled. She ordered Koonthie, her widowed daughter who now lived with them, to fry some puri-patha and some jelebi. Mrs Baijnath said gaily, "Jelthee, Koonthie, jelthee! Beta is back, Beta is alive, arreh Ram, arreh Ram!"

As they drank the tea and snacked on puri-patha and jelebi, Chin told the Baijnaths of how he'd started off as a wine steward and ended up owning a hotel. Of course he didn't tell them about Greta.

Baijnath listened, hanging on every word. "I was right. I knew you'd make it. I was going to make you a partner in my business not for nothing."

Baijnath still owned the accounting firm. His eldest nephew, Mothi, had finished his matric and had studied accounting by post through the University of South Africa. He said proudly, "The boy passed with flying colours and I gradually left the business to him. He has increased the income over ten times. We bought a building in Grey Street, where we now have our offices. Beta, today we are employing over thirty people, ten of them from my family. If only my father were alive today."

Mrs Baijnath said, "Leave all that. You married, Beta?"

"No, Auntie."

"Good. Before you go we must look for a pretty Tamil girl for you. Girl from nice family. We know lot of people now. You so pretty yourself."

Baijnath agreed heartily. He said, "I know just the right girl for you … Oh yes, let me tell you what happened. That time when you disappeared, hell you got us worried, we went here, there, everywhere … Puckree told me – You know Puckree? Gopal Puckree? You used to do his books. He said, you know Baijnath, that boy was very good. When I saw him I thought, I want a son-in-law like that, but he never ask. Maaikeerai, I did not know Gopal was feeling like that. I'm sorry, Beta, I made a mistake. I told you must forget Rani. I told wrong thing."

Mrs Baijnath said, "But he got another pretty daughter. Mogie. Just like Rani."

Mr Baijnath said enthusiastically, "Like twins, just like twins! And she's not married. Tomorrow I'm taking you and your mother there."

Chin seemed unsure. "Uncle, I appreciate what you're saying, but …"

Baijnath cut in sternly, "No buts and all. I'm coming by your house tonight to speak to your mother."

Chin needed more time. "Uncle, please listen to me …"

"What, you don't want us to come by your house?"

"No, that's not what I meant."

"Then that's settled."

Chin said lamely, "Tonight we are going to see Jack and Marnie."

"You mean you haven't seen them and you came to see me first? You see, Maya, this is my son, my own son. You go see your brothers first, Beta, and then we'll come in the daytime."

Mrs Baijnath said, "God must bless you, my son."

On the way to Marnie's business, Rooks asked, "What

was that thing – that pastry with the green stuff inside?"

"Puri-patha – the pastry is called puri and the green stuff is madumbe leaves. When we get home I'll show you the madumbe plant."

"And that sticky, reddish sweet we ate afterwards?"

"Jelebi."

"Absolutely delicious. Why don't you sell things like that at your hotel? People will buy them like hot cakes."

Next stop, Marnie's shop. It was a humble little convenience store, really no comparison to Ahmed's well-stocked shop not far away. They had one over Ahmed, though. Marnie's sold liquor from his store room, which opened out to the yard, safe from the prying eyes of the police. Marnie's wife Chinma's masala-fried reds were a big hit, especially after a "coupla canes". Marnie, himself no mean fisherman, made sure that there was always a ready supply of the bony but delicious fish. Ahmed was furious, and if he had his own way would also have sold liquor, but he couldn't. Allah was watching. He'd reported them to the police, but Marnie had a contact at the station who warned him of impending raids.

Chin's sleek Hudson Terraplane drove up to the store and immediately a crowd gathered. Chin, taking his time, was the last to get out. He was proud of his younger brother. Marnie had stepped out of his dead-end job and by all accounts was making a go of things.

Getting over his astonishment, Marnie told Chinma, "Close up, let's all go to Jack's place."

She said simply, "You go. I'll close later."

Chin was about to say something. Mike nudged him and said quickly, "Let's go, Unnah, this is their busy time and Chinma does not want to lose the busness. Money comes first."

Chinma shot back, "If we got no money, you'll give us money what? Nobody got time for poor people." She continued somewhat defensively, "We got lot of people coming here after work, otherwise they'll go by Ahmed's shop and then we'll lose all that business."

A sheepish Marnie got into the car and they drove off. On Umbilo Road, they passed Cohen's shop. Chin stopped the car. The section of the building he'd once worked in was now converted into a clothing shop. He stood outside for a moment, then walked into Cohen's shop and ordered a duff cake and a pint of milk. Back at the car, he gave Rooks the packet.

Rooks, who by now had had enough to eat, said, "What?"

"That's how I came to own a hotel – but I'll tell you about that later."

As they got to Govender's Butchery, opposite the Tomango Orange Juice factory in Merebank, the astringent smell of discarded, fermenting orange peels and stale pith assailed their nostrils. The permanent odour permeated the whole of the small village of Merebank, but no one complained. They were used to it.

Archee stood at the door, speechless. Then she took both Chin's hands in hers and kissed them. She held his face and kissed him on his cheeks. She couldn't stop crying. Jack emerged from the passageway. He stared, also speechless. Then, still the big brother, he said in measured tones, "Don't stand there. Come inside."

Once they were seated, Jack said, "Why didn't you at least write us? Mother was worried to death. That wasn't fair to her."

Chin didn't respond. Over the long years, he'd thought about this moment and how he would tell his brother off. He'd gone over the exact words he would use: "You treated me, your brother, like a common thief. And it was my money. *My* money! You want money? Here!" And he imagined throwing down several hundred-pound notes at his brother's feet. Now, however, he was not angry – not as angry as he'd been in those first years after leaving home. Strangely, he felt no animosity; just gratitude.

The initial shock and amazement over, Jack pulled out a bottle of cane.

"No thanks, Unnah."

"You own a hotel?"

"Yes … But it's unlicenced. We're not allowed liquor licences."

"We know all that. But you'd be stupid not to sell it on the quiet."

"I do, but …"

Archee was quick to see that Chin had too much respect to drink alcohol in the presence of his older brother. When she'd first entered the Govender household, she'd been struck by Chin's sense of family. She'd been almost jealous of the brothers' strong bond, but Chin's genuine respect for her had ensured a special place in her heart for him. She'd been devastated when Jack had slapped him and would have told him so at the time – but she knew that when Jack was really angry it was both unwise and futile to cross him.

The years had gone by. She'd watched Jack grieve. He did not wear his feelings on his sleeve but she knew, she knew. This moment was the answer to his prayers, the prayers he'd silently whispered to himself over the many days, the many months, the many years. There was nothing in his demeanour now to betray that kind of gnawing anxiety. It was instinctive, this role as the head of the family.

She cut in with the warm teasing that Chin loved so much. "Why you forcing him? He's a big man now. Put your glasses on if you can't see that." And before Jack could answer, she said, "Now, just help me with the salads. After you grate the carrots, cut the chillies." And she winked at

Chin.

There were times after those first few angry years, in his loneliness, when Chin felt that the day he met his brother again, he would embrace him. There was no place for rancour in this family. Now, however, there was an unintentional stiffness on the part of both brothers, although they made every effort to show their amicable feelings.

Archee proudly told him about the progress of the children. Jack's eldest son, Sathasivan, had set himself up in business. After finishing his standard six, he'd tried to get a place at Sastri College but had been unsuccessful. Now he had an office in Lakhani Chambers in Grey Street, where he ran the first black private detective and collection agency in the country, grandly called the FBI – the Friendly Bureau of Investigation. The Americans had failed to win the case they'd brought against him for copyright infringement. That's when Durban had sat up and taken notice of this brash youngster, who had the gall to challenge the might of the Americans. What's more, with no big degrees behind his name, he'd taken on the best white advocates in town.

Archee told him also about all the other children in the family. All of them, it seemed, were doing well at school. Chellamma's eldest son, Gurunathan, was gaining a reputation as a journalist, but she was worried about his political interests. She'd warned Chellamma about how bad the Special Branch could be.

Marnie agreed, "They gave RD Naidu and Billy Peters a very hard time."

The Peters family had lived next door to the Govenders and were very poor. With the trade unionist Billy going in and out of jail, his poor wife was saddled with the huge burden of bringing up their six kids. Billy was also a Tamil scholar: he sang, translating the wisdom of Thiruvalluvar and the great poets Manikaivasgar and Thiruyanasambar, as he stood swaying from too much alcohol on the corner of Trimborne and Discovery Roads. RD, also a trade unionist, rented the outhouse that Jack had built behind his house. Archee told Chin, "That man is influencing everybody. I told Chellamma and Dorrie that they must keep Guru away from him."

"Are they doing that?"

"No. They just laugh. They are spoiling their children, letting them have their own ways."

Mike took Chin into the butchery. The younger brothers, Freddie, Steve and Sonny, were all waiting inside with a bottle of cane spirits, along with Paulus Ngcobo and Niney Chittigadu, Freddie's childhood friend. When they saw each other, Chin and Paulus struck up boxing poses, feigning blows and laughing heartily. Chin didn't recognise Niney until Freddie told him who he was.

"You should have been a fighter too," said Paulus. "You were very good in training. You would have been like your brother."

"Paulus, I hear you are a champion butchery man now!"

Mike cut in, "Unnah, I have never had a drink with you. Neither has Paulus."

Chin wanted a shot, but he was just a little hesitant. He'd shown the necessary respect when Jack had offered him a drink, and here was Mike, his younger brother, not showing him the same respect. How times were changing.

Mike noticed the hesitancy. Amurtham always said that Mike was like his father, "full of mischief." Like his father, he loved life and was always laughing and making jokes. He thrust the glass into his brother's hand as he would have done to a friend. It seemed a perfectly natural gesture and his brother, whom he respected and admired so much, took the glass.

Niney, who was now working as a casual counter-hand in Jack's butchery, plied Chin with questions about Cape Town and job prospects. A law preventing Natal-born Indians from living in other provinces without a permit had recently been passed: they were not allowed to settle permanently in the Cape. Chin told him, "If they catch you without a permit, you go straight to jail."

Freddie, Steve, Sonny and Niney expressed their eagerness to go to Cape Town, because jobs were difficult to come by in Natal. Chin promised to do what he could for them.

It was the first time Chin had drunk cane spirits. The effect was much quicker than with other alcohol. He was conscious that he had to behave in a certain way in the presence of a younger brother. He excused himself. The toilet was some distance away from the butchery, and he walked through the madumbe leaves and cucumber vines. He really had no need to go to the toilet – it was an excuse to be alone. He looked up at a clear sky, where a myriad stars twinkled. There was a big guava tree at the side of the lavatory. Chin used to make his slings from forked guava branches. He went over and closely examined the tree, looking for a smallish forked branch. Ah, this one would have made a perfect sling! He saw himself as a child with the sling in his hands, remembering that sense of power.

Once, long ago, he'd found a similar branch and fashioned a perfectly Y-shaped sling. He'd waited under the inkberry bushes and the mango trees, anxious to prove to Jack that he was a hunter. It was winter. Winter in Durban was marked by a slight chill but was not as harsh as in Cape Town. The inkberry bush was one of a few shrubs which shed most of its leaves, while some of the mango leaves had turned shades of yellow and brown. The light brown slazi bird was perfectly camouflaged among the twigs and leaves, but Chin's eyesight was unerring and his eyes picked it out. He took aim. Perfect hit. The mortally wounded bird fell at his feet.

He held the sling high up over his head and shouted, "Whoa!" He'd proved he was a hunter. He was about to pick the bird up and run to his brother Jack when an almighty quiver ran through the body at his feet. He stared. The death throes of the bird transfixed him. He threw the sling away, but the image of that little creature struggling to ward off death stayed with him.

The memory brought back his conversation with Greta about the little tortoise. His answer to her question then had been glib and unconvincing. He was annoyed with himself for allowing his mind to be badgered by such "extreme sensitivity", as Greta had put it. Was it something to do with the voice within, the voice that Amurtham constantly said was "the voice of God"?

His mind wandered. There were so many contradictions. He was very much a fisherman. He had to admit, however, that while the sight of his catch dangling at the end of his line gave him a certain thrill, it also invariably left him with a sense of unease. He eased his conscience by telling himself that the fish did not feel pain, being a cold-blooded creature. Such contradictory thoughts would suddenly surface, disturbing the tenor of a life smoothed out by financial well-being, by public admiration of his skill as a fisherman – a smoothness, at this moment, helped along by the rapturous welcome he was receiving on his "return from the dead".

He went over to look at the leaves of the guava tree in the faint electric light that filtered through the darkness from the back verandah of Jack's big home. The flowers were giving way to embryonic fruit. He reached out to touch them, then instinctively withdrew his hand. His mother had said to him as a child, "Plants also sleep. Don't disturb them." Sleep fruit, sleep, he thought. There will be plenty of time to be awake in a world that didn't allow you much time to sleep.

When he got back, Marnie was singing "Krishna, Mugunda Murare", one of Chin's favourites. Paulus was drumming on the counter and singing along. Archee entered. "Alright, that's enough, the food is getting cold."

Over dinner, Chin told Mike about his farm in Sandflats. "If you want, you could take over. The workers are still there and you should easily manage the rent. The first three months will be rent-free, so you can settle in."

Mike was ecstatic. This was the opportunity he'd been waiting for. Chin warned him that if he was prepared to take up the offer, he would have to move fast, before the law preventing Indians from settling in other provinces was passed. Mike vowed that he would, and indeed, a few months later, he set off for Sandflats. For Chin, the problem of the Sandflats tenancy was solved. For Amurtham, who saw his act as a brotherly gesture of love and generosity, this was another karmic reward for her family.

Chapter Twenty

DORRIE HAD INVITED the whole family to his place for dinner on Saturday. The kids stared at their rich uncle, who actually owned a hotel, and spent hours admiring his car. Only whites owned hotels and cars like this. Chin lapped up the attention.

Chellamma had proudly told Chin about Guru. "Unnah, he looks so much like you, and he also has so many of your ways."

Chin took Guru aside. "I hear you are a very good writer. Good. Write about sport. Write about the good things, how people struggle and make it in life. Stick to that and forget about politics. It will get you nowhere. I got to where I am by keeping my nose out of trouble. Your mother will tell you about Billy Peters, who lived next door to us. A great man, a brave fighter for people's rights – but he is always in jail. His family is very poor. They sometimes don't have food to eat. You don't want to be like that."

Guru didn't say so, but it disappointed him that his uncle, whom he'd heard so much about, was speaking this way. Later, he confided in his Uncle Mike, who'd been a passive resister together with Jack. Mike said, "That's just big-uncle talk." He recounted how, in his teens, Chin had taken on a white bully who was bigger than him and had given him a hiding. "He is not afraid of whites and I tell you, he has some strong views too."

Chin spent the next day with his three younger brothers, who were now living with Chellamma. Dorrie was a generous man and didn't regard this as a hardship. His own younger brother, Ruthnam, was also living with them. Before that, his younger sister, Bommie, had lived with them for over two years. It was cramped but there was lots of laughter, and that's what Dorrie and Chellamma wanted.

They sat around talking about many things, marvelling at Chin's exciting exploits. Freddie had started work as a printer's assistant. He couldn't become an apprentice because the law prohibited Indians from entering certain trades. His boss, however, was so impressed with his hard work that he taught him virtually everything. Sadly, that made very little difference to his wages. Steve was working as a wine steward and Dorrie had got Sonny a job as a baker's delivery man. Sonny, under the watchful eye of Ngcobo, was taking after Jack and doing very well at boxing. He'd won all his fights and was soon going to fight for the South African Amateur Non-European Featherweight Championship.

Guru entered the room in the midst of the bonhomie and reminiscing. Guru had grown very attached to Sonny. Sonny laughed as he said, "Unnah, this youngster may be a writer but he is the only one brave enough to go near Akka when she has a trance."

Religion had featured strongly in Guru's life. As he grew into his teens, he'd found himself at odds with the smug answers of the faithful. He'd gone through the motions out of deference to his mother's unswerving religiosity. However, he found himself at a loss to explain some of the things that happened whenever she went into a trance. She was able to accurately predict events. How was this possible? This did not prevent Guru from deriving wry amusement from the comic aspects of religious life – rituals were observed with such fervour that it was not uncommon for devotees to break into trance-like states and go into all sorts of gyrations and poses.

On one such occasion, when he was ten years old, Guru was dutifully standing at the back of a small crowd of family members during a prayer at his granny's house. His Uncle Marnie, who was tall and angular, suddenly fell into a deep trance while performing a ritual. His tongue stuck out, his eyes rolled and his body moved in a slow awkward dance – a complete contrast to the impeccably behaved, morally and physically upright, dignified person he normally was. It was very, very funny. Guru giggled. Softly. After all, God was watching … and listening. His uncle seemed oblivious to Guru's irrepressible mirth. This went on for a few minutes. Then, without once looking at him, Uncle Marnie moved through the crowd directly towards Guru, who stood rooted to the spot. Jesus, he must have had x-ray eyes like Superman! He hadn't looked in Guru's direction, how could he have noticed his laughter? Slowly, his uncle blew some ash into his face. An odd feeling seeped through Guru. He didn't feel afraid or apprehensive. Instead he was aware of a comforting calm. He'd stopped giggling. He felt his uncle's hand on his head, a warm reassuring touch, a feeling that would stay with him.

He would always wonder about the strangeness of that moment, even after he'd rejected organised religion. His mother was even more devout in her spiritual pursuits than his Uncle Marnie. She would spend much time meditating and praying and would often go into a trance, especially when some misfortune took place or was about to take place. She had an uncanny intuition – or was it more than intuition? He would wonder for years about these things. There were no easy answers.

When his mother went into a trance, usually late in the evenings, Guru would be the one to fetch the brass tray from the shrine in the prayer room, making sure that on it there was enough ash and a little camphor – all as if it was the most natural thing in the world.

Late one evening, past midnight, the family was roused

from sleep by a piercing scream. Chellamma, in deep trance, gestured almost frantically that they should follow her. She got to the door and said something in Tamil. They couldn't understand her. When in this state, Chellamma always spoke in the purest Tamil, which the family sometimes had difficulty in following. Then she said in clear English, which she'd never spoken before in a trance, "Open the door!"

Just out of their warm beds, they felt the chill of the dark night air. It was quiet but for the distant chirping of a cricket. Chellamma led them under the house, disturbing the chickens that roosted there, and in the dim light of the burning camphor on her tray, pointed to a spot in the sand. "Dig!"

They dug. And there, right before their eyes, wrapped in newspaper, was a revolver. It was the first time Guru had seen a real gun.

The gun had been purchased illegally by Dorrie's stepbrother, Ruthnam. It transpired that the disapproving family of a young lady who had fallen in love with Ruthnam had hired thugs to waylay him in the dark and viciously beat him up. He spent several days in bed, and when he recovered he was determined to get his revenge. Unknown to anyone, he'd secretly buried the gun until he was ready to use it. Had it not been for Chellamma, Ruthnam might have ended up a murderer. As it was, he was later to marry, settle in Johannesburg and raise a fine family.

Yet for all that, Guru was appalled when chickens were slaughtered at some temples to propitiate the Gods. He was also disgusted by talk of black magic whenever some misfortune befell a member of the family. His patient reasoning yielded no satisfactory responses from his mother and his grandmother, who were convinced that people like Veerasamy were capable of dark, evil deeds using supernatural powers.

Chin joked with Guru. "So, my boy, you're going to be a big swamiyaar, eh?"

Guru was adamant: "Never!"

While Sonny playfully shadow-sparred with Guru, Freddie said, "You know, Unnah, I'm worried about Steve and Sonny. They're in love with two sisters whose parents don't want to hear about them."

"Is that so?"

Steve cut in, "He's talking nonsense."

Freddie laughed. "He's our brother, tell him the truth."

Silence.

"Why?" asked Chin.

"Because they say they are too black for the girls," said Freddie.

"Who these people?"

"You know Gounden? That fair-looking man? They're living in Trimborne Road ..."

"Yes, yes. That man used to work at the printers, that man with a pipe in his mouth all the time ..."

"Same family. Unnah, what a big fight!"

And the whole episode was related in detail. Gounden and his wife were appalled that their two beautiful, fair-skinned daughters had fallen in love with these Govender boys who, besides not having anything to offer his daughters, were dark in complexion. A coloured family, the Doves, were tenants of the Goundens, occupying a house on their extensive property. Mr Gounden solicited their assistance. The Doves – all of them, including the women – were to beat up the two brothers and tell them to stay away from the Gounden girls, in return for which they would not have to pay rent for two months. Gounden also promised to give them two bottles of cane spirits.

The cane spirits were provided even before they had undertaken their assignment. An almighty fight took place between the Doves and the Govenders. Eric Dove was huge, a nice enough man when he wasn't drunk. Size did not deter Sonny, and Eric could not catch the youngster with a solid punch. Sonny stunned him with shots to the head. Exasperated, Eric picked up a chunk of hardened cement lying on the side of the road and crashed it down on Sonny's head. They rushed a severely concussed Sonny to the hospital but he recovered, vowing to get Eric, come what may.

Chin was livid. "Let's go there now!"

Chellamma had to use all her powers of persuasion to prevent the brothers from setting off after the Doves and the Goundens. "It's all settled anyway. No matter what their parents say, the girls have made it clear that they are determined to marry our boys."

Chin turned to Steve and Sonny. "Is that so?"

Steve said, "Yes, but we're not marrying right now."

And so an almighty war was averted.

Baijnath was true to his word. He arranged a visit to the Puckree house, insisting that they be accompanied by his mother and his sister. "Baiya, the women are very good at these things."

As Chin walked down the paved pathway to the front door, he thought of Rani. He wondered whether she still looked so beautiful and whether she would also be there. Life had its ironies. Here he was, coming down the same pathway as before, with the distinct possibility of marrying Rani's sister, the little girl who'd clung to her dress when she'd opened the door to him those many years ago. Don't jump the gun, he told himself. Marriage wasn't that simple. He had to marry a Tamil girl, but not just any Tamil girl.

Gopal Puckree embraced him warmly. He had also retired, leaving the business to his eldest son, Magesh. He was delighted to hear of Chin's success and that his daughter, Mogie, was being considered as a bride.

When they were all seated in the lounge, Rani emerged from the passage, together with her husband, who was now balding and quite fat. The shock of seeing her unsettled Chin. The change was unexpected. Instead of the beautiful, lissome girl who'd always been so well groomed, here was a plump, tired-looking woman who appeared not to care about the way she looked. Her every expression, every gesture, every movement was embedded in deep, sad resignation. She gave him a wan smile of acknowledgement. He wanted so much to reach out to her. The years had gone by, but his feelings for her had not dimmed.

Mogie entered, bearing the salutary tray of tea and sweetmeats. She was now in her late twenties, and the resemblance to the Rani he'd known was startling. He could not help but gape. There was an awkward silence until Baijnath said, "Ah, here is our little princess. Mogie, meet Chin – and this is his mother and his sister Chellamma."

Mogie put her palms together, saying, "Vanakam," then shook hands with all of them. As she took Mogie's hand in hers, Chellamma felt a sudden strange sensation overwhelm her. Her body quivered and shook uncontrollably for a few seconds. It seemed much longer. She'd never experienced such a sensation before. Something was not right. Chellamma had a feeling that she'd been given some sort of warning, but how was she to convey it to her brother, whom she loved so much?

Mr Puckree had brought out his best Scotch, Johnnie Walker Black Label, and after the initial self-conscious introductions, they talked and talked. Chin politely refused when Mr Puckree offered him a drink, but the old men got stuck into the Scotch with a vengeance, with both breaking out into song. Mr Baijnath sang "Akiamme Laike Jeeya Beru Maika", which brought back a flood of memories for Chin. Mr Puckree, whose fine singing voice was hampered by short breath and a slight bronchial rasp, sang the Thiagaraja Bagavathar favourite, "Annaaiyam Thandayam". Mr Baijnath, drumming on the table as if he were the legendary Thubla Govindsamy, said, "Beta, I tell you what, we could sing in our days – didn't matter whether you were Hindi or Tamil, we all got together and played music together and we played – I tell you what! We played! Nobody could sing like us, what you say Gopal?"

And Gopal, in between his singing, said, "Pradeep! You too good man, the way you used to send that dolak, hell you were too good man!"

In the car on the way back, Baijnath expanded on the virtues of the Puckree family, and particularly Mogie. "She is just like Rani, Beta!"

Mrs Baijnath agreed volubly. "She's so pretty. She's very fair for a Tamil girl too. After all, Mr Puckree is so dark." Mr Baijnath glared at her and she quickly added, "But his wife is so fair. Maybe Mogie got it from her. She is just like Rani, so fair, so beautiful, so respectful."

Indeed, her remarkable resemblance to Rani eased Chin's anxieties about making such a vital commitment. If she was anything like Rani, she would make a good wife.

Chellamma kept silent as the occupants of the car showered profuse praise on the prospective bride. As they drove, she wanted to say, *Something is wrong … don't rush into marriage* … but Chin seemed quite happy. She ventured meekly, "She's very pretty. If she'd wanted to, she could easily have married here in Durban. Strange that she is marrying so late … and that she is tearing herself away from her family and going so far away to Cape Town."

Chellamma's concern was couched in far too subtle terms

to make any real impact, and she was forced to leave it at that. She consoled herself that the young lady was not only pretty, but came from a good family.

After the visitors had left, Rani sat alone in the room that had once been hers. Balakrishna was in the lounge with the rest of the family, having a drink with Gopal. It would be a few hours before they left for their home in Overport. She was grateful that she had some time to be alone.

She was still in love with Chin. With his smart clothes, he looked the part of a successful businessman, and he'd put on weight, although there was not the slightest fat on his sturdy torso. She had eagerly lapped up the stories of his many successes, which Baijnath couldn't stop talking about. She could have been part of those successes. She could have been a part of his life. Yes, she still loved him. For that reason alone, didn't she owe it to Chin to tell him the truth? If she did, it would devastate her parents, who had decided long ago to let things be, for the sake of the family's good name.

From the moment when Balakrishna had crudely exercised his right as a husband on that first night, Rani's dislike for him had hardened. She'd desperately tried to fix all her thoughts on Chin, imagining him there with her, but there was no escape. Instead, there was his repugnant physical presence, violating her. She gave up her body, limp and detached – but her self-worth, her dignity, even in that wretchedness, remained inviolate. Since then, Rani had put the feelings of her parents and her family above all else. She'd been a good mother to her four children, who had compensated in some ways for the emotional aridity of her marriage.

Her first reaction when she caught Balakrishna in bed with Mogie was that she should leave him. She'd take her children and leave the house gladly to these two, who seemed so suited to each other.

"If it were somebody else, I would say, 'You want him? Take him! You deserve him,'" Rani said to her sister. "Yes, I would leave Bala. You know I don't love him. You know I have no respect, no feelings for him. But you are my little sister, and people are saying all these things about you ..."

"People are shit!" Mogie cut in. Then turned her back on Rani, the one person who loved and understood her.

Rani had always defended Mogie when they said she was not a nice girl. ("What's a 'nice' girl?" Mogie would respond.) Rani had understood Mogie's anger and bitterness when they stopped her from seeing or talking to "low-caste" Mannie Moonsamy, who lived down the road. Rani knew that Mogie's behaviour was saying to the world, "You have no right to do this to me!" Something Rani should have said when Balakrishna's family asked for her hand in marriage.

Rani wanted to say to her sister, "You are harming yourself, not the people you resent." She wanted to say, "By giving yourself to this man who loves himself so much, you are playing into the hands of a monster." Instead, she just looked at this little girl, caught between opposing tensions – her "unbridled" sexuality, as her mother put it in Tamil when she'd caught her masturbating in bed, and the myriad repressions of a paternalistic society, in which sex was meant only for procreation and the cementing of family life. Desire had to be curbed in order to lead a virtuous life, enabling one to move ahead in the next life.

For Rani, the questions were many. What did "moving ahead" mean? Religion said it meant moving towards eternal bliss, which could only come about through detachment, through giving up desire and this illusion of life. Who set the boundaries? What subtle line did you have to cross to go beyond illusion to the point of truth – truth, which they said was represented by that little voice within? For Mogie, there were no such subtle concerns.

Mogie had not come back to their home after that incident, but Rani knew they were meeting in secret. A week later, it was Mogie, out of guilt, who broached the subject when they were alone together: "Akka, please believe me. I have not seen him again."

She was lying and Rani could see it, but she said nothing. What can you do when suddenly confronted with deep ugliness in the one you have always loved and cared for? Does such strong love vanish overnight? Rani was one of those people in whom it didn't.

As Rani had dreaded, Mogie fell pregnant. Her sister was the only person she could turn to. Only then did she confront Bala. "You have done this disgraceful thing to my sister." Amid vehement denials, she continued: "If it were anybody but my sister, I would gladly have left you to your dirty, filthy affair. You have done great harm to my sister and it could harm my whole family. It could destroy my children. It could seriously affect the health of my father, whom you know has a weak heart. If you don't do anything about it, I will expose you … and I will leave you and take my children with me!"

It was arranged that Mogie would stay with Rani and Bala for a few days. At all costs, her parents were not to know about her condition. Rani did not say as much, but she expected Bala to arrange an abortion through a doctor. She'd heard that there were doctors who performed safe abortions – at a price.

But Bala was not prepared to pay the fifty pounds for a safe abortion. Instead, he took Mogie to a back-street abortionist, who charged ten pounds. It was a messy business; they had to rush her to hospital. A gynaecologist was able to stop the bleeding, but told them that Mogie would never be able to have children.

It could not be kept from her distraught parents any longer, but Rani did not reveal who had made Mogie pregnant. And Mogie simply refused to tell.

Rani did not sleep that night after Chin had visited them. Many thoughts went through her mind. This was the man she loved, this man who'd really struggled to get where he was. Her parents could not stop talking about him, and her father looked very happy – much happier than he'd been recently. Chin, and his family too, also seemed happy – except for his sister, Chellamma, who didn't appear to be too pleased. Rani hoped and prayed that Mogie would mend her ways and make him a good wife.

A quick wedding was arranged before two hundred friends and relatives at the Umgeni Road temple.

Among the guests was Monty Naicker, who upon his qualification as a doctor had set himself up in private practice. Monty was now very well known as the president of the Natal Indian Congress. When he entered the room, there was a stir. Everyone wanted to get as close as possible to this man who was regarded as something of a hero. He'd just emerged from jail for the umpteenth time. Later in the evening, at the after-wedding party at the Puckree home, he urged Chin to join the Cape Branch of the Indian Congress. He mentioned the Congress's plans to join up with the African National Congress in the fight against racism. Chin naively asked whether this would not make things more difficult for the Indians. The government, he believed, would not take too kindly to this political union with the African people. Monty was about to tell him the reasons for the impending merger when dinner was announced.

It was the first time Rooks had attended an Indian wedding. He marvelled at the colourful saries and expensive jewellery the women wore, especially the bride, who looked radiant. He was also very impressed with Mr Baijnath's speech. He had no idea that Chin had been an "outstanding accountant" and that Mogie's father was such a wealthy man – and to think these people were virtual slaves when they came to the country!

It was an overwhelming experience – so many people, so much fussing, so much food. He told Chin later, "If this is a small wedding, I'd like to see what a big wedding's like!"

The next morning, tears flowed as Chin, Mogie and Rooks said goodbye and got into the car. They remained silent for a long while after setting off for Cape Town. Rooks sensed both the sadness and the unease. He tried to lighten the mood, joking about the smart turban that Chin had worn, and asking many questions about the involved rituals and the prolonged chanting of the priest.

Chin laughed. "I was baking in the heat, and the fire from the havan didn't make it any easier. I was hoping the bugger would get his act over quickly."

Mogie chipped in, "It was a big act, wasn't it? All these priests want is the money. That's why they go on and on, just to impress people so they can charge more money."

Chin watched his bride from the corner of his eye. She was clearly excited at embarking on a new life, a new adventure, a new start. One thing she wouldn't be short of was clothing. Her big, heavy portmanteau, packed with saries, underwear, cardigans, shoes and jewellery, took up the most space in the huge boot. Fortunately, Chin and Rooks had travelled light.

Rooks seemed to enjoy her company. She was full of fun and her laughter was infectious, but there were some concerns lurking at the back of Chin's mind. The first night had not been what he'd anticipated. He was experienced enough to know that he was not the first man his wife had known. In Cato Manor, when he was still a young man, there was a common understanding that a girl who'd lost her virginity before marriage was "spoilt" and therefore unsuitable for marriage. Masculine pride demanded that the bride enter the pundal chaste and pure, while women could not demand the same from men.

She was not inhibited in her lovemaking, and Chin couldn't say that he did not enjoy the intensity of her passions. There was a compelling sexual reciprocation, the likes of which he'd never expected from an Indian girl – making him realise just how wrong it was to judge people on their race – or, for that matter, on their sex. She seemed quite practised in the sexual arts. He was prepared to admit to himself that he was being hasty in judging her, but the suspicions did not melt away. Was the striking resemblance she bore to her sister Rani merely skin deep?

It had rained, and as the car carefully negotiated the dodgy Van Reenen's Pass, his misgivings heightened. He wanted to tell her, "It's all a big mistake. Let me take you back. This is not going to work out." But he knew he couldn't do that. A Hindu wedding was a sacred covenant, immutable, irrevocable. It was a solemn undertaking before a community of witnesses, every one of whom participated in its sanctification. Whatever his doubts, it was too late now. The knot had been tied and he just had to get on with his life.

They drove through the night. Indians travelling from Durban were only permitted to be in the Orange Free State for twenty-four hours. If they were caught transgressing this law, they'd be thrown into jail. By the time they got onto the long, straight national road that cut through the flat lands of the Karoo, all of them were quite weary. They slept in the car outside a garage in Colesberg.

Chapter Twenty-one

On their arrival at the house in Walmer Estate, late in the evening, Mrs Reddy came to the door with a tray of camphor and a coconut. Mrs Reddy whispered a prayer as she lit the camphor and waved the brass tray three times around the newlyweds. The light from the verandah splayed into the darkness beyond, camphor smoke swirling through it and rising into the bracing night air.

Grace, who was there for the occasion at Mrs Reddy's behest, was asked to break the coconut. After Mrs Reddy had waved it three times around the newlyweds, Grace took it into the garden, where she swung it at a brick placed there specially. She'd never broken a coconut before. It would not have been a difficult task in other circumstances. Her hands shook, but she managed to conceal it from the others. When the bride stepped over the threshold, Grace kept her head down. Mrs Reddy was ecstatic. She'd prepared a beautiful garland of flowers, which Grace was asked to place around Mogie's neck. Grace lifted her head only to make sure she'd placed the garland properly. She could feel Chin looking at her, but did not return his gaze.

Mrs Reddy asked so many questions and told Mogie so many wonderful things about Chin. "I am so happy that Chin married an Indian girl, and you come from such a good family … and you are so beautiful too! My son is really blessed."

Head bowed, Grace walked to the outside room where she would sleep the night.

Mogie had learnt about business at Puckree's Tobacco House and it didn't take her long to learn the hotel trade. She was good with figures: she kept two books, one for the Receiver and the other reflecting the true income. Before, Chin had been so busy that he'd left this to his book-keepers, and he was pleasantly surprised at her good business sense. Mogie relieved Grace of the banking and every morning balanced the previous day's accounts. Grace's accounting was meticulous, but that did not earn her any special commendation from Mogie, as it had done from Chin and Mrs Reddy. Theirs was a strictly business relationship.

Chin continued being the manager of Steynsrust, satisfied to leave Govender's Modern Hotel entirely in Mogie's hands. What he hadn't noticed was that she could be a martinet, although it soon became obvious that the once-smiling workers now seldom smiled. The warm interpersonal relations with the staff, which Chin and Mrs Reddy had encouraged, vanished almost overnight.

Mogie was about to fire a long-serving waitress, Rabia, when Mrs Reddy intervened: "Rabia is not that bad. She makes mistakes now and then, but she's a good worker ..."

Mogie was curt. "Auntie, please don't interfere."

Mrs Reddy looked at her in stunned silence. Suddenly, she felt she had become an outsider.

In the days to follow, in many subtle and not-so-subtle ways, Mogie made Mrs Reddy feel that she was neither needed nor wanted. Mogie resented the strong bond between her husband and this old lady, who acted as if she were part of the family. She was not his mother; she wasn't even related to him – and yet she was staying at their house free of charge, her meals were free and she was even given an allowance. Chin was being far too generous, too accommodating.

Chin had purchased boxes of corned beef from his back-door contact at a ridiculously low price. Mrs Reddy, who always ensured that the hotel workers were given a good meal, was cutting up the corned beef to make some sandwiches for them when Mogie entered the kitchen.

"What are you doing?" It was more an assault than a question.

"I, I, I'm making some sandwiches for the workers," Mrs Reddy stuttered.

"No, you're not," Mogie commanded. "There's plenty of leftovers from last night. We mustn't waste all that perfectly good food."

Mrs Reddy was about to say, "But we've always done it this way," but instead she simply looked at Mogie.

Mogie was in the hotel lounge when Chin came to pick them up that evening. He strolled into the kitchen. It was cold and Mrs Reddy was sitting next to the huge coal stove. She said, "Thumbi, I would like to rent a place nearer to the hotel."

"What nonsense!"

"No, my son. You now have a family. The children will soon be arriving and you need the house to yourselves."

"But you are part of my family."

Mrs Reddy felt like saying that Mogie didn't seem to think so. Instead, she said, "You know, I will always regard you as my son, but I have already spoken to someone. The rent is cheap and I can afford it from the allowance you are giving me …"

"I won't hear another word on the matter." And Chin gently gave her his hand to help her up from her chair and lead her to the car.

As they drove home, no one spoke. Chin sensed the chill of soured human relations, and suspected that Mogie must have said something to upset Mrs Reddy.

That night, after he emerged from the bathroom into his bedroom, towelling his hair, he said to her, "That old lady has given me a lot of money. I would not have been able to buy this place on my own."

Mogie replied, "It was a smart investment. Now she has free board and lodging. She really does nothing at the hotel. I let her do the cooking so that she can have something to do."

Chin glared at her. "What do you mean, *let* her? That is her job – she's in charge of the kitchen. You have a problem with that?"

It was the first time he'd spoken to her like that. Ignoring the rising tension in his voice, she said, "We're running a business, not an old-age home."

Chin almost shouted, "She has been like a mother to me! I don't want her treated any other way. Do you understand?"

It was loud enough to filter through to Mrs Reddy, who was sitting in the lounge next door, crocheting. She put down her needles, wiped her eyes and hurried to her bedroom. The thought that she meant so much to Chin lifted her sagging spirits, and she went to bed feeling wanted, loved. She told herself that nothing would ever come between herself and this boy, whom she had taken to her bosom as her very own.

His tone had been sharp, revealing barely muffled anger. It shook Mogie – she had overstepped the mark. With a look of wide-eyed innocence, she gave him a forced smile. He turned his eyes away in aversion, embarrassed by her glibness.

Mogie was determined not to let this little matter affect the relationship – least of all, dampen their love-making. The practised coquette emerged. "No need to be so angry. Come to bed now."

On their wedding night, she had given her all and, after the initial nervousness and hesitancy, his response had been full-blooded. She'd been afraid that her lack of physical innocence might put him off. Indeed it hadn't. Her doe eyes had been dreamy at the end of an hour of unrestrained passion. She'd wanted so much to say, "There's no one else like you"; but she'd decided that it would not be wise. These days, she eagerly looked forward to her evenings with him. He was far more masculine than Bala, but not so rough and impatient. After prolonged and rousing foreplay, he spent much longer in the actual act of coition than Bala had.

Now Chin slipped under the blankets, but he was in no mood. She put her arm over his chest, running her fingers through the mass of black hair which covered his well defined pectorals. He ignored her hand and reached for his novel – *The War of the Worlds* – and switched on his bedside lamp to read himself to sleep. He could hardly concentrate on his reading, although he gave the impression that he was engrossed in it. Her fake smile played in his mind.

Hanover Street was not the easiest road to drive on. It was narrow, and besides the packed trams you had to dodge reckless pedestrians who kept darting in and out. At the same time, you had to keep an eye on oncoming traffic. In normal circumstances, Chin relished the challenge. But Mogie's forced smile lingered in his mind, taking his attention off the road.

On the urging of Mr Baijnath and his mother, he had agreed to marry a virtual stranger. He'd hoped that he would grow to love this stranger, but that hope was now fading fast. That smile … the ease with which her expressions changed troubled him. This was his wife, the person he was to spend the rest of his life with.

He almost slammed into a grinning, prancing, jaywalking

pedestrian high on dagga, singing "'O Sole Mio", but his reflexes brought him alive and he awoke to his crowded, noisy neighbourhood, swerving smartly at the last second. The pedestrian, still singing, still smiling, bowed like a matador.

His lungs emptied in relief, but Mogie's smile returned again to haunt him, mocking. A smile like a mask, a false smile. He could not but contrast this with Greta's openness and directness, and with the deep humility and genuine innocence of Grace. Grace made no demands. She was there for him, any time. The smile with which she always greeted him was warm, transparent, embracing. A complete contrast to Mogie's mask. Perhaps he was being unfair in making such comparisons, but all the same, events had left him disturbed and uncertain. Love could hardly be built on such uneasy foundations.

Self-exiled from his secure home environment, mixing with strangers at many levels in new environments, establishing completely new friendships and social and business relationships, Chin had gained insight into his own personality and those of the people he was involved with. New relationships, of necessity, began tentatively. One had to make evaluations. He'd once told Greta, who'd accused him of being too suspicious, too judgemental, "Okay, I don't have a right to judge people, but I have a right to protect myself. If I have to make a judgement that errs on the side of my own welfare, then I must do so." Toughness was called for, and he often wondered whether he really had that kind of toughness. He couldn't pretend to put up with what he perceived as phony, but he wasn't sure that he could carry that kind of reasoning through to the end.

Mogie was quick to perceive the shift in their short relationship, and was worried. On the surface, everything seemed normal, and once they got into their stride their love-making still retained its ardour; but ordinary, everyday relations were businesslike. Mogie took some comfort from her conviction that he needed her. Since she'd taken over, profits had almost trebled and the business was being run with great efficiency. Guests complimented them on the spotlessness of the hotel, the clean bedding, the fresh flowers in every room, the nice-smelling bathrooms and toilets, the tasty meals served on time. All the workers were well dressed and if anyone was caught with even a hint of underarm odour they received a warning. The second time around, they were fired.

Chin's friends, especially Rooks, and the small community of Indians in Cape Town had taken to Mogie. Everyone commented on her great beauty and charm, and Chin could not deny that he felt somewhat flattered. At home, she had taken over the cooking – and it had to be admitted, even by Mrs Reddy, that her food was excellent. Mrs Reddy's age was beginning to show. She was becoming forgetful to the point of sometimes not salting the food, or leaving out some spice or other. At the hotel, she continued helping with the cooking, but it first had to be passed by Mogie.

It was true he had come to rely heavily on Mogie. She had taken complete charge of the hotel and its finances were in a healthy state. There was no need to use their overdraft facility at the bank. The cash flow was constant and showed daily profits. Mogie could tell, because she balanced the books daily. At the end of the month, a sizeable amount went into savings and investments. They did not owe a cent to anyone. She insisted on paying cash for most items, and the hotel's credit ratings were excellent. Chin felt good when his bank manager said it was a pleasure doing business with him – although he didn't know how to respond when the manager told him he was the only "non-white" businessman in the area to have received a gold-embossed diary from the bank.

They were both working hard. Greta had left the Steynsrust almost completely in Chin's hands. He had asked for an increase, and although she'd raised her eyebrows at the formal tone of his request, she'd readily agreed. At his salary, he was almost a full-blown partner; but he was worth his weight in gold, Greta told Stomps, who was now staying at the hotel.

Stomps agreed. "I've never seen anybody work so hard."

"He's also got a good mind for these things and I can trust him."

Stomps was about to say, "You can trust me too," but decided that it would sound jealous – which indeed he was.

Greta, still in love with Chin, noticed a change in him. He wasn't his normal charming, smiling self. When they sat around as usual after work, having a few drinks, he was withdrawn and laughed perfunctorily at the others' jokes. Although he put on a show of amiability, this wore off as the evening wore on. When she was alone with him, she ventured, "You're not yourself. What's the problem?"

He was silent for a few moments, wondering whether he should confide in her – he needed to talk to somebody. But instead he replied, "No trouble at all. Everything's fine."

Greta had a feeling that all was not right with his marriage. It gave her some little satisfaction, and she would've dearly loved to have had more information. Perhaps there was a slight chance that he might come back to her. She tried to shake off her thoughts, chiding herself for being unfair to Stomps, who was always there for her. Stomps – ever attentive, kind and gentle – had helped to assuage the pain she felt when Chin stepped out of her life.

It was his fourth double whisky and it seemed as if he were enjoying his self-pity. The Mrs Reddys and the Graces of this world were rare. They were transparent. You could read them like a book. When they smiled they meant it. Was it an exaggeration to say that most people were not like that? It seemed that many were swamped by darkly secretive thoughts, hidden agendas, menacing envy. He'd been on his guard all his life – until that trip to Durban. Life was fine until he let down his defences in Durban. It was a stupid thing to do, putting his whole life at risk, marrying a stranger. He drove to Grace's flat, taking a bottle of Johnny Walker with him. Six doubles later, she put him to bed.

He got up at four, with Grace sleeping soundly beside him. It was the first night since his marriage that he had not slept at home. When he got home at six, he was met by Mogie and Mrs Reddy, who had both stayed up all night.

"Where were you?" Mogie asked.

"I worked late and I slept at the Steynsrust." He hurried to the bathroom, while Mrs Reddy went to her room.

Mogie pursued him. "They told me you weren't there." At about midnight, she had phoned both hotels.

He whirled around. She had confronted the lie, and he was forced onto the defensive. His huge hangover worsened the confusion. He was angry that she had phoned and angry with himself for lying so carelessly. "I didn't tell the receptionist that I was sleeping at the hotel. There was no need to." He could see that she did not believe him.

Mogie was alarmed that there might be another woman, and silently hoped that it was only a one-night stand. She knew that he did not love her, but he was her husband and she was determined not to lose him.

When he came out of the bathroom, a hot cup of coffee was waiting for him. He said politely, "I'd rather not have coffee now. Phone the hotel and tell them I'll be late. I want to have a small nap."

She nodded and sidled up to him as he slipped under the blankets. For the moment, all was forgiven.

Steve, Freddie and Niney Chittigadu could finally afford to come to the Cape – they'd stinted themselves, saving almost every penny of their hard-earned money for the trip, but they did not have permits. Chin scolded them: "This is damned stupid of you. They're very strict. But it's your own look-out – don't drag me into it if you get into trouble."

Much to Mogie's annoyance, Chin put them up in the outside room of the Walmer Estate home, and arranged for Steven and Freddie to work as waiters at the Steynsrust. It was not long before the law caught up with them, however. They spent two months in jail before being "deported" back to Natal.

Niney, however, proved too wily for the authorities. He'd moved in with the family of a young lady he had befriended in Salt River. He shaved his head and always wore a cap. He soon adopted the high-pitched, singsong accent of District Six, mastering the Anglo-Afrikaans patois. He easily got work in a clothing factory, soon rising to the position of foreman, earning far more than he had ever earned before. He kept in regular touch with Chin, who, although wary, welcomed this contact with someone from back home.

Chapter Twenty-two

SINCE THE DAY his Uncle Chin had suddenly come back from the dead, Guru had wanted very much to visit Cape Town. Chin's rise from penniless runaway to wealthy hotel-owner had made a deep impression on him, as it had on the other youngsters in the Govender family. As well as his younger uncles, two of his older cousins had gone there and had come back with glowing stories of the beautiful countryside and Uncle Chin's extravagant style of living.

Over weekends, Dorrie and Chellamma often hosted members of her family. Chellamma cooked large pots of food and the house was filled with the gossip and gaiety of the adults and the laughter of children as they played rounders, hide-and-seek, marbles and gooli-dhunda, or drafts, snakes and ladders and carom if the weather was bad. The adults often talked about Chin and his amazing success. Guru gleaned from these discussions that his Auntie Mogie was not able to have children. Chin had taken her to the best doctors, but nothing could be done. The adults tut-tutted at Chin's unfortunate fate and one of the aunties said, "You see, you can have all the money in the world, but there are things that money can't buy."

Guru felt constrained to defend his uncle, but it was not his place to do so. Most of the people in the district, poor as they were, had large families. The cynical thought occurred to him that it was because of these large families that not many could live the way his uncle could. Guru was determined never to have children if he could not adequately provide for them. His own father worked hard and gave them much more than other fathers in the district. They were among the few who wore shoes to school. Yet there were many things they had to do without. When Dorrie suddenly fell ill and was off work for over two months, Chellamma was hard put to feed the family. There was no such thing as sick leave – if you didn't work, you didn't get paid. Thank God for the small rental they got from the tenants in their two-roomed outhouse, and for the herbs and other vegetables that grew in their garden.

There was very little scope for black journalists. Guru was fortunate to have got a job on the Indian newspaper, the *Leader.* The owner and editor of the paper, Dhanee Bramdaw, had been very impressed with his work on the school paper, the *Nuntius.* The pay was not much, but it was a big help to his father. While working, Guru studied for his matric through correspondence.

Of course there'd been other reasons, apart from money, for leaving school early. Guru had a loathing for rote learning. He hadn't wanted to be one of those "clever" chaps, like Farouk, Govind or Nadaraj, who could recite Ovid word for word. They would surely become wealthy doctors or lawyers, but talk to them about what was going on in Parliament and all you'd get was a blank stare. If "clever" meant mopping up information in detail, then Guru didn't want to be "clever".

Guru loved his work, and was very clear on where he stood as a black journalist. The unwritten code was absolute objectivity and impartiality. But what was objectivity in the South African sense? There were only two newspapers owned and published by Indians – the *Leader* and the *Indian Opinion.* The other Durban daily and weekly newspapers were owned by whites and catered exclusively for whites, with passing references to blacks. The *Indian Opinion* was exactly what its name suggested and did not publish hard news. The *Leader* had a duty to correct the imbalance.

Guru believed that it was the solemn duty of the black journalist not just to report the facts but also to put them in perspective. That meant penetrating the layered myths of South African society, running the risk of being labelled partisan by those on the other side of the fence and their brainwashed victims. It was his responsibility to counter the deliberate and massive disinformation concocted by the establishment media in tacit support of government policy. Years of striving to normalise the abnormal had indoctrinated blacks into believing in their own inferiority.

Guru had long debates with his colleagues and was often aggressively impatient with their smug, shortsighted views. He argued, "Indians need to identify more with the struggle of the African people if they are to secure the future of their children."

Guru was full of admiration for activists like Velliammah Moodley and Thumbi Naidoo, and all those unsung heroes and heroines who had died at the hands of the police. As far as he was concerned, these Indians had showed very clearly that they were patriotic South Africans, and had given a clear signal that they regarded South Africa as their home. More importantly, they had the support of the majority. Most South African Indians, being descendants of indentured labourers, identified with the fight against colonialism and the colour bar. Unfortunately, Guru felt, there persisted the stereotype of the greasy Indian who was only interested in making money, by fair or foul means, and who still regarded India as the motherland. And there were Indians, like the *Leader*'s sub-editor Debi Persadh, who were actively complicit in promoting this unfortunate stereotype.

Guru still remembered the day, some years before, when he'd got his first front-page story as a young cub reporter. It had been Thursday, the day the paper went to print, and Guru had tried hard to control his rising anger. Debi Persadh was only a sub-editor, but he was acting as if he were the editor. Guru was not going to give in so easily. "This is the biggest thing that's happened in our community in years. It's a front-page story."

Debi smiled indulgently. "Politics doesn't sell newspapers. It can go on the inside pages."

Debi had been at the *Leader* for donkey's years, a hack if ever there was one, as far as Guru was concerned. He couldn't string two sentences together in proper journalese, but his cunning ways and his snivelling servility had got him to a position of seniority. Unfortunately, Dhanee Bramdaw, the editor, was away. Dhanee had founded the *Leader* to serve the community as a general newspaper. He was a committed journalist and would surely have used the story on the front page.

Guru's story read:

> This week saw the signing of the Doctors' Pact, which has united the Natal and Transvaal Indian Congresses with the African National Congress in their fight against racial discrimination and colonialism.
>
> In what Dr Monty Naicker described as a singular moment in the life of the Indian community, the pact was intended to unite two major political forces … the historic "Doctors' Pact" was signed by Doctors Zuma, Naicker and Dadoo.

The story went on to give details and the reactions of various community leaders. Some Indian traders were apprehensive that this would further provoke the wrath of the white authorities, who had shown no mercy to Indian activists.

The paper was just about to be "put to bed" when the phone rang. Guru answered it. Dhanee was phoning to find out whether the story had been covered. Yes it had, said Guru, but there was no place for it on the front page.

"Why? Let me speak to Debi."

Guru could hear Dhanee raise his voice on the other end of the line, but could not catch the words. Debi grovelled. He put the phone down, glared at Guru and changed the layout to include the story on the front page. Guru had won the battle, but the personal war was far from over. Debi had felt threatened by Guru's superior journalistic skills, and resented Dhanee's obvious respect for the youngster's talents.

Even Debi was a victim, and it was this, more than his personal, ruthless games of survival, that disgusted Guru. This man had capitulated, allowing himself to be so indoctrinated that he could not or did not want to see the importance of the story in the life of the community. But Guru soon put the ugly personal aspects of the incident out of his mind.

Debi said, "This Doctors' Pact will do more harm than good. This kind of nonsense will land us in even more trouble. Whites won't take it lying down."

His words were to be prophetic in the most devastating fashion. Not long after the signing of the Doctors' Pact, without any warning, unbridled violence was visited on Cato Manor and other districts where Indians had settled. A stallholder in the Indian Market caught a youth stealing and took the law into his own hands. Passing Africans were incensed at the assault and reacted.

It was as if some one had lit a bush fire in tinder-dry conditions. Homes and businesses were looted and burnt, people raped, maimed and killed. Much of the violence was clearly orchestrated by unseen forces. The African National Congress, sensing the scuttling of the new unity with the Indian Congresses by a third force, toured the troubled areas, appealing for an end to the violence. The police watched with folded arms until the government of India threatened to send a warship.

There was triumph in Debi's voice when he accosted Guru. "I told you so. You can't make peace with these people."

Guru lost his temper. He wanted to say, "It's idiots like you who make things worse, you and your superior attitude!" – but he realised it was pointless. Debi and his kind were their own worst enemies. And they couldn't see it. He stormed out, shouting, "Fuck you!"

Chapter Twenty-three

Over dinner, Chelamma mentioned casually that Chin had hinted that he'd love to adopt one of her children. She now had eleven.

Dorrie said proudly, "That will be the day!"

But Guru thought, "Why not? You wouldn't even notice it." Such cynicism apart, he wouldn't have minded being adopted by his uncle. That way, he would enjoy the best of both worlds.

One evening, Dorrie announced at the dinner table that a friend of his was going to Cape Town by train, and that he'd arranged with Chin to put this friend up for three weeks during the December holidays. In return, the friend had agreed to take Guru with him. Guru was overjoyed. He took three weeks' leave from the *Leader.*

Guru was up early the next day to join the queue at the Indian Immigration Offices to apply for a permit to visit Cape Town. The man who processed the applications was a smiling but archetypal bureaucrat who bashed away at a battered Remington typewriter with a great sense of duty and importance. He was very thorough and insisted on every question being answered in correct detail. Fortunately, he knew the Govenders, and Guru was thrilled when he was immediately granted a permit.

The train journey took three days – through the Drakensberg, the Free State and the Great Karoo, which was as flat as a pancake for miles. The Little Karoo was covered in a summer carpet of miniature flowers of myriad subtle hues, in contrast to the Great Karoo's arid landscape. Even this did not prepare Guru for the awe-inspiring beauty of the Cape. The train emerged through the mountains of the escarpment at the edge of the Karoo into the breathtaking Ceres Valley, dotted with the white-washed towns of the Boland, bearing the unmistakable architectural imprint of the seventeenth-century Dutch and Huguenot settlers. In the distance, the shabby, isolated homes of the coloured workers stood like rejected orphans. The train whizzed past row after row of apricot, apple, plum, peach, nectarine and guava trees, and acres and acres of vines heavy with bunches of grapes.

Guru's middle-aged companion marvelled, "This is God's country!"

Guru would have agreed, but as much as he marvelled at the great scenic splendour that unfurled itself before them, his eye also caught the forlorn figures of ragged coloured children, who seemed out of place in this picture of nature's bountiful gifts.

Chin warmly welcomed his nephew as he got off the train in Cape Town's central station. As they drove through the town, Guru couldn't take his eyes off Table Mountain – an actual mountain, right there on the immediate border of the city.

"See that thin layer of cloud on the mountain?" His uncle said. "They call that the tablecloth."

As Chin drove along Hanover Street with its raucous, laughing crowds, Guru couldn't help contrasting it with Durban's Grey Street, where everybody seemed to wear their cares on their shoulders; being here gave him a warm feeling. They turned into Chapel Street, next into Pontac Street and then into Cowley Street … and there it was: Govender's Modern Hotel! The frontage was not imposing – just a plain white bag-washed wall right on the edge of the pavement. The huge carved wooden door opened into a passage, which led to the kitchen on the right and the lounge-cum-dining-room on the left. The lounge was large and comfortable, and in the dining area the tables were covered in starched white linen. Chin took him through the high-ceilinged lounge to his upstairs room – his own private space for the months to come.

Mrs Reddy instantly warmed to Guru – and the feeling was mutual. There was so much about this youngster that reminded her of Chin when he'd first come to Port Elizabeth – his slender but broad-shouldered build, his deeply respectful ways and his enthusiasm for life. She made sure that Guru had his meals on time, personally waiting on him, although she could not move about freely. Her body was riddled with arthritis, but she bore the pain stoically.

Guru was fascinated by the way his uncle dressed. He always wore a suit with a large pocket handkerchief in the breast pocket. His felt hat was kept at a slight rakish angle, and when he smiled he revealed a gold filling in his teeth. Whenever the mood took him, he would talk about his experiences, pausing at appropriate moments to build up the drama, eyes twinkling with hidden mischief. He related the incident with Jack over his pay-packet in such graphic detail that Guru could easily picture the scene. Guru looked forward to such warm moments.

Chin often took the family for drives, and Guru fell completely in love with the natural wonders of the Cape Peninsula. Once, in the unusually long, bracing Cape summer twilight that lasted until about eight, when most people back home would be falling into slumber, they drove past the University of Cape Town. The University was situated in a commanding position on the slopes of the mountain, its views taking in the entire vista of the Cape Flats, right up to the Hottentots Holland mountain range to the north-east and Gordon's Bay to the south-east. Guru felt himself being seduced by the idea of attending the university. There was little future in journalism, and law seemed the next best alternative. He knew his matric marks were good enough – the problem was that his father would not be able to afford the fees.

He felt a touch of homesickness as he thought of how his father had battled to provide for his large family, getting up at four in the morning to deliver fresh bread. As a child, he'd once accompanied Dorrie on his rounds. At a posh white café on the Berea, he'd eagerly lapped up the sight of large round jars of mouth-watering sweets of all kinds and colours: toffees, nutties, candy balls, chocolates. Drooling over a bottle of fruit candies, he hadn't noticed that his father was watching him from the corner of his eye. Dorrie said casually, "Which one do you like?" Guru hopefully pointed to the fruit candies, thinking that his father would buy him a penny's worth – probably about two sweets. Dorrie bought a pound – it must have cost the earth. Guru was the envy of the other kids in the family when he got home, but he gave them all an equal share. He'd never forgotten that moment. Always the strict disciplinarian, Dorrie was also very generous with his children. He would gladly pay for Guru to attend university if he could; but the family simply did not have the money.

Over the next few days, Guru's mind was occupied with trying to find the money to study law. In his youthful optimism, this was merely a challenge to overcome. He was confident that he would do so. At least he would not have to worry about accommodation. Uncle Chin graciously agreed to put him up at the hotel. He also promised to fix him a job as a casual wine-steward during major functions at the Steynsrust when extra hands were needed. Chin reminisced, "I started off as a wine steward, and I can tell you, I made some good pocket money." He laughed as he recalled how he'd messed things up on his first day.

Mogie didn't seem to be too chuffed with the idea of Guru staying at the hotel. She said, "Your family needs the money – why don't you go to work in Durban instead, and give your poor father a hand?"

Behind the facile smile, she was probably resentful of his being put up free of charge at the hotel, rather than genuinely concerned about his family's well-being, Guru thought. As he chided himself for being so quickly judgemental, Chin cut in, "Nonsense, when he qualifies he will be in a better position to help his family." His tone was suddenly curt and impersonal.

Feeling awkward, Guru excused himself and hurriedly went to his room.

He'd bought a newspaper called the *New Age*, the only national paper with the courage to publish the truth about South African politics. Its predecessor, the *Guardian*, mouthpiece of the South African Communist Party, had been banned along with the Party. The *New Age* soldiered on. Guru sought an interview with its managing editor, Brian Bunting, who was immediately impressed with the youngster's political leanings and his capabilities, especially with his reportage at the *Leader*. Unfortunately, they could not employ another full-time reporter. Would he be interested in a part-time job as a sports columnist for twelve pounds a month?

Guru jumped at it. This would be adequate to cover his fees at the university, and his part-time job as wine steward would be handy for other expenses. He phoned his Uncle Jack to convey the good news to his parents. He also phoned Dhanee Bramdaw, who regretted that he was leaving but wished him well with his studies. Dhanee said, however, that his job at the *Leader* was waiting for him if he ever decided to go back.

Guru stood outside Govender's Modern Hotel on a fine summer morning. He'd just had a bath, put on his holiday outfit and was preening himself in the sun. The hotel was in Cowley Street in the shadows of Table Mountain, which towered against an azure sky.

Suddenly the sounds of a "Coon" band filled the air. A raucous but tuneful chorus belted out "Daar Kom Die Alabama" to the accompaniment of tambourines, saxophones and banjos. The minstrels, with painted faces, brightly coloured satin suits and fanciful hats, surged down Chapel Street and turned into Cowley Street, with a crowd of joyous revellers singing and clapping behind them.

Guru was standing on the pavement. One of the minstrels thrust a paper tumbler into his hands and filled it to the brim from a jar of Oom Tas wine – which he would later discover was referred to as "rot-gut". The minstrel winked at Guru and yelled above the singing, "Merry Christmas ou pêl!"

Guru had never drunk before. The happy minstrel urged him on, and he felt he couldn't back down. What the hell! He raised the tumbler like a veteran, saying, "Merry Christmas to you too!"

He spluttered and coughed, but the fortified wine burnt its way down. In a few minutes, he was part of the band, part of the joyous, singing, dancing tide of humanity all the way to the Grand Parade. He would never have been so unselfconscious back home in Durban, where everybody seemed to be watching everybody else and people were so conscious of not making fools of themselves. But here there were no inhibitions, just a spontaneous celebration of life, here and now – just the way he wanted to live.

One evening, some time after enrolling at the university, Guru was sitting in the lounge studying when a resident of the hotel asked whether she could sit at his table to complete the pair of socks she was knitting for her two year-old daughter. It was a strange request, because the other tables were empty. Perhaps she just needed some company. The pretty young lady, Jenny, had finely chiselled features and auburn hair, and her petite looks made her seem younger than her twenty-two years. He was flattered, but it was ridiculous to think that he could get anywhere near anyone so beautiful.

Thank God for fantasies. They are the stuff of emotional sustenance, and nothing stopped him from letting his imagination wander. He pretended to be studying, but his mind was rampant with delicious and impossible thoughts. He was deep in wonderland when he felt a slight brush against his leg under the table. He thought it was his imagination running riot, but then there was another brush – this time a prolonged one. Guru caught his breath. There was no mistaking it. He glanced up surreptitiously, and she was staring straight at him. Her cheeks had a faint blush and she was smiling.

Jenny was the married daughter of Mr Sagadevan Nair, who, like Chin, had settled in Cape Town many years ago. He had become a successful businessman and had married a Scottish girl in the days when mixed marriages were still possible. He owned one of the smartest houses in the predominantly working-class Afrikaner suburb of Parow. He was a smart businessman and regularly entertained important people, including the Minister of Finance, Dr Donges.

Jenny had married a Durbanite, George Nair. Unfortunately, although he too made good as a businessman, George was an "illegal immigrant" under the interprovincial laws for Indians, and soon found himself in jail. "Deported" back to Durban, he decided to leave the country and settle in South America. Within a year, he'd set up a successful fruit import-and-export business. They'd sold their house in Brackenfell, and leased the shop which Jenny's father had given them. Before George left for Rio de Janeiro, he'd arranged that she stay at Govender's Modern Hotel until he'd got himself settled.

Against his better judgement, Guru found himself falling deeply in love. Were Jennny's feelings towards him just as strong? Although she was quick to proclaim her love for him, he wasn't convinced. Was she merely acting out of loneliness and boredom? On the other hand, she once said in the heat of passion that she was prepared to divorce George and marry him. She'd hinted that she had more than enough money to support him at university. Why would she say that if she wasn't genuine?

They had some rousing sex together. She taught him much, after their first embarrassing encounter when he ejaculated prematurely while they were petting. He was still very young and this was a huge step to take. Jenny received letters from George almost daily, expressing the most maudlin sentiments, pleading with her to take the next ship to Rio. She showed him the letters: "I've washed the streets of Rio clean, ready for your arrival, my dearest honeybunch."

The university Students' Representative Council was holding its elections. Political parties were vying for control of the SRC, but the Non-European Unity Movement, which had a sizeable following in the Cape, had decided to boycott the elections. In a heated student discussion, a colleague of Guru's, Claude September, derided the ANC for taking part in these "sham elections which give credibility to the system". He said, "We want total revolution."

Guru cut in, "What are you going to use in the revolution? Rotten eggs and tomatoes?"

The ANC's position was clear – mass mobilisation. Engagement of the regime at every level was important, not just to win little skirmishes but as part of the process of conscientising and mobilising the masses.

Students crammed the Jamieson Hall to hear the election candidates. Candidates representing the United Party, the Nationalist Party, the Labour Party and the ANC made their speeches. The Labour Party, representing liberal white students, seemed to have the most support. Together with the black students, they constantly booed the United Party candidate. The same fate seemed to await the Nationalist Party candidate, Tertius Malan. When he was introduced, there were rumbles which threatened to break into a chorus of derision. Tertius was unruffled. He seemed to thrive on the challenge and immediately exploded into a hypnotic harangue. The irrationality of his speech notwithstanding, his absolute self-belief mesmerised his audience, silencing them. Guru thought, "Hitler must have been like that."

The awed audience was still silent when the next speaker, Devs Mbele, took to the podium. Devs, although still only a teenager, had gained a reputation for being a fearless student activist. Constant Special Branch harassment had failed to dampen his activism. Patiently but firmly, he outlined the ANC position. There was some foot stomping and ululating but the liberals, who were in the majority, won the day and offered the ANC some positions on the executive, which it accepted – much to the derision of the Non-European Unity Movement.

Guru admired Devs and tried to befriend him. The young man was polite, but for some reason which Guru found hard to understand he was cool towards him. Yet Devs was by nature a warm, friendly sort who was always smiling. Guru worked hard to enroll more members for the ANC, and threw himself wholeheartedly into fundraising events and rallies. It was not long before his name went into the records of the Special Branch. Guru accepted this as inevitable and remained undeterred.

Chin spoke harshly to him for the first time after a Special Branch policeman visited Guru at the hotel. "You cut out all this politics nonsense. Finish your studies and then you can do what you want."

For the first time also, when the news of the Special Branch visit got around, Devs called up Guru and offered to buy him a hot dog at the student canteen. He wanted to compliment him for his commitment to the party. Devs asked where he was staying in Cape Town.

"At Govender's Modern Hotel."

Devs seemed unsure of what to say next. "Yeah … I should have thought so. You are a Govender … any relative of Chin Govender?"

"Yes, he's my uncle. How do you know him?"

Devs looked away. "My grandfather used to work with him." He abruptly changed the subject before it could go any further.

When they eventually said goodbye, Devs put his arm around Guru's shoulders, saying, "You've got guts. That's what it takes. I'm with you – don't forget that."

Fortified by his blissful relationship with Jenny, Guru was not intimidated by the Special Branch. He was walking on air, and grabbed every possible moment to be with Jenny. She was equally exuberant about their relationship, but they took great care not to be seen together within the precincts of the hotel. They reckoned without the perceptiveness of Chin.

One day, he took Guru for a drive around Lion's Head. At the view site, he sat down with Guru on a bench looking out over the Atlantic Ocean. His voice was soft and almost pleading. "I've led a difficult life. I've had to turn my back on my family, and I've struggled every inch of the way. The person I missed most during those hard times was your mother – my wonderful little sister." He took in a deep breath. "Now don't misunderstand me. A man has got to live. It's good to have girlfriends, but you are too young to get serious. You are doing a dangerous thing – going out with a married woman. It is my duty as your uncle to guide you. I have no problems if two consenting people want to have fun, but there is no need to hurt other people. You know what this will do to your parents. Not only is Jenny a married woman, she is not Indian."

Guru had deep respect for Chin, and he didn't know how to respond. He wanted to say she had an Indian father, but that would mean he was being trapped into some kind of apology. He just did not look at people in racial terms. It would be pointless engaging Chin in such an argument, so he kept his head down and tried to look as if he were taking his uncle's advice.

Jenny was becoming impatient. She could not keep on delaying her trip to Rio. Finally, she came to his room one evening with a wad of notes in her hand. She had made a reservation on the Dutch-India Lines ship *SS Tegelberg*, which was stopping en route from the East to South America. Aboard the ship were "refugees", most of them businessmen, fleeing the communist uprising in Korea. She said simply, "Either you take this money and we marry, or you go to the agents tomorrow and confirm my booking. I cannot wait any longer."

It was cold and raining. The north-wester was blowing. Wearing his battered but trusty old raincoat, Guru walked out into the night, all the way to his friend Barloo Naidoo's house. The Naidoos were wonderfully warm and friendly people. Mrs Naidoo insisted, as she always did, that he eat with them. He didn't feel like it, but he sat down at the dinner table. Mrs Naidoo reminded him of his mother. How would his mother react to Jenny? She had never once said a harsh word to him, and he wanted to believe that she wouldn't now. Still, Jenny was not Indian and she was married. She was the mother of someone's else's child. No Indian mother would accept that. Besides, did he really want to get married? He was far too young, and there were so many things that had to be done.

By the time he got back to the hotel, he'd made up his mind. He took the bus into town the next day with the wad of notes in his pocket. He walked into the posh offices of the travel agents, feeling immediately out of place. He was unshaven and wet from the steady rain. The smartly dressed clerk looked up from her desk with the practised look of superiority reserved for "non-whites" – especially poor, dishevelled ones. When Guru took out the wad of notes from the pocket of his old raincoat, the look quickly changed and she hurriedly offered him a seat.

Clutching the ticket in his pocket, he walked down Adderley Street to the Cape Town Gardens, where he'd arranged to meet Jenny. He sat on their favourite seat, overhung with a thick bougainvillea canopy which offered some protection from the rain. Eventually he saw her coming along the path that cut across the neatly manicured lawn hedged with roses. She had on a mauve two-piece suit, which neatly hugged her shapely figure. She was about twenty yards away when she saw the look on his face. He'd bought the ticket!

A few years later, looking back on his sometimes impetuous ways, Guru would reflect that it was like a scene from an Indian movie. The rain poured down, the tears flowed – but unlike an Indian movie, there was no music.

Chapter Twenty-four

It was now common knowledge that Mogie was drinking heavily. The marriage seemed to have broken down, but they kept up appearances. Chin was seldom at home earlier than ten in the evening, by which time she would have consumed half a bottle of brandy. Her body was losing its shapeliness. A slight double chin was developing and her face was puffy. With the emerging fat came a dowdiness: she didn't seem to care about her looks the way she once had done.

The sight saddened Mrs Reddy. This was the first Hindu woman she had encountered who drank alcohol. It was also quite clear to Mrs Reddy that Chin was not fulfilling his role as a husband. She felt that one of the major factors contributing to the breakdown of the marriage was that they did not have any children. A marriage without a child was empty. Children cemented a relationship, especially such a tenuous one as this. She herself had no children, but her husband and she had been deeply in love. It was abundantly clear that this was not the case in this instance. She could understand the pain Mogie had to endure on both counts, and her heart went out to her.

After a few drinks, Mogie became over-affectionate. "Auntie, can I get you a cup of tea?"

"No thanks, my child, but you must have something to eat – you have not been eating your dinner lately."

"You must be joking, Auntie. Look at how fat I've become!"

Mogie would put on her favourite records, which she'd brought with her from Durban. She still used her trusted old gramophone, which had to be wound up. The new automatic players, which could play long-playing records and seven singles, could not play her old HMV and Gemini 78-rpm wax records, which had been imported from India by her father and had been wedding gifts. It was odd watching her in her drunken state, winding up the old machine. Her favourite record was a love duet sung by MS Subbaluxmi and Thiagaraja Bagavathar, "Manne Moganaa". She would hum along, smiling broadly at Mrs Reddy, who felt deeply moved by the immense sadness she knew was lurking behind that silly, drunken smile – a smile which failed to hide Mogie's desperation. In a strange way, Mogie became increasingly drawn to Mrs Reddy, and the old lady felt she had to take this lost child to her bosom. She was not to know that Mogie's life would be so enriched by their relationship, even after the old lady had drawn her last breath.

Guru had inherited a liking for cars from his father and wanted to obtain a driver's licence. Chin encouraged him, recalling how Dorrie had taught him to drive – although he would let Guru drive only when he was in the car. One day he said, "I've arranged an appointment for you." Guru was grateful – it was difficult to get an appointment for a driving test.

When the day arrived, Guru got up early. He tried to convince himself that he wasn't nervous, but indeed he was. Chin said, "Just drive around for a few blocks and stop the car away from the licensing office. Give the inspector the keys to the boot." In the boot was a bottle of whisky.

Guru was reluctant. "Marmarcthie, I am confident I will pass – you don't have to do this."

"Listen to me – they fail you as they please, no matter how good you are. I know chaps who have had to go back three times before they could get a licence. This way, you are guaranteed."

As much as the idea offended him, Guru followed his uncle's advice and was duly awarded his driver's licence.

Guru loved driving. Chin had bought another car, a fairly recent, second-hand Chevrolet in very good condition, for use by Mogie. On Saturday afternoons, after she'd had a few drinks, Mogie would get Guru to take Mrs Reddy and herself on sightseeing drives, following the many splendid scenic routes of the Western Cape. Mogie had a good voice and she entertained them with all the old favourites. Out in the open, in the Boland amid the grape vines, or as they drove up Du Toit's Kloof through the huge protea blossoms and the towering mountains of the Hottentots Holland, Mogie's voice soared. It took Guru back to Trimborne Road, Cato Manor.

They choose a spot among the proteas on the banks of the Berg River and laid out the picnic baskets. Mrs Reddy had cooked a pot of mutton biryani – she enjoyed serving the food on paper plates. She had just finished handing Guru his plate when she gasped, clutched her breast frantically and fell heavily. Mogie moved quickly. She shouted, "Open the door!"

Helped by Guru, she picked up Mrs Reddy and put her into the car. "Drive to Paarl!" she shouted to Guru. By the time they got to the hospital, Mrs Reddy had breathed her last.

Mogie sought out a priest. There were no Tamil priests in the Cape, so she got hold of a Gujerati priest, Pandit Ranchod. She wanted to make sure the old lady was given a proper Hindu cremation. Chin was far too distraught to do anything, and he was grateful that Mogie had taken control of the situation so decisively. For the most part, she left the running of the hotel to Grace, whom she was increasingly coming to rely on. Grace asked her permission to take a few hours off to go to the St George's Cathedral to light a candle for the departed soul. Mogie did more; she said she would accompany Grace to the church. As a Hindu, she had been taught to respect all religions. Her Tamil school teacher in Durban, who was also a priest, always said: "All rivers lead to the same ocean."

She located a shop, Ghiwala's, which sold sandalwood chips, ghee and other prayer items necessary for the cremation. For the thirteen days leading up to the ceremony, a prayer was held every evening, during which she sang thevarams and kirtans. She didn't touch another drop of alcohol.

The old lady's death had touched Mogie profoundly. The words of the kirtans and thevarams were no more just words, to be sung with the appropriate piety at ceremonies, more for the benefit of the audience than for the nourishment of the soul. Now, when she sang the words, they found the same resonance within her as the words of her mantra during her silent meditation, which she began to observe every morning and every evening. The words made their way into her consciousness from a reservoir deep within her soul. They had been there all the time, waiting to surface, and when they did they brought with them an all-encompassing peace. Sometimes she would reflect on the excesses of her youth. Those things had happened, but they had happened to another person, someone who had meandered from her own true nature. It was time to bring the true person back; every time she sang the thevarams or meditated on them, that person came closer home.

A shrine was set up, in the middle of which was a garlanded photograph of Mrs Reddy, especially enlargened for the occasion. Mogie baked a variety of sweetmeats and these, together with three types of fruit, were placed in brass trays below the photograph. Chin's friends and the few Indians Mrs Reddy had befriended in Cape Town attended the prayer sessions and the thirteenth-day ceremony. Greta, Stomps and Rooks attended regularly – it was the least they could do to comfort Chin and Mogie.

For Greta, it was a touching sight to see a subdued Chin sit cross-legged before the shrine, with the strange, slightly intoxicating smells of camphor and incense swirling around the room. Occasionally, as Mogie's thevarams reached a mournful pitch, a tear would roll down Chin's cheek. The rituals were intended to assist the soul on its journey of reincarnation, towards the eventual attainment of moksha – freedom from the cycle of birth and death.

Guru had grown out of the religiosity that pervaded his youth. He tried in vain to find some meaning in the endless rituals and ceremonies, which usually bored him. He'd dropped out of Tamil school in the second class. In the Tamil community, there was not as much emphasis on "vernacular" studies as there was in the Gujerati, Urdu and, to a great extent, Hindi communities. He always felt severely embarrassed by barely understanding his granny Amurtham, who spoke to him mostly in Tamil.

Here in the lounge of Govender's Modern Hotel, there was more than a touch of nostalgia in the rituals conducted so fervently by Mogie. He was particularly struck by the rich intensity of Mogie's rendition of the ancient thevarams. He found the thevaram, "Vaazhvaavadhu Maayam", deeply moving. From the smattering of Tamil that he knew, it was something to do with the transience of life.

Later in the evening, when the prayer had finished and everyone had left, he approached Mogie. The change in her was noticeable. The busyness of an outgoing personality had been replaced by a studied calm, an almost impersonal serenity. She called him back into the lounge and instructed him to sit cross-legged with her before the shrine. She picked up the book of thevarams and sang and translated the song, line by line:

Vaazhvaavadhu maayam idhu mannaavadhu thinnam
Life is illusory, what is certain is that your body will become one with the earth.
Paazh povadhu pirravik kadal pasinoy sydha parridhan
The living body is wracked by desire, a vexatious disease …

Mogie paused, struggling to contain herself. The words had struck a deep chord within her. She swallowed and after a while continued, her feelings betrayed only by a slight tremor which strangely enhanced the mellifluous pitch of her voice.

… Cleanse your soul through purity of thought and deed.
Thaazaadhu arram seymin thadam kannaan malaronum
Strive to fulfill the soul's mission to become one with Brahmin, one with the truth.
Keezhmel urra dindraan Thirukkedhaaram eneere
Chant the holy name of the abode of truth, Thirukkedhaaram.

Mrs Reddy had lived longer than most Indians, who were generally struck down in their fifties and sixties, most commonly by cardiac failure resulting from diabetes and hypertension. It was believed that the small Indian community in South Africa had proportionately the highest incidence of diabetes in the world. Doctors were not able to ascertain the reasons for this.

Although, as the priest said, she had lived to a "good age", her death was difficult to accept for both Mogie and Chin. When she was alive she had told Mogie, "Your husband needs you. You are his only family here. In time, whatever is keeping you apart will one day be forgotten. Life is short and as we grow older we realise that soon we will be gone forever. All our troubles then, all our grievances will seem so small. Death is a great teacher."

Mrs Reddy had lit the kamatchi velkoo every evening, both at their home and at the hotel, where it stood in a corner of the hotel lounge before pictures of the deities Krishna, Muruga, Sarawasthi, Luxmi and Ganesha. She had taken care to see that the water in the brass chombus was changed every day and that the lamps and the chombus were washed at least once a week. She had also placed fresh flowers at least twice a week at the shrine. Mogie now took charge of the ritual. She gave up drinking completely and her attitude towards the workers softened. For the most part, she succeeded in holding her temper in check.

Chin, weary of years of tension and unhappiness, welcomed the sudden changes in Mogie. She never questioned him when he was late coming home, which happened less and less, and made no attempt to resume their sexual relationship. She did not pay as much attention to her make-up as she used to. Her dress was a lot simpler, usually a plain white sarie. Almost overnight, she lost weight; her face was no longer puffy, the slight double chin disappeared and the old shapeliness returned. Chin found her new, retiring persona a lot more appealing, and one Saturday evening their intimacy was resumed in the most natural way.

Grace looked on wearily. Her visits to church were now more frequent. She had long felt a pang of guilt whenever she went to church. She had been living in sin, and she constantly begged forgiveness. Yet she could not let go. She dreaded losing Chin, but it was almost as if this turn of events was fated to be. Chin still visited her at the flat, though not as often, and was still very caring. There was nothing that she or Devs lacked; they had all the material comforts they needed. Devs' clothing and studies were paid for. Devs had done extremely well at school, matriculating early and going straight to university to study law. Grace was even able to afford a second-hand Beetle, which Devs took great care of. She knew, however, that Chin had gone back to Mogie, and sensed an increasing distance. Whenever she was alone, she found it hard to cope with the growing emptiness and she turned more and more to the church, participating with vigour in parish activities.

But she needed Chin by her side more than ever, now that Devs was attracting the attention of the Special Branch. She told her son, "Look where politics got your grandfather. It's no good, my son. Put your mind on your studies." The flat had been visited three times by the police. The first time was a shock. They barged in, pulling out all the drawers and throwing the contents onto the floor. Clothes were dragged out of the closets and the place was in a shambles when they left.

Devs was gentle with her. He was careful not to show it, but he deeply resented his father. His birth certificate should have read Devinthiran Govender, but it read Devinthiran Mbele. Once, when he was ten years old, his mother had taken him shopping. He'd seen his father crossing the busy street towards them, and had been about to call out to him, "Pops!" But his mother said, "Shush!", putting her finger to her lips. Devs had been certain that Chin had seen him, but he'd just smiled at Grace as if greeting a worker. Devs never forgot the incident. Grace hadn't said it in so many words, but it was clear that he was not to acknowledge his father in public. This stuck in his gut. Now he increasingly kept out of his father's way, rarely speaking to him, and deliberately staying away from home as late as possible when Chin was visiting. It hurt to know that this actually suited Chin.

But after the second Special Branch raid, Chin made a point of seeing him. He said, "Cut this out. It's a strain on your mother. She's right, your studies come first."

He wanted to shout back, "It's none of your business! Who the hell are you anyway? You're ashamed of being my father, so who the hell are you to tell me to cut it out?" Instead, he just glared at Chin for a moment before walking off.

The Nationalist Government was pressing ahead with legislation entrenching racial discrimination. Among the plethora of laws that had been enacted was the Group Areas Act. Cato Manor had been declared a white group area: 180 000 people had been forced out, to live in makeshift townships without proper roads and basic amenities just outside Durban. It was rumoured that District Six would be next. The Labour Party and the ANC on campus called a meeting. They formed the Students' Democratic Association to protest against the new laws, specifically one that banned universities from registering black students from outside South Africa. Albie Sachs was chairman, Devs was treasurer and Guru, secretary.

They held a protest march to the centre of town. The police moved in with batons. In the melee, Guru received a blow to the head, opening a cut and resulting in slight concussion. Devs carried Guru to his Beetle and rushed him to the hospital. While the doctors were examining him, Chin and Mogie arrived. Mogie held Guru in her arms.

Chin was jolted to see Devs there. He called Devs aside. "How do you know him? How long have you been friends?"

Devs could feel the rising revulsion. He hissed, "You don't have to worry. He doesn't know."

Chin was still very angry. "You see, this is what happens when you take on the government!"

As Chin turned away, Devs said quietly, "Guru is very brave. This country needs people like him."

Chin whirled around and was about to respond but stopped himself.

Mogie thanked Devs for rushing Guru to the hospital. "Aren't you Grace's son?" Devs nodded. Mogie said, "I saw you once with her in town. You should come and visit us at the hotel."

Mogie had heard about Grace's son. And she had noticed the way Grace looked at Chin. Except for the slightly flattish nose and very curly hair, Devs looked like Chin: tall, broad shouldered and good looking. She wanted to get to know the boy. Although Grace bore an African surname, she looked more coloured than African. When she'd once asked Grace about this, Grace had said that her mother's father was an Irishman who had deserted her grandmother when Naomi was a baby. Grace's father also had white blood, but had not known his father and preferred to be known by his mother's name. Devs was old enough to have been born before Mogie had married Chin. That was in the past. There was also much in her past that she was ashamed of. She had no right to feel betrayed, although she felt a deep sadness rather than jealousy that it was Grace and not she who had borne Chin a child.

A few months after the funeral, Mogie asked Guru to resume their Saturday drives. Chin had wanted her to go fishing with him, but having accompanied him a few times, she was bored with that. One Saturday, she asked Guru to bring Devs along. She prepared a hamper of mutton biryani, roast beef and potatoes. It was spring and they drove up the West Coast to see the carpet of flowers, which covered the area for miles. A breathtaking rash of colours greeted them. They chose a spot and sat down to eat. She served Guru some mutton biryani and Devs the roast beef. He said politely, "I'd like some mutton biryani if you don't mind, Auntie."

"No, of course I don't mind, I just thought …"

Devs couldn't stop himself cutting in, "That I'm different?"

For a moment she didn't know how to respond. Guru wanted to say something but before he could, Devs continued: "No, I'm not different." There was a touch of cynicism in his laughter. "That day when the police rushed us in Adderley Street, I also got a slight wound and I was bleeding just like Guru, red blood."

Guru wanted to say, "That's uncalled for."

Mogie said, "I'm sorry that I offended you. Sometimes we say things without thinking. Please don't feel like that. I want very much to be your friend, for you to feel like my own son." She put her arm around his shoulders. She was not aware of the pleading look in her eyes.

In the silent, awkward moment that followed this unguarded sincerity, Devs was quick to respond. He placed a soft hand on her shoulder, and could feel a tender quiver. He knew then that she knew about Chin's philandering ways and that he was Chin's son. It couldn't have been easy for her.

Chapter Twenty-five

Guru was enjoying his studies, especially Roman Dutch Law and Native Law and Administration. In the latter subject, despite the impersonal, apparently objective observations of academia, the long history of ruthlessly calculated African dispossession stood out. His antipathy towards white people would have been greater but for the many committed white activists and liberals he encountered on campus and outside.

He also enjoyed English, and chuckled to himself when test results were put up on the noticeboard – his name was always at the top. It was ironic that the only "non-white" name in the English class regularly appeared above all the other very English-sounding names.

His sports column in the *New Age* was also drawing attention. Since Roger Bannister had broken the four-minute mile barrier some years before, the sports world had been agog. The frontiers of physical performance had been pushed back and the possibilities were limitless. Guru applauded Bannister, but observed that his country had given him the benefit of a normal lifestyle, superior athletics facilities and professional coaching. He asked how great South African sporting achievement would be if its vast black sporting potential were accorded similar treatment. Guru's views did not go down well with the white sporting establishment, particularly on campus, and once more the Special Branch growled.

One Monday afternoon, he had just entered the offices of the *New Age* to hand in his copy when he was turned away by two burly Special Branch policemen, whom he had not seen before and who had no idea that he was a reporter. One of them asked, "What do you want here?"

He hesitated, then lied. "I want to see my friend. She works here."

They told him that the offices were now closed to the public. The government had banned the newspaper. He phoned Devs and they met at the Grand Parade. In the biting cold and steady rain of a particularly harsh Cape winter, they walked into the station for shelter and warmth. They bought hot dogs and coffee from a vendor and sat on a bench, mulling over the excesses of a government drunk with power.

"This is bullshit," Devs said.

"Yeah. That's the end of my stay at varsity."

"Why?"

"I won't be able to pay my fees now. I owe the university about thirty pounds. My parents can't afford that. I was depending on my wages from the *New Age*."

"Why don't you ask your uncle?"

"No, he's done enough already, taking care of my board and lodging. He has his own commitments. Anyway, I won't ask him."

Devs understood, and admired Guru's fierce sense of self-reliance and independence. They sat for a while without talking until Guru said, "You know, the university won't release my results until the fees are paid in full."

"I can lend you the money."

"Thanks, but I won't be able to pay you back …"

"That's okay, I can wait until you qualify."

Guru laughed. "You're a lahnee, eh?"

When the laughter died down, Devs stared at Guru intently. "Look, I'm okay. We, my mother and I, have a benefactor, a rich old uncle. I can help you …"

If Devs had not sounded so serious, Guru would have

treated it as a joke. "Who is this rich old uncle?"

Devs was silent for a moment, as if trying to make a decision. "Never mind. Come, let me take you home."

On the way, Devs said casually, "You know, the movement has gone underground."

"Well, you ban an organisation, what do you expect?"

"The time for talking has ended."

"I should think so. I almost feel like chucking everything and going overseas to join them."

"No, you don't have to go overseas. They need people in the country. You'll be more valuable here."

Guru didn't agree. Devs went on, "They've contacted me. They're establishing cells all over the country. When you go back to Durban, I'll contact you."

He went on to talk about the launch of the ANC's armed wing, Umkhonto we Sizwe. "There's something I'm going to do soon. I don't want to involve you at this stage. It's a bit of a test run."

"What do you mean, you don't want to involve me? I'm involved, whether you like it or not."

"We've got to take this thing gradually. People have to be trained. There's no place for heroes …"

Guru was annoyed. "For fuck's sake, that's not what I'm in this thing for. Or don't you think that I mean it, that I feel very strongly about this?"

"I know you do, but we've got to keep cool heads. You can't just rush in against these guys – they're experts. They'll make mincemeat of us. We've got to undergo training. We're still setting ourselves up in this country."

They drove on. Suddenly, Devs pulled the car off De Waal Drive onto a viewing spot at the side of the road.

"Some of us may lose our lives."

They sat in silence for some time watching the rain fall onto the windscreen. Devs said, "I'm going to tell you something. Promise that you won't mention it to a soul. Promise."

"I promise."

Devs sucked in his breath. The wind had picked up and the rain was now much heavier. It lashed the windscreen. Devs leaned back against the door, turning half-circle in the cosy comfort of his seat. He was staring at Guru. "That rich old uncle … That rich old uncle is your Uncle Chin. He's my father."

It took some time to sink home, and when it did the words came tripping out. "I had a feeling. I just had a feeling! Amazing … why haven't you spoken about it before?"

Devs was looking at him intently. Guru suddenly became very self-conscious under Devs' scrutiny. Shit, he thinks this has upset me. I *am* upset. I'm upset that this thing, this beautiful thing has been kept secret. Mr Chin Govender, big shot, big hotelier. Life was full of hypocrisies.

Devs said softly, "Look, Guru, this may be hard for you to digest …"

Guru cut in quickly, "What the hell are you talking about? I'm just upset because you didn't tell me before."

"There was no need to …"

"No need to! Shit man, we're cousins …" Guru touched Devs' hand, repeating, "We're cousins!"

"Guru, all my life I've had to deal with this thing. I've tried not to hate, you know? That's not easy … but I guess it's given me a kind of strength. You need a lot of strength to live a lie." Devs started the car. "I wanted to be sure I could trust you."

"Do you?"

"Don't be stupid … cousin!"

Before he dropped him off, Devs said he would arrange for Guru to meet the top Umkhonto we Sizwe cadre who had secretly returned to the country.

Guru had always looked up to his uncle, ever since that first day when he'd come back from the dead in his shining new limousine and his Bond Street clothing. Now he was suddenly a man of straw, a philanderer who denied his own son, who was ashamed of his own child ...

Chapter Twenty-six

When Guru got back to the hotel, Mogie had a plate of freshly cooked mutton curry and rice ready for him. The aroma, with the unmistakable bouquet of fresh curry leaves, wafted through to the passage and the dining-room. Mogie was thrilled that she'd managed to get some curry leaves – it was a long time since she'd used them. She'd discovered that an Indian family in Belville had successfully managed to grow a thicket of the sought-after shrub, despite the harsh Cape winters.

Guru did not feel like eating. He told her that he was leaving for Durban. Shocked, she said, "And your studies?"

He explained that the *New Age* had been banned, and as a result he would no longer be able to pay his fees.

"Don't worry about that – your uncle will pay your fees. You are like the son he never had."

He'd been looking away from her, feeling a little guilty that he wasn't telling her the whole story. Now he had to meet her eye, and he was not able to disguise the great pity he felt for her, for Grace, for Devs, the denied son – all this pain to satisfy one man's … what? Vanity, lust, selfishness? He blew his nose to hide his momentary distraction. He thanked her profusely, but said that he had already made up his mind.

She thought, this boy is so independent. "You can treat it as a loan," she said.

He replied that money wasn't the only consideration. For a while now, he'd been reviewing his position. His law studies would take another three years to complete, and then another year in which to serve his articles. Besides, he was sure he would fail Afrikaans, a compulsory subject, in which he had no grounding and which he hated. It would only take two years to become a teacher. He'd thought about it a great deal of late, and decided that the sooner he was of help to his father the better.

That was as close to the truth as he could get. What was uppermost in his mind was the setting up of a cell in Durban and the recruitment of more cadres. He had a very wide circle of contacts there, and could reach more people in his own town. He could get a part-time job with the *Leader.* As a sports writer, he could also support the sports boycott which had just begun, and give as much publicity as possible to the South African Sports Association, which aimed to unify black sport, expose apartheid in sport and gain international recognition for non-racial sport. His articles had long espoused the formation of such an organisation, and he regularly gave publicity to the press releases of Dennis Brutus, the driving force behind its formation. He would begin with recruitment for Umkhonto we Sizwe in Merebank, which had long been a hotbed of resistance.

Mogie spoke to Chin about trying to get Guru to change his mind. When he returned that evening, he told Guru, "What's this I hear about you leaving your studies?"

Guru repeated what he had told Mogie. Chin wasn't easily fooled. "The trouble with you youngsters is that you think you're too clever, you want to change the world, all this political nonsense …"

Guru couldn't contain himself. "This government has made us feel worse than animals!" he almost shouted. "They have taken away the people's land, their rights – they have taken away their dignity. They have destroyed Cato Manor and District Six is next! You will lose your hotel. And you think we should do nothing about it?"

Chin shot back angrily, "What can we do about it? What can you, as an Indian, do about it? Just be thankful for what you have. Look at me, look at all this. We are living well. What more do you want? Indians are caught in between. If the black people get into power you won't have a chance. Look at what happened during the 1949 riots ..."

Guru said quietly, "I am not an Indian. I am a South African."

All his life, Chin had been in control of himself. When his brother had slapped him, his first impulse had been to smash the chair against Jack's face, and it had taken supreme control not to do so. When Mogie's self-centredness had emerged, he had not sent her back to Durban. He'd done all he could, even when she'd insulted Mrs Reddy, to keep the marriage going. He'd always kept control, even in the most trying moments.

Now, he found himself shouting at the top of his voice, "Don't you give me this fucking shit! You little nipper! You grew up yesterday, and now you want to lecture me. Your father worked hard, your mother worked hard. There were times when we didn't know where the next plate of food was coming from. You have everything, and you are still not satisfied!"

Chin wanted to tell him more, to tell him about the offer he had got from Niney Chittigadu. Niney had been baptised as a Christian by the Reverend Manickum, a staunch supporter of the government's policies. The reverend was assembling the first Indian congregation of the Dutch Reformed Church – sardonically referred to as the Much Deformed Church because of its strict segregationist policies. Niney no longer had to hide from the authorities. He, together with other members of the reverend's congregation, found it easy to obtain domicile in the Cape. Niney had introduced the smooth-talking reverend to Chin. Reverend Manickum had promised to see to it that Chin was compensated with another hotel in an Indian group area when District Six became a white area. All Chin had to do was agree to become a member of the South African Indian Council. Reverend Manickum had told him, "You are a very successful businessman, very well known. The government will value your support. Many doors will be opened to you."

Chin had refused the offer – although his friend, Gopi Mansook, who'd passed himself off as a trade unionist, had no compunction in joining and was now reaping the rewards. Chin wanted to tell Guru that he too was totally against the government, but all he could say was, "This shit about not being an Indian. This is ridiculous. Any more such nonsense and you'll regret it!"

Shocked, Guru reacted with equal anger. "Nothing you can say or do will change my mind." Unconsciously, his whole stance was confrontational, almost a physical challenge. He heightened the hostility by turning away in disgust.

Chin grabbed him by the shoulder and spun him around. "What the hell are you if you're not an Indian?"

Guru forgot his solemn promise to Devs. "I am a South African – like your son Devs!"

Chin stared at his nephew. He raised his hand but dropped it even as Mogie ran between them. Guru stood his ground, lips curled and eyes narrowed in utter contempt.

Outside, the deluge continued and the cold north-wester blew the driving rain against the window. Guru ran from the kitchen, shocked at himself for what he had said and the manner in which he had said it. He ran to his room and lay on his bed. He'd never spoken back to an older person in his life. Chellamma had brought them up to respect all elders, especially those in the family. He'd trampled on a sacred convention. What was worse was that he'd upset his uncle and broken his promise to Devs. Alone in his room, he could not shake off that look of deep hurt in his uncle's eyes.

Whether he liked it or not, his uncle's aversion to politics was not unique. Was he not being unfair, expecting Chin to be different from so many others – people who'd been brought up in a certain way and for whom there were more immediate concerns? Jobs were hard to come by. TB was rampant. Over the years, many had been broken into accepting their inferior status as if it were divinely ordained. Survival was all-important; the priorities were food, shelter and clothing.

Yet, despite this apparent aversion to politics, when the call was made for a massive passive-resistance campaign, the Indian community had responded, many of them losing their jobs. They'd gone to jail in droves, prepared to make the sacrifices.

Survival was a huge challenge and his father's generation had risen to it. It took a lot to do that and his uncle, particularly, had succeeded against the odds. Many people either succumbed or resigned themselves to their fate. Chin had stood up to the system. He had achieved so much.

Guru was ashamed of his impetuous outburst and wanted very much to apologise. He was ashamed, too, that he'd broken his promise to Devs. His Uncle Jack had once told him, "Everybody makes mistakes, but there are some mistakes you can't rub out like you can rub out a pencil mark on a page."

Just before Guru could leave for Durban, he heard the chilling news. There'd been an explosion at the Post Office at midnight. Three people had been arrested. Among them was Devs Mbele.

Guru postponed the trip to attend the trial, which lasted three weeks. Devs and his comrades were convicted of sabotage and sentenced to twenty years on Robben Island. When she heard the sentence, Grace let out a long, searing wail. Guru, sitting next to her, held her tightly. Chin was also there; he'd sat almost motionless throughout the proceedings, staring straight ahead. At the judge's words, an audible gasp slipped through his lips.

When Guru drove Grace home, he told her that he'd promised Devs to be there for her any time she needed him. He told her about the newspaper being banned and that he could not continue his studies. He was returning to Durban to become a teacher, and would write to her. If she ever needed any kind of help, she just had to write to him or send a telegram. He also gave her his Uncle Jack's phone number so that she could leave a message for him. Guru's thoughtfulness gave her some measure of comfort.

Guru was more determined than ever to return to Durban to set up a cell there. Devs would have wanted that. But he told himself that he was not going to be reckless. He remembered Devs' words: "There's no place for heroes."

The Umkhonto we Sizwe contact met with him in the pub of the Salt River Hotel. They sat in a secluded corner and Guru ordered two beers. The contact was a tall, grave-looking man. There was something familiar about him. He questioned Guru closely, and then talked at length about MK's strategy. The plan was to hit installations and to avoid endangering civilian life. By the time Guru had had his third beer, he was warming to the discussion. He asked, "What about the racists, the cops, the soldiers?"

The contact paused. He fingered his beer, which he'd hardly touched. He looked at Guru intently. "You like your beer, don't you?"

Guru got the message. He said lamely, "I'm not a drinker, but you can't sit in this pub not drinking – you're bound to draw attention." Realising that he didn't sound convincing, he added, "I seldom have a beer, you must believe me."

The contact said, "Okay." He seemed to sense Guru's acute

embarrassment, and softened somewhat. He said, "When I was studying, I had some wild dreams about how we would punish the oppressor."

Guru asked, "What were you studying?"

"Law at Fort Hare. The cops gave me a hard time and I had to quit."

The penny dropped. This was Welile, Devs' uncle. That was why he'd looked so familiar. Guru wanted to talk about Devs, but Welile stopped him. "In this game, personal life takes second place. There's much to be done."

Guru got his instructions and contacts in Durban. Welile shook his hand and disappeared into the night.

Chin and Mogie drove him to the station. Chin hadn't spoken to him since their argument, and Guru had felt too self-conscious to approach him – he didn't know how his uncle would react if he ventured to offer an apology. Before he entered his coach, Mogie took him aside and pressed thirty pounds into his hands. He protested, but she wouldn't listen. She said, "You must do me a special favour."

He said readily, "Anything for you, Ather."

"I want you to promise that you will not mention this matter of Devs and your uncle to anyone."

He did not know how to respond.

She continued, "Things will work out one day. Don't be impatient. I give you my word that Grace and Devs will be cared for. We will visit him as often as we can. Just leave this to me, please."

In Durban, Dorrie and Chellamma were pleased to see their son again. Chellamma had been having some bad dreams and she was relieved that her son was looking well fed and healthy. Guru did not tell them about his argument with Uncle Chin, nor did he give them any indication of what he secretly planned to do in Durban. He went back to the *Leader.* Dhanee had passed on but his wife was glad to see him, and immediately gave him a part-time job writing about weekend sport. The next day, he applied for admission to the Springfield Indian Teacher Training College.

Throughout his time at College, and afterwards when he began work as a teacher, Guru successfully maintained his cover. Apart from being a recruiter for MK, he ran secret workshops for young activists and helped infiltrate community organisations.

Then one day the Security Police arrested a young female activist for being in possession of banned literature. She was tortured and threatened with rape if she did not point out "your top man". They raided Guru's house, but found nothing. He was placed under house arrest and the Department of Indian Affairs, his employer, fired him because as a teacher he could not be involved in politics.

Within three months, Guru secretly left the country to undergo military training in Tanzania. He was sent back into the country with a unit to blow up the Haartbeespoort power station. South African Army Intelligence was a step ahead. Their informant had briefed them well. Just as Guru's unit crossed the border, they ran into an ambush. They were arrested by a huge contingent of soldiers.

Tortured and grilled for five days at Vlakplaas, Guru and his colleagues refused to talk. They were allowed to "escape". The bullets thudded into their backs as they made a futile dash for freedom. When Guru's corpse was returned to his family, it was in a sealed coffin. The family was not allowed an independent inquest.

Chapter Twenty-seven

MOGIE DID NOT immediately convey the the news of Guru's death to Chin. She'd picked up the receiver when Dorrie phoned. Dorrie, always so strong, so much in control, had been almost unintelligible, and it had taken some time before she learnt of the terrible way in which the youngster had died.

That evening, she broke the news to Chin. She tried to be as gentle as possible. He'd been sitting in the lounge, reading the *Argus*. As she spoke, his jaw stiffened. He stared at her, and then without a word got up and walked to the bathroom. When he came out, his face was buried in a bath towel. Mogie took his limp hand and led him to the bedroom. She sat him on the bed and cradled his head against her breast for a while. Then she left him, closing the door behind her as she went.

This was a double blow, coming after Devs' imprisonment. Not long afterwards, Chin gave up his job at the Steynsrust.

Although she'd known, deep down, that his resignation was inevitable, its suddenness still came as a shock to Greta. He did not give any reasons for his decision. All he said was, "I'm sorry, but I have to leave. I'm sorry."

He never went back to the hotel, even to collect his papers and his money. Greta had them delivered with a little note that read, "Dear Chin, I am sorry you had to leave this way. There is no need to tell you how precious you've been to the hotel and to me. You are indeed indispensable. I know that there will never be another to replace you. All I ask is that you do not forget us completely, and that you'll still join Stomps, Rooks and myself for drinks as often as you can. They all say that they are going to miss you terribly, just like everyone else who works here. Love, Greta."

He left the running of his own hotel entirely in the hands of Mogie. It was as if he'd lost interest in everything. Guru was right. Guru hadn't said as much, but Chin had denied his own son. Devs' imprisonment drove home the denial. Chin longed to be able to speak to his son, to explain to him that he loved him, more than anything else in the world. His thoughts went back to their brief conversations – conversations marked by his son's resentment, which at the time hadn't seemed a serious matter. He had done all he could – the boy was never short of anything. When he'd been the same age, it had been a battle. But he was prepared to do so much more for this, his child, his only child …

It was soon all over the news. The media announced in banner headlines: "District Six Declared a White Group Area." Chin and Mogie had six months to vacate their premises. They had to apply for a council house in the newly declared Indian area of Rylands, in an undeveloped section of the Cape Flats. No mention was made of the hotel – his sole livelihood.

The impending loss of his hotel seemed to make little difference to Chin. Mogie tried to get him to petition the authorities to give them alternate premises to enable them to build a hotel in an Indian area. She begged, she pleaded. It had no effect.

The Reverend Manickum told him that Rylands would be dominated by Muslims, who would surely object to a licensed hotel serving alcohol in the area. "On your own, you are no match for them," the smiling reverend said. "With the government behind you, they'll be no match for you." It would be no problem if he joined the South

African Indian Council. Others who had lost their shops and businesses were sending in their applications.

Niney Chittigadu pleaded with him. "Uncle, don't give up all that you worked for. If you don't take the opportunity, somebody else will."

If he played the game, he would be a very rich man, but Chin showed little interest. Guru's fiery words had not been in vain. If he wasn't out fishing, even in the foulest weather, Chin spent most of his time in his room. His drinking started just after lunch, which he seldom ate. He would play the songs of DK Pattamal, especially "Epadi Paadenaro". It was the melody and not so much the words that touched a chord deep within. The voice and the sound of the veenai were one, indistinguishable even when the one receded before the other – soaring, haunting, reaching into the depths of his being.

Would Devs have liked the song? Would the tune have stirred within him the same deep feeling, beyond thought, beyond the present?

When he'd walked away from home into an unknown future all those years ago, his only material possessions had been the clothes he'd worn. He hadn't taken a penny. But there was something far more precious that he had unconsciously taken with him, something that was there deep down in his soul. He'd carried with him the song of life, the unbroken melody passed on from parent to child, the abiding melody of the soul, of the Atman; the melody his mother had passed on to him, the melody that any parent passes on to a child with unwavering love, enabling a feeling of wholeness, enabling one to reach out, to conquer, to take from life what one needs and even what one wants. Amurtham's unconditional love had nurtured the eternal music of life, the music of the soul, the song of the Atman, intrinsic to his being.

The consciousness dawned now that he had not been there for his son. He had not availed his own son of that precious song of the Atman, denying him his heritage, denying him the silent, primal song of life. In the denial of his child lay the denial of the music of his own life, the abrogation of a sacred trust, the severing of an eternal rhythm.

Every effort was made to keep prisoners on Robben Island cut off from the world – but there were ways to smuggle news through. It was not long before Devs heard of Guru's death. He lay awake for most of the night as pictures of Guru in pin-point focus flashed through his mind. Soon the dam broke and his heavy sobs echoed through the cells.

He wondered how Chin was dealing with the loss. Alone in his cell, Devs thought a lot about his father, mulling over the anger and resentment he'd felt towards him. Time and time again, he went through every detail of their relationship. During his days as a student, his bitterness had deepened. He'd reached a point where he did not want to see Chin again. His father had humiliated his mother, his secret, hidden concubine, a non-person to be desired only for her body. Yet his mother steadfastly believed that his father truly loved her. There was precious little to show for that love.

Devs had had much time now to look back on the tenuous strands of their relationship, and in the quietude of the prison he'd tried to come to grips with the reasons for his father's behaviour. As a child, he'd thought of his father as a strong man, a brave man. In his youth, the doubts had crept in as he became exposed to his father's double life, which he'd reluctantly come to see was shrouded in cowardly secrecy. Now, he was not so sure that these conclusions were entirely true. You had to be strong and brave to stand up against society, but you also had to be strong and brave to achieve what his father had achieved.

He could faintly remember the walks at Sea Point with his father when he was very young. The picture was vague, but the intimacy and warmth of those moments were not easy to dismiss – there were times when he was angry with himself that he couldn't dismiss them. When he entered school, his father no longer took him out. He had cried himself to sleep night after lonely night. When he was thirteen and his father had only briefly popped in and out on his birthday, Devs had flung the present he'd bought for him through the window. Grace had sat him down and patiently explained the difficult life Chin had led. She'd told him about how he'd run away from home without a cent and made a man of himself … was courage merely about survival?

In his cell, he recalled Grace's halting words as she wiped away the tears, "Life forces us to do things … he is not a bad man. I know, I know."

Devs was in his sixth year on the Island when the authorities relented under growing international pressure and prisoners were eventually allowed visitors. The day Chin had hoped for, longed for, dreaded, feared, had arrived. He was at last going to see his son. Chin had persisted with Stomps, finally inveigling his friend into arranging the visit.

At the gatehouse, Chin's letter had been confiscated but its words were written large and indelibly in his consciousness: "I was not brave when it counted."

When it counted.

Chin put his fingers through the grille to touch his son's hands. Devs looked into his moist, pleading eyes and gently touched the protruding fingers. For the first time in his life, as he fought to hold back the tears, Chin uttered the words that lay deep within his memory, the words his mother had uttered so often in his youth – "Aum Naamasivaya, Aum Naamasivaya" … and the melody came flooding back:

Yepadi paadenaro
How shall I sing thy praises, teach me
Adiyaar
My supreme master
Apadi pade naan
That's the way I want to sing
Sivene, apadi pade naan
Almighty Siva, that's the way I want to sing
Aasai konden
To bring my adoration to you through song.

Author's Note:

This is as close to a biography as the structure of a novel will allow. It is based on the life of my late Uncle Chin Govender. Accounts of his life were gleaned from conversations with Chin, my mother Chellamma (his only sister), my uncles and brothers, my eldest sister Gonum (who lived at his hotel for some time), my cousins and Chin's friends such as restaurateur Jack Moodley (still very much alive). I am indebted to Jack Moodley for a first-hand account of the fight for the SA Bantamweight Boxing Title in which Chin's eldest brother, Jack, beat the champion, Jim Slasher. Chin's younger brother, Mike, took over the Sandflats farm, marrying and settling eventually in Port Elizabeth. Steve went on to become a successful businessman and SA Casting (Angling) Champion and the youngest brother, Sonny, went on to win the SA Featherweight and Lightweight Boxing Championships.

My curiosity was aroused as a youngster by whispers in the corridors of the Govender households of a mysterious "Madam" – who appears in this book as the character of Greta.

Most events in the book are true to the last detail, although the names of some real people (such as Guru) and the details of certain real incidents have been changed. For the purpose of constructing a story with a beginning and an end, I have used some licence in introducing fictional events, as well as the imaginary characters of Mr and Mrs Reddy, Rani and Mogie Pillay, "Stomps" Diederichs, the Mbeles and sundry minor characters.

In many ways, Chin's history is typical of the life stories

of descendants of the indentured labourers whom the British Government brought from India to work on the sugar plantations of Natal under slave-labour conditions. Many lives were destroyed, but there were those who made better lives for themselves, largely through their own efforts. Christian missions helped them in the field of education.

Descendants of the indentured labourers contributed significantly to the liberation struggle. A large number have been successful in politics, the economy, the academic fields, the professions, the trades and sport. Among Chin's nephews, nieces, grand-nephews and grand-nieces are Gonny Govender, a pioneering journalist on *Drum* magazine, author and editor who worked for the BBC and on Fleet Street; Kasturie Govender-Pillay, a director in the Department of Social Welfare; Pregs Govender, a former ANC Member of Parliament in the first democratically elected government; Pat Govender, an authority on social marketing; Gopalkrishna Govender, a British TV producer, Prakash Govender, one of South Africa's first black commercial pilots, and many others who have done well in a variety of fields.

Amurtham and Karupanna Govender would have been mightily pleased; but they would be even more pleased to know that the lives of their descendants, whatever their material achievements or circumstances, manifest the belief that the destiny of the Atman (soul) of every living being is eventual union with the Paramatman (the formless God or Truth).

A selection of other fiction titles by Jacana:

Foolish Delusions - Anne Schuster

In Tangier We Killed the Blue Parrot - Barbara Adair

The Dreamcloth - Joanne Fedler

The Hill - Craig Higginson

The King's Shilling - Hamilton Wende

The Silent Minaret - Ishtiyaq Shukri

A selection of non-fiction titles by Jacana:

Darling Mutti - edited and compiled by Joan Marshall

Inside Out: escape from Pretoria prison - Tim Jenkins

Khabzela - Liz McGregor

Mr Chameleon - Tatamkhulu Afrika

Operation Vula - Conny Braam

The Notorious Syndicalist - JT Bain: A Scottish Rebel in Colonial South Africa - Jonathon Hyslop

The Sunburnt Queen - Hazel Crampton

The World in an Orange - edited by Irene Stephanou and Leila Henriques

See a complete list of Jacana titles at www.jacana.co.za